MINOR BODIES

JONATHAN BAZZI

Translated by Alice Whitmore

SCRIBE
Melbourne | London | Minneapolis

Scribe Publications
18–20 Edward St, Brunswick, Victoria 3056, Australia
2 John St, Clerkenwell, London, WC1N 2ES, United Kingdom
3754 Pleasant Ave, Suite 223w, Minneapolis, Minnesota 55409, USA

First published in Italian as *Corpi minori* by Mondadori in 2021

Published in English by Scribe 2026
Published by arrangement with S&P Literary — Agenzia letteraria Sosia & Pistoia

Typeset in 11/16.5 pt Adobe Caslon Pro by the publishers

Printed and bound in the UK by CPI Group (UK) Ltd, Croydon CR0 4YY

Scribe is committed to the sustainable use of natural resources and the use of paper products made responsibly from those resources.

978 1 761380 43 3 (Australian edition)
978 1 915590 46 6 (UK edition)
978 1 957363 76 9 (US edition)
978 1 761385 52 0 (ebook)

Catalogue records for this book are available from the National Library of Australia and the British Library.

Questo libro è stato tradotto grazie a un contributo del Ministero degli Affari Esteri e della Cooperazione Internazionale italiano.

This book has been translated thanks to a contribution awarded by the Italian Ministry of Foreign Affairs and International Cooperation.

scribepublications.com.au
scribepublications.co.uk
scribepublications.com

MINOR BODIES

Jonathan Bazzi (they/them) was born in Milan in 1985. They grew up in Rozzano, on the extreme southern outskirts of the city. They studied philosophy and graduated with a thesis on symbolic theology in the work of Edith Stein. Jonathan has collaborated with various newspapers and magazines, including *Gay.it*, *Vice*, *The Vision*, and *Il Fatto.it*. Their first novel, *Fever*, was hailed as a significant addition to queer literature and won the Sila, Premio Opera Prima, Edoardo Kihlgren, and Bagutta literary prizes.

Alice Whitmore is a writer and literary translator living on Eastern Maar / Gunditjmara country. Her translation of Mariana Dimópulos's *Imminence* was awarded the 2021 NSW Premier's Translation Prize.

For Agata Costanzo,
who was my nonna.

A monk and a butcher fight it out within each desire.

Emil Cioran

All Gall Is Divided

What follows is a story that only now is true.

Prologue

At first, it was a little voice.

One of the hundreds of thousands of little voices that visit, uninvited, each day. Sensations, fragments, pre-verbal trajectories ploughing the soil of the mind, shifting us from where we are or where we thought we were.

Only this voice stayed, and took over everything.

December 2013, early evening. The parabola of a breath.

Inhale, *Do I love you?*

Exhale, *I don't love you anymore.*

Milan on the cusp of the festive season: lights, shop signs, chapped lips, down jackets, fur collars dancing in time with the excited footsteps of last-minute shoppers. Then laughter, hands clutching phones, mouths releasing tiny clouds of breath, although the air is decidedly warmer than it should be, at this time of year.

I'm in the city centre, Via Torino, on my way to work. I have to teach a dance class in less than an hour, at the school on Viale Campania. I have no idea what I'm doing, and no desire to do it, but that doesn't matter. I have no choice — mine is the only income we have. How long has it been, now? Three months, maybe four. It doesn't matter. The arrangement has been tacitly, amorously renewed, countless times: *I'll take care of you; I'll take care of us.*

I check to make sure I've got everything, then kiss him goodbye. The clock on the building opposite the tram stop informs me that I'm running late, as usual.

See you at home. What do you want for dinner?

I hear myself answer: Whatever you want.

I smile and my heart empties, but I say nothing. The voice is whispering again: *Stop lying, it's over.* Fear flows from the diminished ventricles of the heart all the way through my body, carried by the vascular system. How long can life endure at absolute zero?

I killed my love one evening in late December, there among the shop windows and passers-by, because I didn't know how to keep it alive, how to keep loving the same person long-term, over time. No one taught me how, no one teaches us how. It was gorgeous at first — him, us. Every moment of those first eight mesmerising months was gorgeous. April, May, June. *Finally*, I told myself. *You were born for this*. July, August. Then, suddenly, December, this late-December evening, and that little voice.

I start to dismember my love, piece by piece, with my bare hands. I take the eyes from their sockets, the teeth from the gums, remove eyelashes, beard, skin, nails, exposing the bone and living flesh to bacteria. I stood kissing my love, then crouching, kneeling, as I removed the organs, the intestines, the brain tissue. *Nothing*, I tell myself, told myself. *Nothing can remain*. Then I sat on the ground and contemplated it: a bloody pile of scraps.

My love on the butcher's block, then the autopsy table, so I can catalogue it, name its individual parts.

Look at me, a self-made widow. Uxoricide is a crime suffered twice.

Back to the beginning. Start again.

Inhale, *Do I love you?*

Exhale, *I don't love you anymore.*

PART ONE

I wanna be a part of B.A.
Buenos Aires, Big Apple.

Tim Rice & Andrew Lloyd Webber

Eva Beware of the City

Via Volvinio

Be careful when you go into the city. Statt' accort'. You're safest where there's lots of people. Don't trust anyone.

2007, the third week of August, close to sunset. One of those precious few days in the year when it's neither hot nor cold, and the air is fine, diaphanous, as though it weren't there at all. I've just turned twenty-one. I've been here for about ten minutes, at the Via Volvinio tram stop, one stop before Piazzale Agrippa, waiting for the number 15.

Yellow t-shirt, shorts, head in the clouds. I'm thinking about what tv programs are on later tonight, among other things. The tram I'm waiting for is the same one that took me to and from high school every day for six years. Rozzano to Milan, Milan to Rozzano, tracing the long line of Via dei Missaglia. That eternal, sleep-inducing avenue, foggy in winter and sunbaked in summer, draws a boundary that is obvious to everyone, local or otherwise. The place I grew up in and the city I go to every day, as often as I can, are worlds apart. Milan / Via dei Missaglia / Rozzano. City / empty space / extreme southern periphery. Where the poor people live. Not just in public housing towers, but especially there. Rozzano has the largest concentration of public housing in the Milanese hinterland, six thousand buildings housing thirty, forty thousand people.

At the end of every academic year — first the school year, now the university year — my mother honours her personal tradition of austerity and cancels my seasonal public transport pass. To save money, she says, has always said. *You won't use it. You don't need it.* But the real reason she does it is to force me to stay home, to keep me close to her. Her anxiety is a tiny furious animal that she indulges at the expense of my freedom. I'm not a child anymore, but that doesn't matter. *As long as you're living under my roof, you'll do as I say. If you don't like it, there's the door.*

I go to Milan anyway. Because I want to, because I must. Milan is hope, Milan is a magnet. I don't tell her when I get fined for travelling without a ticket. I'm not brave enough to give a false name, or make a run for it. I tear up the fine and throw it in the bin as soon as I get off the tram. I've lost track of how many times it's happened. Sooner or later, they'll come for me. Payment demand, property seizure.

Jail, most likely, since I own nothing.

2007, the third week of June. I'm on my way home from the city, waiting for the tram, resting against the chrome rail that separates the footpath from the street. To pass the time, I'm flipping through a fat illustrated volume: *New Trends in Figurative Art*. A bargain-bin find, fifty per cent off. My favourite artist is Vanessa Beecroft: part stylist, part magician, part parapsychologist (all pretence, those in the know assure me). Everything about her work resonates with me. The gaunt, ethereal designs, the staged performances featuring groups of meticulously choreographed women, the overexposed polaroids, the obsession with food and the body, the chromatic ties linking skin, wigs, underwear. When I grow up, I want to be Vanessa Beecroft.

I bought the book with the pocket money my nonna Liliana still gives me every week. Lilli, as she's known, came to Rozzano from Campania in the Sixties. She earns my allowance cleaning signora Antonietta's house, behind the Piazza del Comune. Imagine it: a woman her age, cleaning someone else's toilet, for the sake of her selfish piece of shit grandson. But I needed it. I need it. I have to prepare for my future. Please, nonna: work for me.

My family, however, is a faulty circuit. Occasionally, my mother keeps my allowance without telling me. Nonna entrusts her with the money, but it never reaches its final destination. When I discover the deception, and demand an explanation, mamma dismisses it, says she forgot, she was distracted. Nonna calms me down — *leave it, next week I'll give you extra* — and I make futile plans to steal the money back, plus interest.

It's true, though: I have to prepare for my future. After graduating from high school, I couldn't decide between philosophy and fine arts. I finally chose the former. My teachers were clear in their advice: *If you want to study philosophy, it has to be at San Raffaele, otherwise don't bother.* San Raffaele is a prestigious private university, the best in Milan. The philosophy campus is housed in a seventeenth-century villa — think baroque frescoes, mosaic floors, formal gardens — in Cesano Maderno, north of Milan. I apply, and I'm accepted, with a scholarship to cover my tuition costs.

I enrol, then drop out after six months. I could do anything, but I end up doing nothing. Instead of proving myself among the best and brightest, I slink back into the shadows of indecision.

After a semester at San Raffaele, rubbing shoulders with the children of the Milan elite, only one thing left a lasting impression. One of my professors, Roberta De Monticelli — *she's very good*, a graduate student once told me; *it's a pity she believes in angels* — introduced me to the secret history of Europe's female philosophers. Simone Weil, Jeanne Hersch, Edith Stein, Etty Hillesum, María Zambrano. Voices largely absent from university curriculums. All the famous philosophers are men, male philosophers taught by male professors, although the female professors teach them too, of course. Everyone, regardless of gender, is expected to kneel before the Great Masters of Western Philosophy. I remember Professor De Monticelli — slender, wearing a different shade of velvet suit every day, hands crowded with esoteric-looking rings, cropped blonde hair reminiscent of Kenneth Branagh's Hamlet — commenting on my very first classroom presentation (before each lesson, we were asked, in pairs, to summarise the previous lesson): *So young*, she said, *and already poised to steal my job*.

Even her approval isn't enough to stop me from dropping out. San Raffaele is an excellent university full of polite, boring students dressed in polo shirts and expensive coats. I struggle to keep up with the demanding workload. We're expected to read lecture notes in English, whole passages in Latin and German. I'm slow, too slow — is there such a thing as teacher aides for university students? I didn't study any of this at high school. I went to a liceo artistico, an artistic high school, where I was allowed to rearrange my thoughts in a way that was creative, accessible, real. I survived my oral exams by memorising a few pages of notes at a time, learning things by heart so I could recite them in front of the class without stuttering.

I'll never be an intellectual. My grandparents were illiterate. And my mother is happier when I'm drawing, anyway.

It's decided: I'll study painting at the Accademia di Brera. I can start in September.

There's an entrance exam, but I'm confident I'll get in. I went to a liceo artistico, after all, and my grades were excellent. Everyone was always telling me how talented I was. *I wish I could draw like you.* Do I love drawing, or do I just love standing out? True artists draw, or paint, or write, for themselves, above all. Their creativity is an impulse that cannot be ignored. Even if they were completely alone on the planet, they would still make art. I am light years away from this kind of purity of spirit, this kind of seriousness. Still, whatever my future holds, I know I must go to Milan to find it.

I'm repeating this fact, this mantra, in my thoughts when something appears in my peripheral vision.

Three boys, one big and dark with a shaved head, the other two pale and skinny, walking one step behind. They look about my age, maybe even younger. Before I have a chance to do what I always do in the presence of strangers — dodge the encounter, retreat to a safe distance, observe — they have sidled right up to me. Are they about to ask me for a cigarette? A lighter? Directions? The bigger one, the leader, has his hands in his pockets.

Hi.

I return the greeting, smiling, but only barely. A slight raising of the sides of my mouth, like the lifting of a protective veil.

I've got a knife, he says.

Then he adds: We're not going to hurt you.

I feel like I'm fainting, the tendons and cartilage in my knees melting towards the earth. I've imagined this situation so many times, and now it's really happening. Despite everything, this sort of thing never happens in Rozzano. My mother was right, I should have stayed away from the city. My stomach feels like it's falling through my body, like I'm on a roller-coaster. My diaphragm is lost to gravity, there's just a deep void beneath my lungs.

Give us your wallet.

I've got no money, I spent it all on this.

And I lift the book to show them, electric-blue title on white. Proof of my honesty, my good faith — an anchor, something small and innocuous to hold on to, to bring me back to the physical realm.

I'm telling the truth. I think I've got about forty cents in here.

I pull out my wallet and show them that, too. It doesn't help. They change tack.

Do you have an ATM card?

No.

Where do you live?

Rozzano.

We're coming with you.

What?

To your place, to meet your folks.

This can't be possible. This can't be happening. When we get home, will I be brave enough to shout for help? The scenario plays out in my head. My mother tied up, bleeding. *The money's in the safe, in the bedroom, behind the Van Gogh print. You'll need the key, it's in the jewellery box with the ballerina on it.* Ivano, my mother's husband, also immobilised, cut, tortured with the knife

I still haven't laid eyes on. Or maybe a struggle, three against one. A brawl inside our tiny home, forty square metres shared between four people. My mother, my sister Nora, and I sleep in the only bedroom, in two single beds — the one they share is a trundle bed, stored underneath mine. Ivano sleeps on the sofa. Ivano will think of something, surely. It's his job to protect the family. The father, the man of the house. Not like me. I'm incapable of defending myself. I'm not a real man. But what if Ivano isn't home? What if they threaten my little sister? She's only seven.

The whistling of metal on metal announces the arrival of the tram. A little tap on my elbow, a signal.

Let's go.

We board the tram, which is heaving with people. No one looks at me. I'm only invisible when I don't want to be.

Stay quiet, don't make a sound, the big one says. The others haven't spoken yet. We sit down, and he asks for my phone. He opens my text messages, types something, and hands the phone back to me. He's decided this is how we're going to communicate.

Pretend everything's normal. We're coming to your place so you can give us the money.

I text back: *But my parents are home, also what money? We're broke.*

Say we're your friends and you need the money to buy something you want.

They won't believe me.

I don't write the truth, which is that I don't have any friends, apart from Melissa and Ismene. And the concept of asking for money 'to buy something I want' doesn't exist in my family.

Do what I say or this ends badly.

The tram stops, then accelerates again. Suddenly, an idea. I can fix this.

You should know — I text into my phone — *my father is a policeman.*

A little smile. His, not mine.

I shouldn't have told them that. I've made it worse. The son of a pig: a symbolic opportunity as well as an economic one. I could back-pedal, tell them the truth, which is that I never see my father, he barely knows I exist. Or I could attract the attention of the other passengers, start screaming, throw myself to the floor, pretend to have a seizure. But what if he really does have a knife? Even if I made a scene, it would be so easy for him to stab me, slip the blade into my spleen, my pancreas, my heart. I decide to comply. I won't resist. I'll be a docile hostage, let myself be remote-controlled: anatomy without will. Do whatever you want with me.

In an attempt to distract myself from my fear, I type: *Are you guys from Rozzano too?*

Nah, I'm from Via Padova, they're from Gratosoglio. He gestures at the white public housing towers moving past the tram windows, then adds: *We don't shit where we eat.*

We don't communicate at all for the last few stops. All four of us are concentrating on what comes next.

Via Cabrini: end of the line. We get off the tram with everyone else. Me and the big guy first, the other two following behind like bodyguards. We're about a hundred metres from Via Giacinti now, from the apartment where, twenty-one years ago, my parents tried and failed to make a life together. My beautiful little mamma, eighteen years old and pregnant. A classic shotgun wedding (abortion was a sin, a slight against Christ). My father left when I was two and a half — he had other women, lots of them — and my mother fell into a heavily medicated depression. She stayed in Via Giacinti, in the apartment that was briefly theirs, with the son she suddenly had to raise alone. She stayed when, not long after that, I went to live with her parents and adolescent siblings in Via Verbene, a kilometre down the road. I lived with them for a decade or so while my mother spent her twenties working from five in the morning until late at night, cleaning offices and tv studios. Occasionally, I'd get to see her on weekends.

Here we are: Via Giacinti. We stop at the corner of my building.

The big guy says: If you call anyone, if you do anything stupid, we'll come back here and find you. Get it?

I nod convincingly, reassuringly.

I run up the stairs as quickly as I can, two steps at a time. Mamma is in the bathroom taking a shower. Ivano is in the lounge room watching tv: a football match, by the sounds of the commentators. Nora isn't here, she must be at nonna's house, or visiting her schoolmate who lives in the building next door. No one notices me come in. I go straight for the video camera my father gave me for Christmas. He bought it on sale at Media World. It doesn't seem to work, I think it's defective — or maybe I'm the defective one, incapable of figuring out how to use it. Six months after Christmas, it's still in its box, gathering dust in the wardrobe. An easy sacrifice. I also take my nonno's gold watch. Nonna gave it to me after he died of a heart attack, five or six years ago, right in front of her. It's a horrendous watch, the kind an old pimp or drug dealer would wear. I thought about pawning it, but it's lucky I didn't. Today, nonno's legacy will save my life (I've always had a thing for fate, and the supernatural). Finally, I collect my confirmation bracelet and a small gold pendant — plated, not pure — of a praying angel, to flesh out the offering, and fly back down the stairs, barely touching the cracked steps. I turn the corner and join the three figures standing wide-legged in a cloud of cigarette smoke. I hand them my treasures, hoping it's enough. Their tone is completely different now, their faces relaxed, almost friendly. It's hard to tell where their satisfaction ends and their guilt begins.

So sorry about this, the big one says. We really needed the money.

We wave goodbye, like friends, and they turn and walk casually back towards the shelter of the tram terminus. I don't go back upstairs straightaway. I take a walk around the building first, a kind of celebratory lap, to calm my nerves. All the things I could have done, but didn't, are suddenly swimming in my head. I could have stayed upstairs, called the police, called my father, asked Ivano to go down instead of me, stuck my head out the window and shouted at them to go fuck themselves. All the things I could have done, if only I were capable of standing up for myself. And yet, sacrificing nothing but my dignity, I solved the problem on my own. For the sake of my family, I grovelled on my knees, and saved us all.

Years later, when my mother learns what happened, she'll say: *You should have told me. I would have gone down there and sorted them out myself.*

Twenty-one years old and still in need of my mother's protection. That's the natural hierarchy of things: men at the top, then women, then people like me. Weak, soft, always willing to yield. At best, we can aspire to be victims, or emotional blackmailers. Poor wretches to be pitied.

You should have told me. Instead, I stay silent. I don't leave the house for three or four days after the exchange (let's call it that, for lack of a better word). Leaving the confines of Rozzano is unthinkable — if I return to Milan, there's a chance I'll run into them again. They could be waiting at any tram stop, any crossing, any street corner.

Be careful when you go into the city. Statt' accort'. You're safest where there's lots of people.

But the danger of Milan, or the memory of its danger, soon washes away. Rozzano is an unacceptable refuge. Less than a week later, a fresh fine is ripped from the tram inspector's booklet and delivered into my unrepenting hand.

Via Noto

A flock of soap bubbles. Small, tiny, a messy formation drifting lazily away, up and into the dark tree line, to die against the vertical expanse of black leaves. Ismene is pouring vodka into an enormous plastic cup.

Say when.

Melissa runs her tongue along the edge of a cigarette paper. She lifts her eyes before she starts rolling.

When.

It's past ten in the evening. We've just eaten overcooked pasta with supermarket pesto, and now we're sitting under the fabric veranda of a caravan in the Pian dei Boschi camping ground, in Pietra Ligure. We take turns dipping the pink plastic hoop into soapy water and pressing it to our lips, releasing the strings of bubbles with our breath. My friends are in charge of the music: only groups whose names begin with The. The Libertines, The Kooks, The Killers. My music is banned.

No whiny music tonight, Melissa insists. I'm begging you.

You mean, no women.

Jesus, I mean like the stuff you put on this morning.

Cristina Donà?

It sounded like a bleating goat, whatever it was.

Ismene interrupts: Did you hear about Britney Spears?

What about her?

Check it out.

Holding the cigarette between her lips, Ismene shows us the photos on her phone. Britney with a shaved head (she was sick of people touching her hair, according to one trusted source). Britney wandering in the street, face crumpled in postpartum depression. Britney attacking a paparazzo's car with an umbrella.

Poor thing.

That'll be me, one day.

You're pretty much there already, babe.

Laughter; tree branches stirring in the wind, casting moving maps of shadows against our bodies. As they get drunker, Ismene and Melissa start blowing cigarette smoke into each other's mouths. Heads of messy hair moving towards one another, white clouds travelling between their lips, like a magic show. I'm scared they're about to kiss. Ismene throws herself to the ground, in bikini top and shorts. She stretches her arms over her head, half-closes her eyelids.

Take a photo! Do I look like Marilyn?

We oblige, spilling rolls of toilet paper around Ismene's head like soft white waves. A flash: the veranda explodes with light.

This is the first independent holiday of my life. My first time going somewhere without my family. The only way I could afford it was to come here, to the same place I've been visiting since I was born — since I was forty days old, as nonna Bina likes to remind me. *When you cried, I used to take you to those trees up there, see?* The trees are poplars, spruces. *I'd rock you in my arms and say: listen, my love, do you hear the cicadas? And you'd fall asleep.*

This year, though, it's just the three of us: me, Melissa, and Ismene.

We all went to high school together, then Melissa and Ismene both enrolled to study art history at Milan's best public university, La Statale. Every day, they take the number 24 tram to the Via Noto campus, all the way at the end of Via Ripamonti (when people ask them where they study, they're in the habit of replying in unison: *The arse end of nowhere*). They've grown much closer since high school. A partnership of convenience — it's important to have an ally by your side when navigating the transition from school to university.

Melissa is my best friend. We met in our first year of high school. Ismene came along two years later. I knew I wanted to be Melissa's friend the moment I saw her. She's very beautiful: huge eyes, copper hair, a Natalie Imbruglia look-alike. It's fair to say I value appearances above all else. I have the moral compass of a magpie. To quote Marina Tsvetaeva, the Russian poet: *I loved people for their beauty; the rest, for the most part, I could always make fit.*

After spending all morning at school together, Melissa and I would spend entire afternoons talking on the phone. It's incredible, the quantity of words adolescents have inside them. Our interminable phone calls drove my mother mad. *Can't she call you for a change? What does she think, that I pull the money for those phone bills out of my arse?* She'd set a time limit — twenty minutes, max — and when it expired, she'd start shouting at me to hang up. If that didn't work, she'd unplug the phone, forcing us to finish our conversation on MSN Messenger. My mother also hated me visiting Melissa in Buccinasco during the summer break. I'd walk there most days, five or six kilometres each way, past the Forum di Assago, through parks and industrial estates.

Why do you always have to go to her? Is she in a wheelchair or something? My mother is suspicious of anyone who might use her, use us. She's obsessed with symmetry, equality, except when it comes to her own relationships with men.

These days, Melissa and Ismene are a two-for-one deal. They go everywhere together. Their relationship is practically symbiotic. They're even enrolled in the same classes: cultural-heritage legislation, art and landscape, history of modern art. They study for exams together, go shopping together in the afternoons. After a while, they begin to influence each other aesthetically: animal prints, fluoro, leather handbags, fast fashion matched with pale foundation, rosy cheeks, thick eyeliner. Think Avril Lavigne styled by Tim Burton. Years later, we'll discover this look earnt them a cruel nickname at university: the creepy clown sisters.

Summer, 2007. We're only here because my nonna Bina finally caved, agreeing to let us borrow her caravan for five nights while she stays with her boyfriend Gian (she pronounces it *Jean*, à la française) in the next village over. Gian's real name is Giancarlo. He's the nightwatchman here at the camping ground, which is how nonna met him. Jean Blue Eyes, she calls him. Melissa and Ismene approve, to a degree. *He's a handsome guy, until he opens his mouth.* Gian is from rural Piedmont, peasant stock. Widowed, with two daughters. Nonna Bina started dating him a year or two after my nonno died. My other nonna, my mother's mother, disapproves of Bina's eagerness to replace her dead husband. *I've always said that woman was a slut.*

Nonna Bina tries to keep her relationship with Gian a secret. She doesn't want people to know she's seeing the nightwatchman.

Pian dei Boschi is small. People talk. When Gian gives her a lift back to the camping ground on his scooter, along the ocean road, she gets him to drop her off a few hundred metres from the gate.

Before handing the caravan over to us, nonna gave us a talking-to: *I want you to treat this place with respect. I don't know if you know this, but people around here would do anything to get their hands on this caravan. That's not a caravan, they tell me, that's a villa. Villa Pian dei Boschi.*

Five nights in Pietra Ligure. I show Melissa and Ismene the places I know, places I've known for more than two decades. A mini tour of my childhood memories: the street vendors lining the waterfront, the secret alleyways, the discount supermarket, the newsstand where, every summer, I'd buy books and magazines with the pocket money I'd been saving all year for that very purpose. I'd lounge in the hammock, strung between the two trees dividing our camping lot from the one next door, and read those crisp books and magazines for hours on end. The hammock was a luxury I had to defend tooth and nail from the incursions of my cousin — my father's sister's son — who would join us at the camping ground every year in the brief intermissions between resorts and cruises. Three years my junior, he was much more beautiful than me: cupid blond, with thick red lips. The superior grandson. He lived with both parents in a three-bedroom, two-bathroom apartment in the affluent suburb of Milano 3. He had access to all the video games, Coca-Cola, and gummy bears he could dream of. He also suffered from faecal incontinence until he was an adolescent. I'd physically eject him from the hammock whenever necessary, secretly hoping he'd crack his head on the stones below.

In these last days of June, Melissa, Ismene, and I are

marvellously free. It's strange seeing my friends here, in my little summer kingdom, where I was always the loner, the antisocial child sitting by himself. Those days are over; everything is different now.

Pietra Ligure, in the province of Savona, is the realm of summer camps and grandparents on babysitting duty. We go around taking photos with Melissa's digital camera, then post them on MySpace. Giant plastic sunglasses, H&M tank tops, my new tattoo (a Hebrew letter on my neck, inspired by a class I took with Elena Loewenthal at San Raffaele). We barely go to the beach at all — we prefer the pool at the camping ground, the same one in which my nonno once tried to teach me to swim, without success.

I show Melissa and Ismene the yoga poses I've perfected over the past two months.

Ooh, what's that one called?

Peacock pose. I can't remember what it is in Sanskrit.

I started getting into yoga straight after high school. When I dropped out of university, yoga became my sole focus. My obsession. I practise every day, including weekends. I've stolen money out of my mother's purse to pay for yoga classes. She never notices, since Ivano is always pilfering her money anyway.

I take the tram from Rozzano to a yoga school in Corso Sempione, in central Milan. Years later, I'll learn that the school's founder, Cosetta Sandoni, was charged with fraud not long after my time there. The school is located in Sandoni's grande-bourgeois apartment: three magnificent storeys connected by a spiral staircase. I remember Sandoni sitting in a circle with us on the rose-coloured carpet, at one of our weekly Indian Philosophy sessions (one hundred euros cash for the full course, paid in advance), with her cloud of teased blonde hair and a layer of clear gloss on her lips, saying: *Sorry, but you'll never get me to give up steak.* She liked to use me as a model during her yoga classes — *Ladies, look at this! This right here is true yogic discipline!* — and would invite the other students to take photos of me in various challenging poses. I recall crashing to the floor more than once while attempting to reproduce a backwards drop into wheel pose for the benefit of someone's phone. *What the hell was that?* Sandoni would ask when it happened. *You'd better not pull a stunt like that at open day, my dear.*

Here, in Pietra Ligure, Corso Sempione feels worlds away. Poolside, I slip easily from pose to pose, my body tracing a smooth sequence of arches, twists, and stretches on the warm terracotta tiles. People walking past stop to watch me. I'm abnormally flexible; poses come easily to me. Someone once hypothesised that I was an avatar, the reincarnation of a certain Hindu deity. More recently, ligamentous laxity was suggested as a likely cause.

Freak show, Melissa says, applying sunscreen to her calves.

In the evenings, we drink and smoke. Ismene brought weed, which she keeps hidden inside the cap of her body wash. We take turns reading the descriptions of our zodiac signs — Aries, Scorpio, Gemini — from a book published by the Kabbalah Centre (the spirituality school Madonna made trendy). Aries, it tells us, is *a rebel without a cause.* Scorpio is associated with the root chakra. Ismene throws her head back and cries: Are you saying I think with my cunt?

I shush her. The camping ground has been silent for hours; all the lights are out.

Meli, turn down the music a bit. The old ladies who live here will bust my balls.

She disappears through the plastic-and-fabric wall of the veranda, then re-emerges, saying: So, I don't get it, what are you doing next semester?

I told you, I'm enrolling at Brera.

You should keep going with philosophy.

I miss drawing.

Yeah, and at Brera you'll miss philosophy. You always do this. You fall in love with something, then decide you hate it. Like with music, remember?

She's right: I studied singing and guitar from fifteen to nineteen, at a music school near Famagosta. My teacher was an ex-opera singer from Brescia. We were constantly fighting over what songs I should learn. I wanted to sing Alanis Morissette, Carmen Consoli, numbers from *Evita*; she insisted on Elton John and George Michael. Even after an appointment with a speech therapist, who confirmed I had thin, feminine vocal cords (her words), my teacher refused to let me sing songs by women. *There's a repertoire for boys and a repertoire for girls*, she told me. *We don't allow hybrids. The days of the castrati are long gone. Your voice just hasn't broken yet.*

It was actually here, at Pietra Ligure, that I wrote my first original song, inspired by J.T. LeRoy's *Ingannevole è il cuore più di ogni cosa*. The plan was to record something I could send around to musicians and independent record labels. But I got shy, and gave up. I quit music altogether. That's what I do: abandon the things I love without even saying goodbye.

You'll love this, I say. There's this passage from Oriana Fallaci's *A Man* that's literally about me. I posted it on MySpace. Let me find it.

Melissa inspects her recently shaved legs for regrowth, and mutters: Great, here comes the Fallaci.

And that curse stemmed from your inability to conclude the things you set in motion, to materialise the things that you dreamed. The more obstinate and unshakeable you seemed when a thought became an obsession, a monomania, the more you proved inconstant and impatient in the task of carrying it out. For a certain period, you would fling yourself body and soul into the project, tormenting your existence, ruining the existence of others, ignoring obstacles like a tank overriding every object or creature it finds in its path, then abruptly the pirouette: you gave it up and you never spoke of it again.

Melissa says: Good shit.

Ismene says: Let me guess, is that one of Menna's books?

Menna was our high-school literature teacher. One time, just before graduation, he asked everyone in the class what we wanted to do when we were older. When my turn came around, I answered confidently, triumphantly: *I want to write and draw and sculpt and make music. I want to express the immensity of thought and feeling through boundless, multidisciplinary, flowing creativity.* Menna nodded and said: *Is your family rich?* I shook my head. *Then you'll have to learn to go hungry*, he said.

Ismene, reaching to refill our cups, declares: According to Kabbalah, it's called *multipotential.*

Seriously though, I don't know how people can stand to do just one thing for the rest of their lives. Aren't you curious about what it would be like to do something else?

Melissa says: Sure.

Ismene says: But don't you get tired of starting from scratch over and over again?

I don't know. Maybe I've got more mental stamina or something. It almost feels like I've got all these miniature energy reserves inside me, each one activated by a different stimulus, but none big enough to sustain me on its own. What I know for sure is that I have to get out of Rozzano, as soon as possible. It's impossible to think in that apartment.

Is it that bad?

It's just so loud. The only place I can study is the bathroom, with headphones on. There are always two or three tvs going at once, plus the constant shouting. Every time they fight, there's a chance it'll finish badly. Like, really badly. Ivano is the world's number-one biggest arsehole. Last week, after my little sister's dance recital, he told her: *I liked you in the modern bit, but in the classical bit you looked like a retard.* She started crying, obviously.

Did you say anything to him?

I take a sip of vodka, then another, and change the topic.

Don't you two ever think about moving out?

Ismene says: How would I pay my rent?

Melissa says: Exactly. Anyway, my parents are super chill. My mother does my laundry, irons my clothes. Imagine having to do all that on your own?

A flash of light illuminates my thigh. I look down: my phone is one big green-yellow firefly.

Who is it?

That guy I was telling you about.

What was his name again?

Pietro.

So, you like him?

Don't know yet. We've only chatted on GayRomeo.

What a surprise. What are his photos like?

Not bad, it's hard to tell.

What does he do?

A set designer, I think. Something like that.

How old?

Older than me.

Well, let's hope this one works out.

Melissa doesn't understand, and frankly disapproves of, my dedication to online chat rooms. She's been going out with the same guy, Christian, for the past five or six years. They met at a youth centre in Buccinasco. He plays in a grunge band (I think he thinks he's Kurt Cobain) but makes a living working at Lucky Music, the giant music shop near Romolo station. Ismene is more open to online dating. She likes the idea of meeting new guys, but says all the straight chat rooms are full of losers.

I've only ever met boys online. Never in the real world. With one exception: Pasticcini (he supposedly earnt the nickname thanks to a love of party drugs), the housemate of a guy I went on a date with one afternoon. We stopped by his apartment — their apartment — in Viale Misurata so my date could get changed for a dinner he had to go to later that evening. While I was waiting in the kitchen, Pasticcini wandered in, wearing only pyjama bottoms, and heated up a bowl of frozen minestrone. He was the most beautiful thing I'd ever seen. The next day, I texted my date asking for his number. Pasticcini and I went out maybe three times. The last time we met, he took me to the top of Torre Branca, and I fell in love (a hundred metres in the air, the romantic process accelerates considerably). Then he disappeared. The ones I like always disappear.

I was born to fall in love. Love may well be my one true aspiration in life. The problem is, I'm not very physically attractive. The guys I meet always end up ditching me for someone better. My first boyfriend — we were together for all of three weeks — took me to the Villa Palestra gardens on our second date, where he told me: *You're not handsome, but you're fascinating.* The first part of that sentence stayed with me. Every time I see myself in a reflection or a photo, I start enumerating the flaws: receding hairline, spindly little muscles, completely anonymous eye colour, crooked lower canine (pushed out of place by an emerging wisdom tooth), cheeks eroded by the hormonal storms of adolescence (and the overzealous application of acidic skincare products), protruding chin, too much body hair, not enough facial hair. My ridiculous, uneven tufts of beard make me look younger than I am. Insipid twenty-somethings like me are only appealing to old men, so that's who I often end up resorting to. I take what I can get.

Whenever I'm ghosted by a boy I like, I waste several days expecting him to change his mind. Waiting for him to call. Each time, it feels like I've been sucked into a tiny, airless box I can't escape. I feel like I'm imploding. For three or four days, my whole life stops. It doesn't matter how many times we've gone out — we might have only met once, for a coffee or a drink or a brief conversation during his lunchbreak. (*You're worse than a woman,* Melissa tells me.) During these periods of expectation, my head feels like it's been filled with some unshakeable, muffling substance. I tend to write a lot, to try and clear it. Poetry, mostly — repetitive lines of obsessive, cloying verse that, later, I find too embarrassing to re-read. Eventually, slowly, the disappointment starts to recede, and I start the process all over again: I go online, cast my sad line out into the sea of chat rooms and dating sites, and fish for the next object of my monomania. If I'm feeling romantic, I look for thirty-somethings with blue eyes, connoisseurs of art, cinema, literature. If I'm horny, age doesn't matter — sixty-five is my upper limit. I want them tall, muscly, well endowed. I don't even care if there are no photos of their faces. It's just about getting back on the horse; who cares if the horse is ugly? At such times, I'm only interested in one question: how soon can we meet?

At two or three in the morning, Melissa, Ismene, and I finally crash. We fall asleep without even realising it, fully clothed on the old, mite-infested caravan mattresses. A loud banging wakes us the next day. The sun is already high. I jump to my feet.

Shit, what's the time? Meli, are you awake?

Her arm emerges from the blanket, reaches for her phone: Ten something.

Shit — Ismene's croak from inside the pillow.

Nonna Bina is out on the veranda, banging and yelling. An ambush. What is she even doing here? She's meant to be away with Gian.

Nonna Bina opens the caravan door and thrusts her head inside.

Hey! It's an absolutely pigsty out here!

She pushes the door wider and gestures, arms outstretched like an orchestra conductor, towards the outdoor table, which is carpeted with dirty plates and cups.

We'll clean it up this morning, signora.

No!

Nonna is out of her mind with rage. Her eyebrows, drawn in pencil, arch madly towards her forehead. Her eyes are wide and white under their sparkling orange porticoes of eyeshadow.

You'll clean it now! Im-me-di-ate-ly! I told you: the rats! If you don't clean up after yourselves, this place will be infested with rats!

Nonna Bina fetches buckets and rags and walks them up the slope to the bathroom block, to fill them with water. She's wearing a blue floral sundress and flip-flops. When she returns, she comes right up to me, brandishing a mop like a spear. But I'm not the one she's angry with.

What is it with young women these days? she says. She's so angry she can barely catch her breath.

All they want to do is smoke and drink.

Piazzale Cadorna

The trick is to squeeze the overhead rail with your free hand as though your life depends on it. Reading standing up is an art form, especially on these old trams — some drivers brake and accelerate so aggressively you can almost feel their frustration pulsing through the machinery.

As we pass the Arco della Pace, my mother's parting words return to me, and I lose focus on the words dancing against the page. We had a fight last night, which isn't exactly unusual for us. The same old criticisms: *Plenty of kids your age have their shit together. Consuelo's son is studying and working at the same time. What's stopping you?* I replied that, for her information, I know plenty of kids whose parents pay for their tuition, buy them a car or a scooter, pay for their petrol, and give them extra spending money on top of all that. Like Melissa, for example: her father is the only one in the family with a job — he works at a milk factory — but she still isn't expected to pay for anything herself. My mother always cuts me off: *I don't give a shit what other people do! I can't afford it!*

A few years ago, though, I finally got her to admit the truth: *I've made enough sacrifices for you*, she told me. *Sorry, but I'm not depriving myself of a new pair of shoes because you want to borrow money.*

I've only recently come to the realisation that we're not actually that poor. Ivano buys a new car every two years. (*What's that got to do with anything? It's his money, he can do what he likes with it!*) My mother only ever cries poor when I'm the one asking for money. I'm the burden, the unwanted son, the product of a family that never existed. When my mother got a new husband, had a new baby — a daughter, this time — her priorities shifted. Resources had to be diverted. Make the best of what you've been given. It's not too late to start again.

My mother has been attempting to direct me towards more concrete ambitions — money, a job, things she understands — since I was a teenager. Always, in her arguments with me, she starts off inquisitorial, then softens.

Why don't you just look around for something part-time, sweetheart?

When I was fifteen, she got me a job assisting a building manager in the affluent part of Rozzano. A few afternoons a week, I'd help him file mail and receipts as the winter sun sank into premature evenings. He'd been having trouble keeping on top of things since his wife got sick (cancer, advanced). While I worked at a desk in the lounge room, facing the wall, I'd hear her coughing behind me, growing smaller and smaller, curled up on the couch in a blue or pink dressing-gown, watching tv — rom-coms, usually, or celebrity talk shows — with the volume turned down. When she died, the building manager texted me to let me know my services were no longer required. I was relieved; money was never enough of a motivation, for me. I hated working. I was born poor, but with the soul of an aristocrat.

Around the time I met Pasticcini — I would have been seventeen or eighteen — I worked part-time clearing tables at a self-service restaurant in the food court of the Fiordaliso shopping centre. It was my idea, this time: I decided I wanted to save money for university. The recruiter seemed impressed by this, when it came up in the interview.

Why philosophy? she asked.

I want to stir people's consciences, I replied.

She smiled, and jotted something down in her notepad.

At a certain point, one of my managers at the self-service restaurant — a pale, bald guy in his forties, who resembled a kind of horrendous anthropomorphised insect — developed an obsession with me. He started stalking me on dating sites, asking me out continuously. I was interested in a different workmate: the store manager, a Luca Tommassini lookalike. One day, though, the desire for some quick cash put an idea into my head. I texted the manager: *I'll give you a blowjob for 100 euros.* Within half an hour, his car was outside my house. He drove me out of Rozzano, to an isolated area populated by parked trucks and abandoned sheds. Afraid someone might see us, I took his small, soft thing in my mouth without preamble. He smelt like intimate wash. I remember his cheap white underpants, the grey pubic hairs glued to my tongue. Him moaning, high-pitched and breathless; me gagging. He finished himself off, hand moving frantically in front of my face as I rested my head against his almost-hairless, white thigh. When he dropped me home, he handed me fifty euros. Half of what we'd agreed. I wasn't brave enough to say anything to his face. A few hours later, he wrote to me in the chat, as usual. I wrote back, threatening him: *Fucking scammer. I'm reporting you. To our boss, definitely, then maybe the police. I will ruin your life.* He returned, mortified, to give me the other fifty. He pulled up beside me, on Viale Lombardia, and handed it to me without even stopping the car.

I quit the self-service restaurant soon after that. I think I was there for about a month, in total. In that short time, I'd lost weight, and the dark circles around my eyes had grown even more pronounced than usual. My mind has its own autoimmune system: it knows how to pit my body against itself. Even my mother was worried about me: *Please, for the love of god, just stay home and look after yourself.*

The tram continues on its seismic course towards the city centre. It's hard to keep my eyes on the page, with all the violent jolts and convulsions.

'The flower,' said Bernard, 'the red carnation that stood in the vase on the table of the restaurant when we dined together with Percival, is become a six-sided flower; made of six lives.'

My stop is coming up. I close the book — Virginia Woolf, *The Waves* — and slip it into the messenger bag strapped across my shoulder. I stole it from the library, like I do all my books. We don't have a bookcase at home, so I keep them all piled on a shelf in the hallway cupboard. Every time she gets the ironing board out, my mother complains about the space they're wasting, and slams the cupboard doors loudly. So I sell the ones I've read to the second-hand bookshop in Navigli. Two lire apiece: peanuts, but better than nothing.

I check the time on my phone — I'm not late yet. After my yoga class at the far end of Corso Sempione, near Piazza Firenze, I jumped on a number 1 tram towards Cadorna. The sun was, still is, brutal. I detest summer in Milan. From June through to October, the heat is like a miasma. The nights are even worse than the days — the cement holds on to the sun's warmth and returns it threefold after dark. I'd like the temperature to be permanently fixed to eighteen degrees, like the inside of a museum. In Rozzano, we survive the summers by seeking refuge in the air-conditioned Fiordaliso shopping centre. The cooler temperature is compromised, though, by an unbreathable layer of funk, a microclimate of recycled air that makes you feel somehow dirty, infected. I don't know what's worse, the natural heat or the corrupted, artificial cool.

I check the time on my phone again: eighteen past six.

I'm meant to be meeting Pietro at six thirty. If I'm honest, I still haven't decided whether or not I'll go through with it. His new photos have put me off. He's one of those guys who upload only a select few, carefully curating his online image. I'm worried they might be misleading, chosen to capture angles and aspects that don't actually exist. Anamorphosis, optical illusion, special effects.

We continued messaging after my return from Pietra Ligure, and finally decided to meet in person. So here we are. We're meeting today, in Piazzale Cadorna, just outside the Metro station, at the end closest to Castello Sforzesco. I'm tempted to turn around and disappear. I could so easily ghost him. Head straight home, or take a detour via La Feltrinelli bookshop in the Galleria Vittorio Emanuele II. I could just pretend nothing ever happened. I've done it before, with other guys. It's a consequence-free crime. If anything, it's their fault for failing to keep me enthralled — if you didn't sweep me off my feet, seduce me, intoxicate me, then you deserve to be stood up. Plenty of guys have done the same thing to me. Although I must admit, when I'm about to ghost someone, I never let myself remember how it feels to be on the other side of it.

The gay chat rooms I frequent are full of interesting people, but the most promising ones never write back. The few exceptions make me so anxious that I self-sabotage until, finally, they give up on me. The last one was Matia (with one *t*), an architecture student at Politecnico. He looked like a brown-skinned Keanu Reeves. I liked him so much that, for the entirety of our date — an aimless walk that began at Porta Romana and ended at Crocetta — I tried to make myself seem more interesting by disagreeing with everything he said, disguising my adoration with intellectual barbs. A strange kind of alchemy: my soft, famished heart becoming its antithesis. After our date, he stopped responding to my messages.

This time, it's even less promising, because Pietro is already taken. It was one of the first questions I asked him: *Do you have a boyfriend?*

Yes, he answered.

Are you happy?

Blissfully.

They've been together for more than a decade. Usually, I stop replying to the unavailable ones fairly quickly, regardless of my level of interest. Even if they're very attractive. Not out of respect, but out of a need to feel special — that is, for fear of being treated as a hobby, a side project.

I pause among the thick red columns at the entrance to Cadorna Metro station, beneath the spectacular vaulted roof designed by Gae Aulenti. There, half-staring at the river of human bodies flowing in and out of the station, I make a decision. For no particular reason, I decide to stay. To meet him, see what he's like.

I continue past the fountain and sculptures — Oldenburg and

van Bruggen's *Needle, Thread, and Knot* — towards the agreed end of Piazzale Cadorna. It's an unwritten rule of online dating that, once you've arrived at the specified place — a street corner, a bar, a number on the front of a building — there's no turning back. Not everyone honours the rule, of course. One time, a guy came to pick me up in Rozzano, at the foot of the Telecom Tower. When I got into the car, my would-be date — tall, pale, with a thick mane of red hair — took one look at me and said: *I'm so sorry, I just got a phone call.* He brandished his phone, as if it were evidence. *It's an emergency.*

I retraced my steps home, accompanied by the thought that I wasn't even worth his pity sex.

A dark green car, Pietro had said.

That must be him. I cross at the lights, arm raised, hand open. He gets out of the car. Red cap pulled all the way down to his eyebrows, large tortoiseshell glasses, greying beard. Two small, attentive eyes. Blue, in his photos — I'll soon learn those were contact lenses. Small, crooked teeth; when he smiles, he takes care not to expose them too much. He looks like he could be a machinist, or a computer programmer. He looks timid, or maybe just composed.

Pleasure to meet you. I'm Pietro. I thought you'd be taller. (He has a nice voice.)

Are you saying I'm short?

No, I wouldn't say that. So, where should we go?

No idea — wherever we want.

Not here, anyway.

We get into the car. He starts the engine, and manoeuvres his way out of the carpark with a confidence I wasn't expecting. I love being driven around by men. I never got my driver's licence, and driving — controlling the movements of a large, mechanical vessel — is a skill I've decided lies beyond my reach. I have assumed an existential position: passenger, guest, parasite.

While Pietro is distracted, I look at my phone. A pixelated envelope unfolds into a message from my mother: *Where are you?*

I lie, as I often do: *At an exhibition with Melissa. I'll be back for dinner.*

I slip the phone back into my bag.

We stop at a red light, and Pietro asks if I'd like to go to his place.

My housemates will be there, he adds, as if sensing my hesitation. Then we can meet my friends in Porta Romana, if you like. Have something to drink. If you want. Or we can do something else.

I wind the window down all the way, letting the hot breeze dry out my eyelids and the inside of my mouth.

It's late June, 2007. The traffic lights change colour.

We drive on.

Autostrada dei Giovi

The headlights are getting closer.

They're approaching from behind, there's no way to dodge them. We're naked, caught in the act. T-shirt, shorts, belt, hands fumbling in shame. Too late: I hear car doors opening. I cover myself — we cover ourselves — as quickly as possible. Suddenly: torchlight, a harsh, day-bright glare entering from the side windows, illuminating the interior of the car and our hot bodies, sticky with sweat and saliva.

Laughter. One of them is saying: Let them get dressed.

Absorbed in the task of putting my clothes back on, I don't hear anything else.

It's two thirty in the morning. Pietro was driving me home when he pulled into the emergency stopping lane on the highway. We kissed, on the lips and elsewhere, and rubbed ice cubes on each other's necks and chests (we'd taken the ice from the service station, smuggling it into paper cups we stole from the soft-drink station). An initiation rite, impressed on the nervous system, a sensory memory to be relived in the hours and days to come.

Not even ten minutes had passed before a patrol car noticed us, and pulled up behind Pietro's car.

They open the back doors: Alright, boys, move it.

Three policemen — I can only see the lower halves of their faces.

We step out into the muggy darkness. The only lights around are theirs. In my haste, I've only managed to slip my toes into my shoes, leaving my heels protruding obscenely.

One of the policemen says: Don't you have a home to go to?

There's a good chance that one of us, either me or a policeman, will escalate things. Whenever I find myself in conflict with an authority figure — police, carabinieri, soldier — I feel an overwhelming urge to provoke them, insult them, shout in their face. I want them to know how much they disgust me, all of them, as a social and symbolic category. How much I despise their abuses of power, their micro and macro aggressions: the sarcasm, the sexually lewd comments, the jokes about sex workers and fags, the impunity, the complicity of the herd. I feel nothing of the reverential fear they expect — their uniforms look like Halloween costumes to me. My father is one of them. I ate lunch in their mess halls for years, eavesdropping on their conversations, the things they said when they felt most at ease. I'm well acquainted with their mindsets, their tones of voice, the kinds of words they use. As my mother used to say: *Your father was born to be a cop.*

Standing in the emergency stopping lane, they start to frisk us. They ask to see a licence and registration. My urge to resist is dampened by Pietro's docility, contained by the soft walls of his composure. He retrieves his driver's licence and a registration document from the glove box.

Do you have everything? I ask him, as if I know what I'm talking about.

Yes, I think so.

He follows two of the policemen back to their car. I stay with the third policeman, who watches me in silence. In the distance, the lights of the Forum di Assago are a constellation — they draw my gaze beyond the empty expanses of grass and asphalt that stretch away from the edges of the highway.

Earlier in the evening, after our rendezvous in Piazzale Cadorna, Pietro and I went to his house to pick up Jacopo, one of his housemates. Then we met up with some of their friends at the bar in Piazza Buozzi, their weekly haunt. Pietro's friends turned out to be a lot of fun. One, in particular: they call her Corte, because of her apparent resemblance to Paola Cortellesi. She works as a sales assistant at Zara, but wants to move to London. She studied art history, like Ismene and Melissa, and passionately regrets it. She tells me that, after graduation, she asked her thesis advisor for some professional advice, wanting to know where she should look for work, and his response was: *I saw they were advertising for massage therapists at Policlinico. Maybe you could do a short course?*

I also met one of Pietro's closest friends, Viola (nicknamed Minnie). She's a semi-professional actor and voice actor. She lives in a tiny village somewhere between Milan and Lodi — I can hear it in her accent — with her father, and a dog named Merletto. She's in a relationship with a middle-aged theatre director who is rather well-known in Milan.

Whenever I go to gay bars, I'm struck by the strange, enmeshed relationships gay men often seem to have with their straight female friends. Enormous intimacy and closeness punctuated with an element of disdain, or ridicule. I put it down to a need to objectify the feminine — to reclaim the suffering they endure for failing to comply with the norms of masculinity by punishing someone else. Namely: their *fag hag*, their *fruit fly*, their *fairy princess*.

I think about this to distract myself from what's happening. From these black fields, briefly illuminated by the rare car headlights speeding past us on the highway. Why are they taking so long? I realise I completely forgot to tell my mother I'd be home late. She'd tried to call me when I was out with Pietro and his friends. She claims she can't sleep until I come home. She won't even remove the keys from inside the front door, so I have no choice but to knock and wake her when I arrive. She opens the door in her underwear, face glazed with sleepy resentment.

Pietro's boyfriend was calling him all night, too. Pietro eventually excused himself and took his phone outside. I watched him through the window of the bar, pacing a small section of the footpath. When he returned, his smile was tainted with something.

Who knows what his friends were thinking. Nobody said a word about it.

Car doors open and close behind me. I only hear them, I can't see what's happening. Are they leaving? Are we free to go? Pietro reappears a moment later, his eyes downcast. All good, he says softly. We get back into the car. He places his licence and registration documents back inside the glove box. Familiar gestures, returning everything to normal. Outside, the policemen are laughing. They approach the car just as we're about to leave.

Get a motel next time. Let us know if you need some help with the crowdfunding.

Pietro adjusts the rubber mat under his feet, turns the key, and we drive off.

The lights of the Forum, to our right, grow closer. Our shame is a vaporous presence that travels with us inside the car.

We take the exit to Rozzano.

For a minute or two, neither of us say a word.

Via Porpora

The snake has brown and yellow markings. I can see its shining skin moving between the leaves and the thick, curved branch.

It manoeuvres itself into a corner, unsettled by my presence, head swaying with an elegance no one ever associates with predators. It takes a moment to notice the small body being lowered into the terrarium. We bought the mouse from a shop in Viale Umbria, opposite the food co-op. During the car trip home, it left small pellets of shit in the white cardboard box we transported it in. They call them 'feeder mice'. They cost two euros each — less if they're on sale.

The python is awake now, outstretched. It suddenly descends, or lets itself fall, fixated on the movements of the rodent now pawing frantically at the glass walls of the terrarium. The briefest of dances: the snake strikes to take the mouse. It constricts the small white body, then begins to eat it. Its jaw stretches wide, as wide as possible, and the mouse opens its mouth, too, its teeth useless now, its eyes bulging in their sockets like gel about to be squeezed out of a tube.

The snake is fed a live mouse every three or four weeks. It would rather starve to death than eat pinkie mice, those tiny, hairless creatures frozen and packaged a few days after they're born. Pinkie mice are much more convenient — they can be kept in the freezer, and defrosted just before feeding. But this python doesn't seem to recognise them as food. It's an instinct thing, Pietro says.

After ingesting the rodent whole, the snake has a visible bulge in its body for several days. It remains immobile, curled in on itself like a belt in storage, slowly digesting its prey. All of it: fur, teeth, nails. Once that's done, it's ready for its next meal.

In the terrarium next door, two bearded dragons — a couple, male and female — chase each other around the ornamental branches and stones, which they like to use as sunbeds under the UV light. Their mouths turn upwards at the corners, so they always look like they're smiling. Unlike the python, the dragons are fed fruits and vegetables, although a few times a week they get crickets or mealworms.

The praying mantis, as brilliant as a green leaf, is hanging upside down from the roof of its terrarium like a stalactite. When it feeds, it grabs a cricket like a cob of corn and devours it quickly, head first.

Pietro is passionate about reptiles. His bedroom houses three large terrariums. The python and the bearded dragons are kept inside, while the praying mantis lives outside, on the balcony. (When they signed the lease, Pietro made sure he got the master bedroom.) The walls are painted black, and all the furniture and bedding is dark. A huge IKEA bed sits in one corner, under the window. Two frosted glass light fixtures hang from the ceiling. On the walls, a playbill for Ibsen's *A Doll's Hous*e, a poster of Tilda Swinton (Pietro's hero, the best actor in the world), and an X-ray of a human torso.

Is that you? I ask.

Yeah. I get one every year. I've got a heart defect, so I'm at risk of myocardial ischemia. It's like having a time bomb hidden in my chest.

I don't know how to respond to that, so I say nothing. I try to concentrate on our surroundings. The bedroom is huge, almost the size of our entire apartment in Rozzano. Pietro has lived with the same two housemates for a couple of years now: his childhood friend Jacopo, a precariously employed fiction editor, and Matt, an AcquaGym-obsessed Irish-Italian who works at a private after-school care centre. Their two-bedroom apartment is on Via Porpora, a ten-minute walk from Lambrate railway station.

Everything happens so naturally, so quickly. Two weeks after our first date, Pietro asks me if I want to move in.

I can't afford to pay rent, I say.

Don't worry about it.

Are you sure? What do your housemates think?

They'd be thrilled to have you.

He wants me there, and I'm happy to go along with it. The twin paths of our needs and desires intersect neatly. I say yes, obviously. And just like that, my fantasy becomes a reality: I'm moving to Milan.

No one says a word about Pietro's now ex-boyfriend. All that's left of him is a nicely framed photograph, standing on the floor against one of the black walls in Pietro's bedroom. Every time I see it, I scan for comparisons: are we similar, identical, completely unalike?

As soon as I get a chance, Pietro says, I'll give that photo back to him. I promise.

△

Back in Rozzano, I pack my things into suitcases in preparation for the move: my best clothes, the few books I haven't sold, the CDs of female singer-songwriters I bought in my adolescence. I transport them in several trips, via public transport. On one occasion, when my parents aren't home, Pietro comes with me to Rozzano to help. He drives, and parks out the front. We get out of the car, hoping no one spots us. (*Look who it is: the cop's fag son.*) We walk through the smashed-up front door of my building and head upstairs. In Pietro's presence, the one-bedroom apartment seems even smaller, as though my new proximity to Milan has revealed the true poverty of its proportions. Everything looks miniature, shrunken; the ceilings seem low, the doors narrow. Like we're Snow White in the dwarves' house, or Alice after she tastes the Eat Me cake.

I'm moving out. When I officially break the news to my mother, she's speechless. For the first time in her life, perhaps. Now who will she take all her stress and frustration out on? How will she cope without me, the thorn in her side?

The transition happens quickly, without much ado. Like ripping off a Band-Aid. A quick goodbye — *ciao, mamma* — then it's time to fly the nest, and soar.

Another world is waiting.

Pietro makes space for me in his wardrobe, buys me a new pillow. His enthusiasm corroborates my own. These domestic adjustments, the tweaking of his environment to accommodate my presence, are rituals to mark my rebirth.

Often, in memory, important periods of our lives are condensed into a symbol, into a single detail — an image, an object, a figure

— that preserves their essence perfectly. For me, the move to Milan is a piece of baklava in a polystyrene tray. That honey-drenched pastry, purchased at midnight from the takeaway kebab place on Via Salieri, has become a kind of talisman. It says: you are allowed to leave the house at any hour of the day or night, and buy yourself something to eat. Anything you like. Nothing can stop you — not your mother, not anyone. It feels like a sense of endless space is opening up in front of me. The rules I used to live by were arbitrary, and now they have been demolished.

I confuse my love of Milan with love for Pietro. It's a kind of wilful deceit; I'm lying to myself, sinning against my own soul. The truth is, I'm not in love with Pietro. I'm not even attracted to him. I am the son of a beautiful woman — for me, looks are everything, absolutely everything. Beauty is my personal teleology. I use its reflections, its auras, its opalescences, to orient myself in the world. Still, Pietro is kind, and warm, and good to talk to. Intuitively, in my gut, I know I can trust him.

I decide to stay with him. Give it time. I've been waiting so long for a love story to come along; every time I think I've found one, it dissolves in my hands. This is the closest I've ever come. With any luck, time will work its spell on me. Little by little, out of habit and routine, maybe love will grow.

Sex isn't too bad, as long as the lights are out. At twenty-one, the body needs little encouragement: blood flows where it's meant to, when it's meant to. Arousal is a biochemical reaction I can trigger easily. I never initiate sex, but I don't decline it either. It's just a matter of enduring the first few moments, the transition from distance to contact. I have sex with Pietro as an act of gratitude, of recognition. I offer him this body that he desires because, until now, this body has always been seen as a means, never as an end.

I've always wanted to be someone's boyfriend. *My boyfriend* — when I say the words, I feel them filling my whole mouth; when I write them, they pulse through my fingers. It's the idea of it more than anything.

I take care to move in the peripheries of my own consciousness, avoiding the empty, diminished centre. I try not to think about the fact that I don't love him. It's almost muscular, the willpower involved. I choose not to look at things too closely, let the edges stay blurry. And when doubt creeps in, meowing like a kitten, I drown it with both hands. I keep my true convictions submerged.

I surreptitiously transcribe one such conviction, expressed in a quote by Edith Stein (a pupil of Husserl's, who later became a nun and was killed in Auschwitz), into the Notes section of my Facebook profile:

It is possible to agree with others on the properties that characterise a human being, and their value, and it is possible to demand 'respect' for this value. But that I must love a person for the sake of their value, this cannot be expected of me. If and how I love someone is based on the manner in which their way of being connects with mine, and this is as absolutely unique as one's way of being itself.

It's as if I've been split in two. A disassociation event worth examining.

But no — that logic is wrong. A belief is only ever valid for one part of us, and we are made of many parts. As children, we're taught that the heart is a single organ, one solid, red, unambiguous thing. Whole. Pure. But that's not true: the heart is full of corridors, passageways, twists and turns. The heart is porous. Nothing is absolute, nothing stays the same at all ages, in all conditions, at all latitudes. Could contradiction in fact be the true language of the world? For me, at least, it is.

From Rozzano to Milan. The euphoria this transition evokes in me comes from many places, if not the most fundamental place. Pietro has offered me a safe place to live, a decent home. He has shared his friends with me, his money. He's trying to make it as a scenographer, with mixed results. To make ends meet, he sometimes takes jobs in focus groups for market research companies, giving his opinions on new yoghurt flavours and toilet paper textures. He might earn forty, fifty euro for two or three hours of his time. In any case, his family can always help him out if he needs it. Unlike mine. We come from completely different social classes: his mother is deputy manager of a bank, his father owns a rental car and courier company. He has nothing to worry about.

I move into Pietro's apartment in late August, 2007. Soon after, I pass my entrance exam to the Accademia di Brera. In celebration, I start taking classes at a more expensive yoga studio. This one has two locations, in Corso Vercelli and Via Solferino, and is frequented by the likes of Anna Dello Russo and vaguely recognisable ex-MTV veejays. I also become vegetarian. For the first time in my life, I am in charge of what I do and do not eat. I even get back into singing lessons, with a more accomplished teacher this time, who uses an American methodology called Voicecraft. Only the best for me, from now on. I'm greedy for life. I let myself dream again. I can do anything, be anyone — even a popstar.

My reignited multipotential is made possible, too, by my mother, who begins sending me my father's child support cheques (the conditions of the divorce state he has to pay until I'm twenty-five). Three hundred and ten euros a month, taken directly from his policeman's salary. He's never made peace with it.

By the time autumn arrives, I am Milanese. I am no longer a newcomer, an interloper. Pietro quietly handles the rent, and all our living costs. He takes care not to make me feel like a burden. He offers me the stillness I need to think about my future. A solid, stable base from which to take flight.

Finally, I have left Rozzano behind. The asphyxiating one-bedroom apartment that somehow housed four of us. The violent arguments between my mother and Ivano. The Sundays spent rotting in front of the tv in our pyjamas. The swathes of time swallowed up by the computer screen, scrolling for profiles on Gaydar, GayRomeo, Me2. The pathetic pieces of shit who would call me a fag every time I left the house (last time it happened, the guy slapped me in the face when I met his insults with silence). The aimless afternoons spent wandering Fiordaliso. The brief moments of teenage elation promptly transfigured into languor, depression, putrefaction. The pervading feeling that this, and only this, is what you deserve.

I didn't grow up with my father — the playboy, the philanderer — but I must have inherited my sense of ambition from him. The feeling that the world and everything in it belong to me, are fated to be mine; that I can aspire to more than seems possible. Even at the expense of others, when necessary. I'm not above standing on the bodies around me in order to climb a little higher. High enough, maybe, to peer over the fence at the kingdom next door, and hatch a plan to conquer it. Expansionism: Milan is my promised land.

Some make it to the city through sheer hard work. Not me. I'm not tough enough for that. Instead, I have traded my body for freedom.

Finally, I decide on my life path: yoga and fine art. I will be an artist.

In November, I start at the Accademia di Brera. I enrol in Alberto Garutti's classes in painting, although he doesn't teach us how to paint, because he's not a painter himself — he's best known for his public art installations. One of his most famous works, *Ai nati oggi*, is a pair of lanterns in Sint-Veerleplein square, in the centre of Ghent, Belgium, that flash every time a baby is born in one of the city's four maternity hospitals.

The classes are held in an empty white space, like an apse. Their structure is simple: one by one, each student presents their work before the class so it can be torn to shreds by their peers. It's a methodology that has been tried and tested over decades. Garutti's aim is to teach us how to survive in the dog-eat-dog system of contemporary art. He provides us with tips, strategies, advice. But in the end, it's a matter of natural selection. Some students cry, some have panic attacks, some tell Garutti to go fuck himself. The ones who endure, however, have an excellent chance at making it — many go on to become accomplished artists.

Our class becomes a kind of family. Garutti is the father figure we must appease, win over, seduce, if we want to belong. I'm incapable of doing that. As with most of the older heterosexual men in my life, I find Garutti inscrutable. I stand on the sidelines, watching the hungry vectors of other students' ambition whiz past me, dodging them when needed.

In the first three or four months of class, I only present two pieces of work. The first is my old Nokia playing a recording of the Ashtanga yoga mantra — *vande gurūnām caranāravinde samdarśita svātma sukhāvabodhe* — repeated, by me, at a slowly increasing volume, beginning with a whisper and ending with a scream. The judgement is unanimous: pathetic. The second piece is a video, projected onto the large white wall of the classroom, in which I read an excerpt of Tomasi di Lampedusa's *The Leopard*, edited to emphasise the pauses caused by my stuttering. This one fares a little better. Later, though, in a private gesture of self-absolution, I conclude that the whole process is absurd. Faced with the fierce ambition of my peers, I let myself shrink to nothing. Invisible, I take up residence with the other atoms. I'm useless. I don't know how to break though the membrane. I retract deeper and deeper into myself, until I abort my own birth.

I quit Brera. Soon after, I also quit the singing school. (Multipotential, or just chronic indecision?) I continue with yoga, and start attending the Kabbalah Centre. I wear a red wool bracelet to protect me against the evil eye. I go to events in hotel conference rooms. I attend monthly gatherings to connect with the new moon. Maybe this is my calling: to teach Kabbalah. To travel the world as a custodian of millennia-old wisdom. All sorts of people come to the Centre: dentists, entrepreneurs, celebrities. Intoxicated, I spend all my money on merchandise: handbooks, candles to cultivate the energies associated with various times of the year, all twenty leather-bound volumes of the Zohar, like a bilingual encyclopaedia set, with the Aramaic text on one page and the English translation on the other. It doesn't matter that I can read neither English nor Aramaic. It's not about understanding what's written. All I have to do is scan a certain passage every day — the daily paragraphs are communicated via email — and tune in to the energy conveyed by the text. The volumes are sent to me from London. They cost me almost six hundred euros, in total. For the first time in my life, I have the money. So I spend it.

Pietro is sceptical, but doesn't really try to stop me. All spiritual cults are the same, he says: their aim is to brainwash you into joining a pyramid scheme. They're basically entrepreneurial projects founded on emotional dependence. Maybe he's right, maybe not. All I know is I'm fascinated by Judaism, and this seems like the easiest way in.

I actually tried reaching out to a real rabbi, but apart from the circumcision thing, there's also the question of starting a family. Progressive Judaism is accepting of homosexuality, but, as the rabbi explained, my partner — boyfriend, husband, whatever — would have to convert to Judaism and pledge that any future children would be given a Jewish education. When I raised the idea with Pietro, he shot it down immediately.

So the Kabbalah Centre it is. Even there, though, it's only a few weeks before obstacles start to arise.

I learn about the custom of tithing: in order to remove the limitations that might block the flow of blessings into our lives, we are encouraged to offer ten per cent of our income to the centre. I ask the people in charge if that also applies to people who don't have jobs. Does it apply to kept men, like me?

It's up to you, they reply. But keep in mind that the more intense the effort, the greater the effect.

Shortly after our conversation, they arrange a Skype call between me and one of the Centre's senior teachers. Like all the women, she wears a wig and uses a fake name — something from the Bible. She's wearing a white shirt and a headset; it looks like she's in a call centre. In the background, I can see dozens of other people sitting at computers, doing exactly what she's doing. My mystical guide, my mentor, wants me to enrol in a new course that's about to start (the courses are structured like video-game levels: Kabbalah 1, Kabbalah 2, Kabbalah 3). She looks directly into the camera, articulates her words carefully, raises her voice at key moments. She convinces me. Two hundred and eighty euros for a level-up.

Melissa and Ismene say I have the life of a middle-aged housewife.

To be fair, though, I don't spend all my father's child-support money on Kabbalah. I also use it to celebrate the end of my captivity in Rozzano. I buy books, as many as I want, and keep them all. I visit museums and galleries. And one day, on a whim, I decide to get my tongue pierced.

I go to a piercing place in Ticinese. The needle is pushed through the muscle, slowly. A simple steel piercing, with a little jewel (you can always change it later, they tell me). My tongue balloons. I can't speak for a week because of the tender, swollen flesh filling my mouth. For seven days, I eat nothing but gelato.

The first night, I bleed all over my pillow — the fancy, ergonomic, hypoallergenic one Pietro bought me. The next morning, the bloodstain looks like a Rorschach inkblot. I keep the piercing for a while, then remove it. It's unbearable. They did a bad job, it's asymmetrical, too far to the right. All my attempts at aesthetic improvement seem to end in failure.

Pietro doesn't have piercings, but he has tattoos. Six, for now. There's a theme to them: they represent the word *art* in different languages. Eventually, he wants to cover his entire body with all the languages of the world. The universal human need: to create is to elevate life to its highest potential. To take possession of it.

I've only got one tattoo, for now: a *yod* underneath my left ear. I plan to cover my arms and back with depictions of female divinities from various spiritual traditions. Bastet, Diana, Lakshmi, Teresa d'Avila, Rachel the Matriarch, Andromeda. A gathering of my muses — or rather, of the strong women I've dreamt of transforming into, over the years.

I tell Pietro: Once I've saved enough, I'll start. Do you think a thousand euros would do it?

And then: If I can't save it, could you lend it to me?

Pietro is often away for work — he has to travel to different set design studios and workshops — which is good for me. It means I get a lot of alone time. I can be autonomous, enjoy the house as if it were my own, fill it with my habits, leave imprints of myself on it — my language, my rituals.

In the evenings, after dinner, I stay up late talking to Jacopo in the kitchen. (Our other housemate is almost never there; he only comes home to shower, change his clothes, and, rarely, sleep.) Sometimes, on my way home from yoga, I stop by Mundial, the grotty bakery opposite the station, and buy two pieces of focaccia, dripping with cheap olive oil, and a can of Coke Zero to share. We eat and drink and smoke and talk, perched on the fat vintage armchairs surrounding the dinner table, watched over by Pietro's posters and sketches on the walls.

How'd it go today?

Want some of my pasta?

Are you seriously telling me you've never read Harry Potter?

Months later, I'll learn that Jacopo — barely five foot three, size thirty-eight feet, permanently rosy cheeks — is in love with me. The very first day he met me, he asked Pietro never to bring me back to the house. *Never. Please. I can't do it, I like him too much.* When I share my discovery with Melissa, she says: *I'm sorry, is this guy blind, or … ?*

Perhaps the kind of people we attract says something about us. Maybe all fondness — even the unrequited kind, the blind alleys, the dead ends — cracks some secret code in us. What does it mean, then, that Jacopo — in poor health since adolescence, capable of spending whole weeks shut in his bedroom, allegedly still a virgin — is obsessed with me?

With time, the situation gets worse. In the spring of 2008, Eris hurls her Golden Apple of Discord: Pietro and Jacopo have a falling-out. After years of friendship, they stop speaking to one another. Their only communication is via MSN Messenger. Jacopo gets petty about the rent and bills, starts demanding Pietro pay double what he was before. In lieu of love, he demands money. It makes no difference that Pietro is almost never home, that I'm the one occupying his room and using his share of the gas and electricity. *It's a matter of principle*, Jacopo claims. He also starts accusing me of leading him on, gossiping about me to our common acquaintances. He's convinced I was sending him secret messages through the songs I listened to while washing the dishes, when Pietro wasn't home.

You let a whore into this house.

The apartment becomes unliveable, divided into warring factions, each barricaded in a bedroom. A hostile, cold war that could erupt at any moment. Pietro and I are left with no choice: in April, we move out.

Δ

Pietro doesn't want to waste money on rent anymore, so the new plan is to take out a mortgage and buy a place. As expected, his parents offer to help him out.

We spend weeks trawling through real estate listings online. Finally, we find it: a one-bedroom apartment on the Naviglio della Martesana. Sixth floor, no lift. Walking distance to Gorla Metro station. One hundred and forty thousand euro. All ours. A whole place, just for us — aren't you happy?

My job is simply to let things happen to me. To follow whatever process is in motion. To sit still while things grow around me — all the beautiful vines and mangroves that I invoked, the ones I prayed would emerge from the earth and descend from the skies to take me away from myself, from my old life, like enchanted bridges, or staircases.

I am the protagonist of a virtual-reality experiment, an empty shell, a hologram. I am the demiurge. I am twenty-two years old. When I think about my life, I avoid dwelling on the grafting points, these artificial wounds, edges sown together unnaturally, by force. Mine is a love story that lacks for nothing. Except love.

Only a small, quiet part of me knows the truth of this.

Piazza dei Piccoli Martiri

The trolley moves through the lanes of IKEA, past the walls and walls of homewares, and you tighten your grip on the handle, straightening your arms. Your feet lift off the earth — forty centimetres, fifty — feet dangling like a rag doll's, like they're made of cloth.

It took you some time to learn how to defy gravity, but now it's second nature. The secret is in the lower *bandhas*: two internal 'locks' or seals, one formed by contracting the perineum, the other by retracting the abdomen, that create a kind of internal lever, subtly channelling the body's energies upwards, making it lighter. Your zeal for mastering the art of arm balances, the hours of practice in and outside of class, has caused inflammation in your wrists, sprouting ganglion cysts the size of cherries. You slather them with arnica ointment and massage it in. Your teacher recommends green clay. A fellow student suggests wrapping a coin tightly against each cyst with a bandage. Pre-modern remedies for the haunted body.

You lag behind, a child playing with a shopping trolley. You climb even higher on the handle, spreading your legs, a precursor to a flying splits. Ahead, you can see the others talking and laughing, picking up items, turning them over to look at the prices. Chopping boards, colanders, frying pans.

Where did you go?

I'm here! The trolley flying to meet them.

With each month, your body hardens, the muscles tone. Your shoulders broaden — the hunch of adolescence is no more. Finally, you possess the upright posture of *Homo sapiens*.

For you, yoga is another way of drawing. You observe the positions of the greatest teachers in the world — Chuck Miller, Eddie Stern, Kino MacGregor, their dazzling, hyperactive bodies gleaming from the pages of books and magazines and websites — and reproduce them, your precision improving with each attempt. You take photos of yourself in poses, and show them to people. Your ego inflates, grows into something glorious.

Couches. More couches. Mirrors, shoe racks.

Pietro worships IKEA, his Swedish temple of furniture. He'd come here every day if he could. He loves *stuff*, in general — anything that has structure and mass. Pietro loves everything I'm indifferent about, and everything I hate.

Spring, 2008. Pietro is buying the last missing pieces of furniture for the new house. Minnie is with us. We see her often — she stops by whenever she has voice-over work at the studio behind our apartment. I like her. I like how quickly she gets worked up about everything and anything. Most of the time, her visits involve sitting on the couch and talking to Pietro for hours, chain-smoking cigarettes until the two of them disappear into a dense, stinging nebula that fills the apartment and makes my breath catch in my throat. I think to myself how dedicated they are to giving themselves lung cancer, and it almost feels like a wish.

I stopped smoking because of yoga. I started relatively late, anyway, compared to most people I know, and the habit never really stuck. I quit as an act of self-purification. To continue felt nonsensical, like spending time and money on a nice hot bath then walking back home through the mud.

No cigarettes, no drugs: when I get the flu, I heal myself by swallowing whole garlic cloves and chewing thick slices of raw ginger. I wear activewear all day, every day, even in formal situations. I'm hypersensitive to anything that limits the movement of my joints — I wear only stretch fabrics with soft, pliable seams. Nothing must impede my prodigious flexibility.

After meat and fish, I begin eliminating all animal products from my diet. *Yoga is a life practice, both on and off the mat.* Pure, I must be pure. Sometimes, I let myself stumble off the path. Pietro tempts me, and I surrender. I find myself at the McDonald's on Corso Buenos Aires, devouring the biggest burger on the menu: half a kilo of sin. Bacon, ketchup, nuggets, fries. The artificial flavours and saturated fats leave me buzzing. For a few days afterwards, I binge on dairy — burrata, stracciatella, grilled tomini — before the regret hits. My teacher's warnings rattle around inside my head: *Do you know how many years, how many decades, it takes to eliminate a single particle of fried food from your body?*

In the Ashtanga yoga tradition — the strictest, but also the most egotistical, according to its critics — yogis must practise six days a week. The commitment is firm, ineluctable. We're allowed one day of rest a week. The only valid reasons for breaking this commitment are high fever, new moon (energy deficit), and full moon (excess energy). We practise for two or three hours every day, like athletes. If something comes up and I'm unable to make it to class, I feel furious, desperate, like everything is ruined. I get the urge to smash plates and windows. Sometimes I actually do it, a tumbler slipping from my hand like a little glass grenade. *Look what you made me do!* I take everything out on Pietro. I slam doors, I don't speak to him for days, I get out of the car without saying goodbye. It's all his fault — his laziness and defeatism are infectious. I'm racing towards perfection, towards optimal efficiency, and he is slowing me down just by being there. He is my handicap.

On public holidays, when the yoga studio is closed, I practise at home on my own. Sometimes the motivation comes easily, other times it doesn't. If it's too cold, for example — yoga was born in India, it's meant to be practised in forty-degree heat — I have to turn the heater up all the way, until it's roaring like a jet engine, and lower all the blinds, so the room is filled with warm air. I try to recreate the climate of Rishikesh, construct my own yogic temple in the middle of Milan. The windowpanes fog up; condensation forms little puddles on the floor. Everything is contaminated — I have to sweat it all out. Pietro complains, says I'm running up the power bill.

It's not my fault this apartment is so draughty, I answer. *You should have chosen a better one.*

As we're walking through the homewares section, Minnie updates us on her love life. Ruggero, the theatre director she's been with for four or five years, treats her like shit. They were in the mountains last week, in Valle d'Aosta. A couple's getaway. They had a fight, and as punishment he locked her outside on the balcony.

He locked you outside on the balcony?

For an hour and a half. Without my phone. It was freezing. I should fucking leave him.

You don't necessarily see it at first glance, but Minnie is a walking paradox. Her nun-like appearance — straight, shoulder-length chestnut hair, porcelain-white skin, cheap glasses, United Colors of Benetton knits — belies an inexhaustible, chaotic energy. She plays with contradiction, by turns demure and obscene, fearful and foolhardy. Still waters run deep, as my nonna Bina would say. And in fact, Minnie's star sign is Cancer: a water sign, governed by the moon. Just like the moon, there's a side to Minnie that is perpetually bathed in light, and then there's a dim, mysterious side, from which signals arrive only intermittently. Her life is always running on two parallel tracks: alongside her relationship with Ruggero flows a constant river of new flirtations and re-emerging ex-boyfriends. She feeds off the thousands of mini dramas, laughs about them, cries over them. All the while, her long-term partnership is forever on the verge of breaking down, but never does. Pietro does his best to encourage the inevitable split — he hates Ruggero. But the truth is, Minnie relies on Ruggero for contacts, job opportunities, and that is hard to give up. She assists him on projects at all the big theatres: the Piccolo, the Franco Parenti. Despite everything, she wants to get married, maybe even have kids, but he keeps resisting, delaying. Minnie perseveres, indulging the odd distraction on the side. Maybe she does love him, in her own way, or at least did, used to. For now, she takes whatever Ruggero has to offer and fulfils the rest of her needs elsewhere.

Summer, then autumn, 2008.

The neighbourhood around Gorla Metro station — Turro, Piazza dei Piccoli Martiri, Viale Monza — becomes my new ecosystem.

Vibrant and shabby, the area is home to large South American and Chinese communities, and to Pasticceria Scaringi, my new breakfast spot. In five minutes you're in Loreto, ten and you're in Porta Venezia. Even before it becomes trendy — before it earns the nickname NOLO, short for North of Loreto — the neighbourhood is beginning to fall prey to property speculators. A few metro stops down from us are the headquarters of disgraced celebrities Lele Mora and Fabrizio Corona. When I discover it, I'm ecstatic. I slow my pace whenever I walk past, wanting to be noticed — could this be the start of a new career? There's always activity outside the building, tv personalities coming and going. One day, I spot Iva Zanicchi wearing a fuchsia suit. The evidence is clear: this is the centre of the universe. I have officially crossed over to the other side.

Viale Monza is safer and more well off than neighbouring Via Padova. The only time it's not so safe is in the early evening, when the Metro station floods with pickpockets stalking home-bound commuters. They shadow people as they disembark from trains, follow them through the turnstiles, then pass them on the stairs, slipping a quiet hand into bags and backpacks. You don't even notice them — they're as swift and discreet as ghosts. The Metro staff do nothing, remaining aloof inside their little booths, pretending nothing's wrong. I carry my backpack on my chest, like a marsupial with its young, and miss Rozzano. This, too, is Milan. Milan is everything at once.

My new home — I open my arms wide, embrace it all.

On my Facebook page, I write (after Pia de' Tolomei): *Rozzano made me, Milan unmade me.*

Unmakings aside: I have an apartment in Milan. When we paint the walls, I choose the colours myself: acid yellow in the lounge room and kitchenette, lobster red in the bedroom. I get to choose the furniture, too. Naturally, Pietro pays for it.

Pietro takes care of everything. When he fails — when he denies me something I want — my body overflows with anger. On Saturdays, when we do the shopping together, I demand certain, specific foods in accordance with my strict new diet. I've become fanatical about nutrition. When we eat out, despite giving the waiter extremely precise instructions about how my meal is to be prepared, I inspect the food closely before eating it, sniffing the plate like a hound dog or a truffle pig. I examine the colour, the consistency, the reflections thrown by the oils, looking for the telltale opacity of butter. *You can't trust them.* The rare times I do the shopping on my own, I go to the organic supermarket and pluck items from shelves without even looking at the price. If Pietro touches any of my organic fare, I lose it. *Eat your junk.* By which I mean: your delicious snack foods, your chips and biscuits packed with mono- and diglycerides of fatty acids. All that stuff I can't have. Pietro eats everything and anything. Gradually, his appetite grows, becomes uncontrollable. My orthorexia is matched by his emotional eating. His body begins to change, and I withdraw even more from his attempts at intimacy, shrugging off hugs and touches with feigned playfulness. In bed, in the evenings — and in the mornings, on his days off — I lie there and silently pray he's not in the mood..

There's only one thing missing from our domestic scene: a pet.

Not the reptiles and insects Pietro had in Via Porpora — he got rid of them before we moved. Those enormous terrariums would have taken up precious space we needed for furniture. The bearded dragons, python, and praying mantis disappear, and I don't ask any questions.

What we need is a puppy. I time my request as well as I can —

in the evening, in bed — and use my little girl's voice: Pietro, can we get a puppy?

His response is terse: No. Absolutely not.

I persist: A kitty?

I said no. Anyway, I'm allergic to cats.

What about a hairless cat?

Hair has nothing to do with it, he tells me; he's allergic to something in their saliva. But the possibilities are endless in the mammalian kingdom: one Sunday afternoon, at a reptile market somewhere on the outskirts of the city, I'm mesmerised by a clutch of Vietnamese Pot-bellied piglets. They're for sale, crammed into a tiny cage.

Pietro, look, the little black one is gorgeous — can we get him? Please?

I imagine myself walking a little pig on a leash, like George Clooney.

Then I imagine us in our one-bedroom apartment, with a farmyard pig the size of a couch, shitting and pissing all over the floor. We'll have to get rid of all that excrement. Inevitably, we'll have to get rid of the pig, too. If only we had a garden — Pietro, can we look for a place with a garden?

In spite of myself, I give up on the pig. I return to the cat idea, and double down. I spend entire days researching breeds on the internet, and finally I find something: Devon Rex. My favourite breed, I decide on the spot. They're unusual, unlike anything I've ever seen: sinuous bodies covered in short, wavy hair; gigantic eyes and ears. They look like they were designed by Egon Schiele. Their name, the internet tells me, comes from the region where the breed's mutation first arose: *a cat belonging to Miss Beryl Cox — a white and tortoiseshell female living near a disused tin mine in Buckfastleigh, Devonshire — gave birth to a litter in which one kitten stood out for his long legs, pixie face, and curly blue-black coat.* I wonder: what kind of creature did Miss Cox's cat breed with down there in the mine? The legend has a gruesome, chthonic element to it that I'm drawn to.

Pietro takes some allergy tests and learns that, actually, his reaction to cats is only mild. And this lithe, stark breed is growing on him — he likes them, I can tell. It's all but a done deal. Online, I track down a veterinarian in Milan who breeds them. *You're lucky*, she writes, *two were just born, a male and a female.*

The male has already been reserved — in any case, I prefer the female. I've always liked women better.

Eight hundred euros, including sterilisation, the vet-slash-breeder explains to me over the telephone. Or a thousand without sterilisation.

I meet her on my own, without Pietro, at an apartment in Via Plinio — the home of the owner of the mother of the kittens. The vet is in her fifties, with platinum-blonde hair streaked with blue, and faded tribal tattoos on her arms. Her breeding program seems fairly laid-back, more like a hobby shared among various friends and acquaintances. She leads me into the bedroom and lifts the duvet on the bed. Underneath are two tiny, wrinkled aliens, about twenty centimetres long. They look like figurines carved in rosewood. They're sleeping, snuggled together in the shape of an upside-down heart. Yin and yang. This, right here, is true love. The vet mentions weaning, and vaccinations. My kitten will need to spend at least another month with her mother before I can take her home.

You have to be vigilant every time you open the front door, the vet says as she's seeing me off. These cats are escape artists. They like to run away. They're hyperactive, curious. Their temperament is even more peculiar than their appearance.

Once the month is over — the sweetest waiting game imaginable — I return to the apartment in Via Plinio to pick her up. From that moment, Rosaspina (Spina, for short) becomes the centre of my universe. I cradle her in my arms morning, noon and night. I leave the house as little as possible, if at all. She couldn't weigh more than a kilo and a half. Grey, with a violet sheen, her fur like some kind of velvety bouclé fabric. Emerald-green eyes, the colour around the almond-shaped pupil lightly textured, like the skies of Dante's paradise in Gustave Doré's sketches. Her large ears are two pointed parabolic dishes, like a Furby's, or like Gizmo from *Gremlins*.

She's stunning, the breeder says as she hands her over. It's a pity she's a little small for the breed's standard, otherwise you could show her.

Small? Why? Is she a runt? Is she sick? Underdeveloped? No — only petite, miniature, doll-like, like all the rarest and most special things.

I'm completely enchanted by her. Bewitched. I take hundreds of photos of us together and post them on Facebook. She is the most beautiful, dazzling reward for the compromise I've chosen. Compensation for my sacrifice.

After ten days, the breeder calls: You wouldn't want to take her brother, too, by any chance?

She explains that the guys who reserved him had a change of heart, backed out of the arrangement. The kitten is all alone, practically an orphan.

If you don't want him, she says, the sire's owner will take him to Switzerland.

Rosaspina's brother is going cheap; she'll let me have him half price. I'm ecstatic at first, then I rethink it. My thing is absolute love, monomania. I crave the exclusivity of an only child. And then there's his face, which I don't like at all — he's much less beautiful than his sister. But Pietro wants him. He's addicted. Rosaspina has turned him into a cat person. So we take him.

Rosaspina and León: two siblings under one roof.

The perfect family.

Moving into a new physical space means moving into a new headspace, attuning to a new psychic pitch. The fresh start offered by the change of apartment sets a virtuous cycle in motion. Pietro finally dedicates himself to a project of his own: designing sets, props, and costumes for theatrical workshops in retirement and nursing homes. He secures some online funding and decides to go into business with Minnie and Lorenzo (another actor friend of theirs). The original idea — let it be known — was actually mine. I have a gift for identifying and correcting the paths of others. I give them the directions, and all they have to do is apply themselves. Persist. Do the one thing I'm incapable of. By helping Pietro find his calling, I convince myself I'm doing my part to correct the imbalance in our relationship. To avoid eating the *bread of shame*, as the Kabbalah calls it: the fruits of a fortune that has not been earnt. *Do ut des*: reciprocity, mutual benefit.

For months now, Pietro had been gritting his teeth through a particularly ungratifying collaborative project. Entire weeks on the road, loading and unloading sets and props from the minibus, breaking his back for someone else's dream.

Why don't you start your own thing? I suggested.

Pietro has never told me this — not in so many words, at least

— but he trusts me. And the conditions for success are all there: Minnie, Pietro, and Lorenzo's families all have contacts and acquaintances across the region. A dense and reliable network: in Italy, this much is essential. So they decide to take the plunge. They start a business. They register for a tax identification number, make it official. One corner of our apartment becomes an office, a dream factory in which to assemble the future.

Minnie finds an excuse to visit our apartment practically every day. This is how it will always be. Until it isn't.

My relationship with Pietro is sustained by the wide, strong circle of his friendships. Minnie, Lorenzo, Giulia, Massimo, Fabio, Corte — I am more their boyfriend than his. I feed on their voices, expand to meet them: their stories, their laughter, their raucous lunches and dinners. When they leave, the apartment feels empty. *Don't go, you just got here!* I want to get on my knees and beg them to stay: *Please don't leave me, don't leave me here alone with this mistake I've made.*

I renounce individuality. I am not in a relationship with one person, I am in a relationship with my new life. This is a collective project, a collaborative love story.

Via Festa del Perdono

Autumn, 2008. I re-enrol to study. At La Statale, this time. A public university. Like cures like, as the saying goes.

The tuition is a lot cheaper, but not free. Even if you're eligible for a scholarship, you have to pay the first semester's instalment. It will be reimbursed a few months later. My mother objects: *And if we can't pay it? What do we do, steal it?*

The money set aside from my birthday isn't enough, so I ask Pietro. I say: Would you maybe be able to lend it to me? But we both know he's never getting that money back. I enrol in communication sciences. It's decided: I'm going to be a journalist. Hotly anticipated weekly columns, memorable interviews with the greats of our time, must-read books that top all the nonfiction bestseller lists.

This bold new vision of the future lasts a little less than a month. After two weeks, my aesthetics teacher (he dumbs down the course for non-philosophers) unexpectedly projects a series of slides on Edmund Husserl, the so-called father of phenomenology — *back to the things themselves*; i.e. thinking is not about limiting oneself to the study of books, to the repetition of old ideas — and I feel a flame of nostalgia ignite in me. Husserl is followed by Max Scheler and his 'material ethics of value': *the values of things are given to us prior to and independent of pictorial representations*: i.e. the cosmos is brimming with meaning. My destiny appears to me, as if in a clear beam of light. Ladies and Gentlemen, this is it. My true calling.

For real, this time.

It's decided.

I go to the student administration office and request the paperwork to change degrees. I'm going back to philosophy. Shortly after I begin attending classes, I find a new mentor: Laura Boella, a professor of moral philosophy specialising in Hannah Arendt and empathy. Professor Boella renews my obsession with female philosophers. I start dreaming of the possibilities: I'll be her research assistant, her protégé, then, eventually, her successor. I devour every one of her books — *Thinking Hearts; Unforgivable*; *Feeling the Other* — and attend all her seminars and labs. She teaches me about the relationship between Heidegger and Arendt, the relationship between freedom and action, Arendt's notion of catastrophe and its implications for environmental ethics. If it weren't for Professor Boella, and the thinkers she introduced me to, I'm certain I would have given up on philosophy again. Their words are the place, the only place, in which I can exist. The words of women philosophers, who have expressed their ideas through minor, non-canonical forms — letters, diaries, prefaces and commentaries annexed to the work of others — without renouncing their first-person subjectivity. Using lived experience to intercept eidetic structures and essential meanings: Simone Weil's work on the dignity of labour; Edith Stein's 'dark night'; Hannah Arendt's exile, her stare into the abyss of Nazism. And, at the heart of everything, the fundamental, irrevocable female body. I feel a spontaneous, exalted kind of reverse sexism blooming inside me.

I attend classes at the campus on Via Festa del Perdono, then head to the Via Noto campus to study for exams with Melissa and Ismene. There and back, it adds up to an extra hour on the tram every day, travelling from central Milan to the end of Via Ripamonti, right at the edge of the city, towards the southern periphery, just a few hundred metres as the crow flies from the border with Rozzano. It's a ridiculous and unnecessary commute — I could just study at my own campus, near the Duomo, like everyone else. I have a wealth of libraries and study rooms at my disposal. But I'd be studying alone, and motivating myself would be impossible.

I have an overexcited, pliable mind. I am a distracted little monkey. In order to follow through with anything, I need company, other people like pins to keep everything in place. Others are my exoskeleton. They contain me, they quell the constant feeling of dissatisfaction. From this dependence stems the incipient urge to demolish the myth of my own autonomy: I am the most social creature on Earth; I am pure performance. Without the presence of others, all I can do is light fuses. I am incapable of finishing anything.

At the Via Noto campus, I'm a fish out of water. A philosophy student who spends all his time with art-history students. I'm an intruder, a stowaway, forever afraid the porters will notice I'm not meant to be there and kick me out. I learn the styles of various painters and sculptors by osmosis (Gaudenzio Ferrari paints his Madonnas with red hair; Perugino's have tiny rosebud mouths). Over the course of any given afternoon, I hear more about schools and movements of painting than I do about philosophy. But I do better, it seems, when I'm the exception. I require a strong figure–ground contrast.

Melissa and Ismene set up our study space on the fifth floor — the top floor — in the media library, where there are PCs we can use to access the online materials uploaded by our professors. Our little nook is always crowded with disposable coffee cups from the vending machine, and dirty Tupperware from lunch. In the warmer months, I hang the sweaty contents of my yoga bag out to dry on the fire escape, purple and yellow cotton dancing in the wind, while around us sweeps the morose silence of the outer suburbs, nothing but warehouses and construction sites and empty fields.

We waste a lot of time, but the routine of our study sessions eventually has an impact. I depend completely on the presence — both concrete and ideal — of Melissa and Ismene. It's only thanks to them that I sit, one after the other, every single one of my first-year exams. When I falter, when my mind starts getting scattered because there are too many thoughts in there, Melissa is the one to bring me back to Earth. She has what seems to me like a superpower: the ability to focus on one thing at a time. She simply decides what to apply her attention to and gets on with it. Everything she does follows a straight, logical line, from A to B. My line, on the other hand, is a labyrinth of digressions, alternatives, and second thoughts. Melissa keeps my tendencies under control. It feels like an abnegation, like putting blinders on, but it's the only way to move forward. In order to progress, I have to suppress a part of myself. Success demands omission, sacrifice. Adulthood as amputation.

Δ

Via Noto is a small campus, like a small town. Everyone knows everyone. At Festa del Perdono, I'm utterly alone, despite the constant tide of human bodies surging around me (in some of my lecture theatres, there's not even room to sit on the floor; *every boy and his dog is a university student nowadays*). I walk in, take notes, then leave, speaking to no one, avoiding eye contact like I'm navigating a hall full of Gorgons.

Via Noto is different. We spend the breaks together in open, ever-changing groups: Gianfranco, Alessandro, Elena, Nina, Silvia, Silvia, Silvia (every second art-history student is named Silvia), Camilla, Tobia. Melissa and Ismene's favourite friends become my favourites, too. I'm the kind of person who can be either very timid or very talkative, depending on who I'm around. A chameleon, a mood ring, easily contaminated by the energy of others, which suggests that my own energy, my own identity, is non-existent. There is nothing to me. I have no control over things, I simply *join in*. My social life is entirely dependent on the initiative of others; it's only by chance that I have any friends at all. Companionship is a fluke of circumstance, or else a second-hand gift.

Via Noto has a kind of genius loci, in the form of Gabriele. Gabriele is a forty-something alumni who graduated about twenty years ago, the son of faculty staff. We often see him racing through the corridors, up and down the stairwells, dripping with sweat in the summer months. He has a prodigious memory for facts and dates, and knows practically everything there is to know about fifteenth- and sixteenth-century art history. He tours the classrooms brandishing an old tourist guide that's falling to pieces, full of loose pages and unidentified stains. He's in the habit of forming obsessions with certain female students, and although he's been warned to contain himself, he makes the occasional inappropriate comment before running to the restroom to masturbate — he confesses as much, in a completely neutral tone of voice, after the fact. Among our group of friends, Nina is the object of his obsession. Nina has an enormous rose tattoo on her arm, is passionate about contemporary art, and is writing a thesis on vandalism. One afternoon, during a break, Nina, smoking her hundredth cigarette of the day, tells us in hushed tones that, last night, Gabrielle came into the Via Tadino gallery where she's setting up her exhibition and pissed everywhere. He'd already left by the time she discovered the scene of the crime — *can you imagine? I wanted to die.*

I like being at Via Noto. I need it. But Gabriele ruins everything. Melissa and Ismene find him annoying, but not unbearable. Apparently I'm the only one who finds his presence paralysing. Now I understand why: I'm scared of Gabriele. Why doesn't someone keep him in check? Can't we organise some kind of petition, collect signatures, hold a protest? Hasn't anyone thought of calling the police? The porters and professors are against it: this is the only place Gabriele feels safe, where he can remain calm; we need to be patient with him. My heart, so full of performative compassion, is as cold as a stone.

Eventually, couples begin to emerge. Pietro and I start hanging out regularly with Melissa and her boyfriend, Christian. We drive out to the mountains and stay at Pietro's parents' place in the hills of Piacenza, where we while away the weekend together eating polenta and going for walks. In Milan, we often invite each other over for dinner. Christian and Pietro get along well. They share certain 'masculine' interests: being in the woods, picking mushrooms, things like that. Melissa grows fond of Pietro, too. Me? I love Pietro like a friend, or a big brother, or a mentor, or a father. Whatever you do, please don't call him my *boyfriend*. I can stomach *companion* — a nice, gentle word that keeps everything at arm's length.

In the mountains, we take photos of ourselves walking along trails, with meadows and valleys yawning all around us. The photos look like scenes from *Dawson's Creek*. The only thing I want to erase from them is Pietro. I want to cut him out and replace him with someone else. Over time, what began as an experiment between us has settled into something immovable. It has set deep roots, like a weed, and keeps growing, completely independent of me. What began as a flexible, flowing thing has solidified into a wall, a tower, a fortress. My small, private decision transformed into a contract, a conspiracy. Everyone took me at my word — they believe us.

They all think I'm in love with him.

On the upside: I live in Milan.

I return to Rozzano as little as possible, for Saturday or Sunday lunch, when I know Ivano won't be there. I go alone: I will never introduce Pietro to my mother. I'm embarrassed, both of Pietro and of the place I grew up in.

I don't pay rent or bills in Milan. As if to compete with Pietro's generosity, my mother always sends me home from lunch well stocked. My nonna contributes, too. Between them, they prepare enormous canvas bags — the kind they take to the market — brimming with food: parmigiana, torta di scarola, spaghetti with olives and capers, all neatly packaged and secured with Scotch tape and elastic bands, so the oils and sauces don't spill everywhere (it happens anyway). Each week we replay the same scene, a miniature version of the migration from South to North that brought my maternal grandparents to Rozzano. From the margins to the centre, to the land of hope.

For my family, Milan is a distant, alien place. When my nonna says *a Milano*, she makes a grand gesture with her hand that suggests enormous distance, across oceans and deserts. My mother won't even ride the Metro. She's terrified of being underground — it's like being in a coffin, she says.

Be careful when you go into the city. Statt' accort'. Don't trust anyone.

Occasionally, when I'm in Rozzano, I visit my other nonna. My father's mother. She's no longer with Giancarlo, the nightwatchman at the camping ground in Pietra Ligure. She tells me she caught him chatting to other women online. Now nonna Bina lives with a dog.

Not long after the departure of Gian, Pepe arrived: a frenetic mongrel, medium-sized, pitch black with a white belly. Nonna Bina's daughter, my aunt, picked him up from the pound. A dog to replace a man.

The days I visit nonna Bina for lunch, she sets the table in the dining room, like she would for Easter. The food is amazing, although I habitually find Pepe's long, thick black hairs distributed throughout the dishes — at least three or four strands in each. I can't bring myself to mention it to her, I know she'll be embarrassed, so as soon as she turns away or returns to the kitchen I remove them with my fingers, transfer them to a napkin, fold the napkin neatly, and continue eating. If I miss a hair or two, it's not the end of the world.

I think of it as a kind of communion: the body of Pepe, amen.

Rozzano no longer exists for me. If I can't see it, it's not there.

I visit, I pass through, but as far as I'm concerned, Rozzano is a ghost.

People tell me it's changed. *The usual shit, but now it's full of foreigners. They eat the coypu in the canals, and live ten to an apartment.* These dreaded interlopers come from China, the Middle East, South America. The shops I knew from the Nineties have all but disappeared, and in their place have emerged nail salons, hair salons, halal butchers. But, at a glance, Rozzano looks exactly the same. The peeling façades of the public housing towers still form gigantic, almost geographical shapes against the horizon, entire atlases sketched in crumbling plaster. Which is ironic, considering no one here ever travels anywhere (my mother has gone as far as Lugano, an hour's drive away, and even then only a handful of times).

The distinguishing features of Rozzano are repeated all over Milan, not just on the outskirts but in the city centre, too. Baggio, Quarto Oggiaro, Corvetto, Giambellino, Via Gola, Barona, Stadera: marginal spaces lurking like spiders even within the boundaries of fashion Milan, finance Milan, publishing Milan. The city's external and internal peripheries. 'Difficult' neighbourhoods. Museums of poverty.

Milan's public housing towers, concentrated near the city's industrial zones, were built in the Fifties, Sixties, and Seventies to house the waves of new workers migrating from the South. Entire neighbourhoods, entire municipalities of public housing. When the factories closed, the communities erected around them lost their meaning. Since then, no institution or administration has been able, or willing, to transform them. What began as hasty solutions scattered across the urban fabric — or at its hems — soon deteriorated into ugly, outdated stains, places to be avoided, shunned, denigrated. Self-fulfilling prophecies.

All of Rozzano's public housing towers look the same: tall columns of tiny balconies crammed with broken furniture and cheap clothes-drying racks, overlooking a central courtyard like a stage on which all kinds of sordid dramas play out, day and night. Arguments, altercations, acts of jealousy or retribution. Gunshots, stab wounds. There was even an execution, once, to avenge a granddaughter abused by her father-in-law (I read about it in the crime pages). There are also plenty of decent people in Rozzano. But here, their presence needs to be stated, specified.

To be fair, some efforts have been made to fix Rozzano's public housing. At a certain point, aesthetic renovations were undertaken: a fresh lick of paint in a different colour, minor restoration of the crumbling facades. We're not animals, after all. A handful of buildings were done up — the most prominent ones, the ones visible from the ring road — but the project was abandoned when the money ran out. All it amounted to was a kind of suburban-scale window-dressing. A farce. Meanwhile, the rest of the buildings continued to fall apart.

So many years passed between renovations that, by the time the project was renewed, even the redeveloped buildings had begun to deteriorate again.

Rozzano is a closed loop, a sealed ecosystem.

Qua le cose so' fatt' senz'ammor', my nonna Lilli likes to say.

Here, things are done without love.

It's enough to make you want to explode; *ce fann' schiattà in cuorp'*.

Rozzano never changes. And even when it changes, it looks the same to me. Whenever I return, my feet seem to move on their own, like in the Hans Christian Andersen fairytale. It's as if, underneath the asphalt, there were a magnet dragging me along, like the ones in the floor of the fancy dollhouses I craved as a kid.

I know everything about this maimed, ill-tempered village. I know too much about it, every street, every corner, every shortcut. I know all its parkettes, down to the last flower bed. I have my own secret paths, long detours carved to evade the company of my peers, the Rozzanesi youths who cosplay as rappers, wearing clothes pilfered from market stalls, for whom I will always be an anomaly, a freak, a punching bag.

I try to erase Rozzano, extract it from my cerebral cortex. I return for lunch on weekends and leave as soon as the meal is over. I complete the short trajectory from the number 15 tram terminus to my mother's apartment at a brisk pace. No reminiscing, no nostalgia. I form the opinion that the climate, the air itself, is different in Milan. Superior. More nourishing for the psyche. Milan is better in every way; Milan saved me. The city is not a paradise, an oasis for the blessed few, but a melting pot where everything is commingled. Hybridity is an opportunity for rebirth. The constant fusions of the city — the wealthy alongside the destitute, students and lawyers and entrepreneurs all walking the same streets — allow for the possibility of disappearing and reappearing at will. Camouflage, dissolution. Freedom.

Sitting on one of the brand-new, ice-white park benches on Via Mercalli, I read a line in my Environmental Ethics coursebook from Californian essayist Rebecca Solnit: *democracy is based upon trust in strangers.* Big cities, she writes, are unique in possessing public spaces where this trust can flourish.

I frame her sentence with a single, neat pencil stroke.

Next to it, I leave a small heart.

Via Morgagni

I turn the key in the lock, and glance up before charging down the stairs. The passionflower vine has now colonised the entire façade of our apartment building. The virus-shaped blooms, lurid purple and white, keep multiplying, punctuating the dense green vine that creeps unchecked against the wall. *Flower of passion*: the favourite plant of the man who, to everyone but me, is my boyfriend. And to think that I was the one who gave him the plant in the first place, when we first moved here.

A familiar, throaty scream rings out: Bastardi!

The woman responsible lives in the building opposite, ten or so metres from our front door. An ectoplasm in a dressing-gown, white hair loose, grazing her knees. Already, this early in the morning, she's on the attack, half-obscured behind the thick wall of leaves shielding her balcony.

She spits on the ground, then elaborates: I'll blow you to smithereens!

She gets like this when she thinks she's being spied on. All it takes is a neighbour lingering too long on a balcony, or at a window. She heads inside for a moment, then returns wielding something — a rifle? a watering can?

I'm always on high alert. Horror stories follow me around like stray dogs, leaving a miasma everywhere I go. There are rumours, shared in hushed tones at the mailboxes, about our neighbour: one evening, many years ago, she was on an evening walk with her husband, on one of the streets lining the tracks of Central Station. They walked there often, out of habit, just to get out of the house. It was an unusually windy evening — apocalyptically windy, even, as if the world were about to collapse. Three or four men ambushed the couple in an alley, in a parking lot, in an underpass, and tried to have their way with her. Her husband froze — *can you believe it?* — and didn't even try to fight them off. A dog would have been more help. Somehow, she managed to escape on her own with only a few bites and scratches. *The Lord was watching over her.* She's never been the same since, the poor creature. She left her husband, naturally. That homunculus. Now she stays locked indoors, and never leaves the building. Not ever.

Another scream rings out: Mind your own damn business!

I emerge from the vine-shrouded entrance and begin walking in the direction of the Metro. Sucked back into the world. Being a part of things — that's all that matters to me.

Months become years. 2008, 2009, 2010. Pietro eats as if trying to fill a void. He eats when he's bored, when he's anxious, when he needs consoling, then attempts to counteract the weight gain with laxatives and fat-burning supplements. He empties his half of the pantry (we shop and eat separately), then lathers his body in slimming and anti-cellulite creams. He starts a series of strict diets, each lasting less than a day. Is this what happens when a person is starved of affection? His thighs and belly swell, his tattoos stretch — there are still only six; at a certain point, he abandoned the idea of a multilingual art collection. He hates his body, and so do I. He looks decades older than he is. Like so many sons of aged fathers, he is becoming an old man before his time. His personal hygiene lapses: nails bordered with black dirt, holes in his socks, infrequent showers, sad tufts of uncombed hair emerging from the sides of his skull.

In a long-term relationship, our self-image always ends up being influenced by, or even borrowed from, our partner's perception of us. If we're unappealing — or, worse, invisible — to our partner, then what do we have to hold on to?

At Christmas, we both write letters, adorned with cartoons, to Father Christmas. Within the cosy, domestic space of the couple — real or imagined — we regress to childhood. Pietro asks for invisible braces for his teeth, and liposuction. I could be his remedy, but instead I am an infection. I am bacteria poisoning his blood, I am a gangrenous limb. I'm afraid he'll make the connection, realise the correlation between his suffering and my indifference. How must it feel to build your whole life around a lie?

He starts to deteriorate mentally. He grows more obsessed with furniture and interior design. He's always been interested in it, but now it turns into a kind of mania. When I return to the apartment after a day of yoga and study, the layout is always different. Our home is a puzzle, a psychotic complement to our artificial relationship. Pietro is constantly rearranging, assembling and disassembling, making and regretting purchases. The couch ends up in the bedroom, the fridge makes a gradual migration around the apartment. He goes to IKEA every second day, hunting bargains, returning and exchanging goods. He discovers that the return policy is generous: six months, and the item doesn't even need to be faulty. A change of heart is sufficient. The sound of hammers against nails and drills in screws is ever-present. There is no peace, no consistency. The cats are continuously forced to update their mental catalogue of leapable, squeezable distances. It's as if Pietro is searching for a secret order, a perfect form that might repair the environment I'm sabotaging from within. Diverting the dark, foreboding subconscious onto a more practical plane. I complain — *don't you have anything better to do?* — but the beam of my attention is turned elsewhere. Towards my studies, my exams, my yoga. I'm much more focused on ensuring I'm as loved as possible elsewhere, everywhere.

I leave home at six in the morning, for yoga practice, then head directly to university. I don't return until seven or eight in the evening. When I get back, Pietro has already prepared dinner: hyperbolic plates of spaghetti drenched in Barilla sauce, at least three hundred grams of pasta per person, which I burn off easily, thanks to my vigorous daily workouts on the yoga mat.

You're too skinny, he says.

I think: *You're just jealous.*

Jealous of my small biceps, my slender ankles, my tight, compact abdomen, the defined pectorals that are now beginning to show under my t-shirts.

To me, Pietro and the house are opportunities. Tools. A clear violation of Kant's categorical imperative: *Act in such a way that you treat humanity, whether in your own person or in the person of any other, never merely as a means to an end, but always at the same time as an end.*

I avoid being seen with Pietro in public. I lie, make deliberately conflicting commitments, invent emergencies, all to get out of spending time with him. I'm embarrassed of him. I'm ashamed of the person I share my life with. We shouldn't be together. We have absolutely no reason to be together.

In the meantime, my hiding place grows more and more

precarious. The consequences of my intricate lies begin to close in around me. Pietro complains I don't help him with the cleaning — an epiphenomenon of my withdrawal, a symptom that can safely be named — and says he can't take it anymore. If I don't start pulling my weight, it's over. Crumbs and dust bunnies accumulate, the toilet seat turns crusty with piss. The house is disgusting, unbearable. I consider returning to Rozzano. Then he relents, repentant. These are the only occasions on which I greet his embrace with relief, although always as briefly as possible, in the densest darkness I can create. A brief moment of tension, against which I close my eyes and wait for it to be over. Like magic, the bond is renewed; Pietro is content.

One day, he asks: How would you feel about staying together, but living separately?

Being with Pietro sans apartment? Not a chance — what would be the point? This is my home now, my life. I think this, but I would never say it. It's not hard to convince him: I'll be better, I'll make an effort. I promise.

If we argue without making up, he takes refuge in bed, burying himself in blankets, swollen with tears. He stays there for days at a time, never showering or changing his clothes. I let him wallow. *Drama queen. Attention whore. He'll get over it.* I consider the possibility that he could do something stupid, like kill himself. I think about what I'd say to the police, the speech I'd give. *I had no idea he was so low. We were so happy. He* — a pause, a lump in my throat — *he was my whole world.*

At the lowest points in our relationship, the moments when I think it might really be over, I call my mother. She tells me (all of a sudden a marriage counsellor, an agony aunt) that it's normal. At a certain point, she says, despite how much two people love each other, they need a common project, a common goal. *Despite how much they love each other.* I decide to take her advice. I'll try anything. Pietro and I must remain united, welded. I just need to add another layer of binding. Introduce new elements to the relationship. Muddy the waters.

A common project, she suggested. At most, we'd make the occasional trip to a garden centre on the outskirts of the city, or go shopping for kitchen accessories and fantasise, in the aisles of some warehouse superstore, about our dream house.

Pietro starts seeing a life coach. Then a homeopath. Every surface in the apartment is soon crowded with tinctures and supplements, the contents and therapeutic purposes of which I don't bother to verify.

I ask him why he doesn't just go to the gym. He tells me it's too late for that. He's too far gone, he needs liposculpture — to prove it, he grabs a handful of fat from either side of his pelvis, and shakes the flesh in his hands.

In a sudden burst of optimism, he starts taking online Tai Chi classes. He's seeking my approval, my encouragement. Instead, I take aim and fire: Do you seriously think this shit is going to help you?

I'm not sure what he's been diagnosed with, exactly. I'm not sure if he's seeing a therapist, or a psychiatrist.

Every time we argue, I think I should just take my opportunity and leave him. Get it over with. But I don't want to go back to Rozzano, to that rat-hole of an apartment, the four of us crammed in like sardines, pinching pennies, listening to the screaming matches that intermittently drown out the sound of multiple televisions. Besides, I do feel something like affection for Pietro now, after all this time. The rituals of everyday life have grown into and around us, like mould on old fruit, creating a second skin that binds everything together: us, the apartment, our friends, our possessions. We are all one body. When I so much as think about leaving, alarm bells start sounding all around me, like an animistic symphony: the coffee cups, the furniture, the car, the cats — *my* cats. All singing in unison.

How can you
even contemplate
living without us?

The thought of detaching myself is like a razor slicing me from my guts to my throat.

Not now, I tell myself. Just a little longer.

A few more days, that's all.

A week, at most.

A month.

A year. Another year.

Often, after dinner, when Pietro is watching tv, I go to the other room to use the computer and chat to guys online. Some of the guys I know, others I don't. Regardless, they are avatars on which to project my pent-up desires. When Pietro is out working with Minnie and Lorenzo, I make plans to meet up with some of them — for a coffee during the day, a beer at night, or just sex, without preamble, here in the stairwell of our building (*shh, be quiet, come inside me*), or out in the courtyard, among the bushes and bicycles, three or four guys at a time, just to feel something, anything. But when the time comes, I never follow through with it. The most I end up doing is masturbating for them on camera, letting them transcribe their intentions in the chat, like the script from a porno: *What do you want to do to me? How do you like it? Lower the camera angle. Turn around, open your legs. That's it. Fucking slut.*

I did cheat on Pietro, once. Early on, ten or eleven months after we met.

Before moving into our own place, we lived separately for a month and a half. I went back to Rozzano, and he moved in with his parents. It was a necessary evil, a force majeure: renovations needed to be done on the new apartment. During those six weeks, we only saw each other two or three times. The distance between our bodies translated into greater expanses of empty time, more space for fantasies to luxuriate. I started chatting — online, naturally — with a guy. We made arrangements to meet for a coffee in the late afternoon. He arrived by bike, directly from work: khaki trousers, sandals, white shirt unbuttoned to his chest, revealing neat tufts of chest hair. He was tanned, bearded, slender, with dark eyes. Handsome, but not exactly my type.

Igor. Pleasure to meet you.

He dismounts from his bicycle and wheels it beside him, like a prince with his steed.

Shall we take a walk?

We talk, and I follow his lead, without paying much attention to the direction we're headed in. Corso Buenos Aires, Via Cadamosto, Piazzale Lavater. We find ourselves outside his apartment building.

Would you like to come up?

He works in the art and publishing worlds, frequents fancy nightclubs like Plastic. His small apartment reeks of money: parquet floors, expensive magazines, vinyl records hanging on the walls. I can feel my heart beating in the roof of my mouth and in my throat. *Yes* — my whole body is a single, oceanic *yes*. Taut, poised. *Multipotential*. In the presence of this urban prince, this young modern lord, I imagine what it would be like to stay here with him, to live in this palace, to be part of this life, this genuinely Milanese life of dinner parties and magazine subscriptions and aperitifs with gallery owners. I wonder how it would feel to be worth something, to have a front-row seat to the city. When he suddenly kisses me, the sensation is less an electric shock than an epileptic seizure. Some enormous, undeniable reaction occurs when our two bodies make contact.

I didn't want to do that, I'll repeat to myself afterwards, but we both knew it was inevitable. This is what I came for. I came all the way here, from Rozzano, for this purpose.

When he kisses me, I don't stop him. I can't. I don't want to. This is how a body feels when it's alive. This is a real kiss — it feels like the first kiss of my life, the first kiss in history, his mouth desiring, devouring. It's been so long since someone kissed me that way. Everything happens in a matter of minutes, both of us still partially clothed, in front of a window framing the pink clouds of Milan at sunset.

He asks: Can I fuck you?

Next time, I say.

He says: Sure.

My suspicion hardens into certainty — he doesn't give a shit about me, about this. I make him come with my hands and mouth, quickly, on his single bed, awkwardly positioned in the little space available, then we clean ourselves up with the tissues and citrus-scented wipes conveniently located on the bedside table. We put our clothes back on, eyes directed at the floor. What if he asks to see me again? A wasted thought. He only lifts his head to say: You remember the way out, right?

As I leave his beautiful apartment in Via Morgagni, the smell of what I've done seeps out of every pore in my skin. The sky is a gorgeous gradient, streaked with shafts of sunlight, and I am disgusting. My mother's oracle has finally been fulfilled: I am my father's son. I let this happen. Now I know how it feels to betray someone.

I try to forget about it immediately, bury everything in handfuls of dirt. I don't tell a soul. If I don't love Pietro, then why do I feel so bad? Where is all this caustic guilt gushing from? And what happens if, against all odds, the guy does get in touch with me again?

I make a promise to the asphalt under my feet, to the air: *Never again.* I slip on a pair of headphones and let Vasco Brondi take me away from myself. Nothing happened. I'll fix things. I'll just keep showing up, day after day.

Right there, on the footpath, I celebrate the funeral of my desire.

Autumn, 2010. Time keeps passing. Let's look at it objectively: you're twenty-three, almost twenty-four. The age when you should be stumbling on a love story, or at the very least sounding out the world around you, looking outwards, giving destiny space to work its magic. You've renounced your sins, you've made sacrifices. Now it's time to get your life back on track. While you're still young, while your meat is still fresh. Think about all the lives you could have — better lives, more suitable lives, lives filled with dinners and dates and nights out. The names of potential lovers form a nightly procession across Pietro's computer screen. Votive figures, beguiling prayer cards: the DJ, the contemporary dancer, the fashion photographer. You tell yourself you can't have it all. You place your trust in Saturn, the planet of limitation, deprivation.

And above all else, have restraint, which is the bond of perfection.

You periodically review your reasons for staying with him: Milan, the apartment, the free meals (let's not sugar-coat this), all the time and space you could ask for, all the peace and quiet you require. The companionship — it may not be love, but it's still worth something. Four years, now, of cohabitation. Forty-eight months. One thousand four hundred and sixty days. Approximately thirty-five thousand hours of endurance.

I'm so sorry, Pietro. I really don't know how to do this.

I need to be free, not just of you, but also of the expectations of others. My mother's, even though she's never met you. Your friends'. Mine. The constant roar of voices, opinions, demands. It's my body against all of theirs, my sixty-six meagre kilos against their tonne of inquisitive flesh. I have to push back, explain myself, lay out with care and persuasion my reasons for wounding a heart as good as yours.

But why? they'll say. *I was so fond of him.*

I wish I could disappear into thin air, *poof*, with the flick of a magician's cape, without getting my hands dirty. I find myself thinking that, if only you would just die suddenly — if only that defective heart of yours would just give out — then everything would be so much easier.

I keep thinking I'll reach a breaking point, but it never arrives. Arguments and crises aren't enough: they swell and pass like storms, and the old arrangements remain in place each time, thick roots cemented into place with tar.

Then, as if everything weren't already terrible enough.

January 2011.

Sirens. Flashing lights.

Your phone ringing and ringing, with no answer.

Via Mac Mahon

Minnie dies on the second-last day of January.

It's actually the traffic lights that kill her. The strike to the back of the head.

It's a Sunday evening. The Sunday traffic restrictions were only lifted about an hour ago, and cars are circulating as normal again. Minnie and Ruggero are standing on the footpath, at a pedestrian crossing. Fresh from a weekend out of the city, they make a last-minute decision to spend the night in Minnie's brand-new apartment (a purchase made possible thanks to a little help from her father, an entrepreneur from Lodi). The apartment is a tiny studio in Via Mac Mahon, in the north-west of the city, the same neighbourhood my mother's sister lived in when she first escaped from Rozzano. Minnie hasn't moved in permanently yet, there are still a few details left to organise, but the bulk of the move is done. She's proud of her new place, she talks about it all the time: her first home. She recently bought a couch, and last week we visited the apartment to see it in situ.

Do you think it's too dark? She was holding the thick catalogue of fabric samples, scrutinising them. *There's still time to return it.*

She and Ruggero divide their time between his place, in Zona Fiera, and hers. This evening, 30 January 2011, as he's parking the car not far from her building, he says: Shall we order a pizza?

Sure.

I'll go.

I'll come with you.

You sure?

She's sure. Minnie is sure.

They decide to walk to the pizza place. It's just around the corner, a couple of minutes away. They stop at a red pedestrian light, at the corner of Via Monte Generoso and Viale Monte Ceneri, in the fog and drizzle. It's freezing cold. Two cars approach the intersection, one on Via Monte Generoso, one on Viale Monte Ceneri. Two cars like two bullets fired into the rain, on the second-last day of January. One of the cars should stop, but doesn't. They collide. One of the cars is lifted off the ground by the impact. How long does it all take? A second? Less than a second? Minnie and Ruggero see it happening, they have time to react. They move in different directions: he runs forward, towards the thin puddles in the road, and she turns back the way she came. There's no time to coordinate it, their movements are instinctive. Ruggero's instincts are right. Minnie's aren't: as she retreats, the traffic lights follow her. The pole, hit by the flying vehicle, collapses onto her. It's as if she measured the distance to the inch. The pole crashes cleanly into her skull, but only the back of it — her face remains perfect, intact. Her cousin assures us of this when he returns from identifying her body at the morgue.

She was twenty-nine years old.

Pietro has a few things to drop over at Minnie's place: a script, some paperwork. As he arrives, he sees a crowd of people under the Viale Monte Ceneri overpass. Red and blue lights turn everything violet.

There is Minnie — Viola — lying on the ground, dying, as Ruggero holds her. Dying in the arms of a man she might not even love. He is screaming, or crying, or perhaps he is silent, whispering small words to her. The emergency services arrived quickly, but uselessly. She didn't suffer, everyone says, repeating the words to each other like a prayer. She probably didn't even feel it.

I don't see any of this firsthand. I was at home, alone, when it happened.

Pietro had gone out immediately after dinner, calling: *Can you wash the dishes?*

An hour passes, then two hours. I try calling him to ask something. Once, twice, four times. The phone rings and rings, but he doesn't pick up. I sit down to revise for my theoretical philosophy exam. I set myself the task of re-reading at least half of my lecture notes. This is what I'm doing when my phone rings.

There's been an accident.

Pietro's voice sounds stuck in his throat.

Where?

...

Are you there?

Viola's gone.

Minnie's dead, and for an entire week, nine endless days, mourners come and go from her mother's house in Melegnano. I visit, reluctantly. I've always been useless in the face of other people's pain. But there's no getting out of it.

I arrive, and so begins the sequence of rehearsed moments I so desperately wanted to avoid. First comes the hug at the threshold of Minnie's mother's house, which I cross alone. Pietro and the rest of our friends are already there, arranged quietly on chairs, armchairs, couches. The hug is warm but artificial, as if performed for the benefit of observers. I suppose all suffering involves some degree of acting. Nothing about Minnie's mother — the hands clasped to her chest, the sharp bob framing her face — seems spontaneous. Maybe Minnie was a born actress. Maybe all she wanted was to turn a family trait into a profession.

I'd never been to the Melegnano house before. Now I see Minnie's childhood bedroom for the first time. A bed, a desk, a small bookshelf filled with photocopied scripts. She went to a liceo linguistico, a linguistic high school. That must be where she caught the theatre bug, I decide. No, I'm told, I will be told — it happened earlier. She started doing plays in middle school.

As I'm standing awkwardly in Minnie's bedroom, her mother walks in.

She'd dreamt of moving to Milan for so long, she says.

Pietro and I return home. It's early February. The days are heavy with shapeless grief — our own, others' — as we prepare for the funeral. The date is continually postponed, an everlasting wake, until someone finally makes the call: until this is done, there can be no healing, no moving forward.

In the meantime, we fuss over the details: which dress to put her in, which rose should keep her company in the casket.

Voices chase each other around in circles, repeating themselves.

So, one of the two drivers was drunk?

I don't want to see her. I want to remember her the way she was.

They're investigating it. Manslaughter, drink driving.

Do you think she should wear the hat?

The hat or the headband?
They both claim they had a green light.

The day of the burial arrives. I take the train alone, from Cadorna to Minnie's town. Pietro is already there. The large church, with its tall pews, is filled with friends, actors, classmates. The priest's words are less contrived than expected. He spares us some of the more edifying rhetoric, the one-size-fits-all homilies designed to transfigure our grief into some kind of mindless metaphysics. The triumphant organ, the smell of incense collecting in the nostrils, has a certain effect on the nervous system. The colour grey predominates — the only appropriate colour at a Catholic funeral, aside from predictable black.

Poor Minnie.

At Pietro's best friend's funeral, deep in the heart of the tragedy that has stopped everything in its tracks, one thought won't stop playing in my head: *I can't leave him now.*

In spite of their shock and pain, Pietro and Lorenzo have to make a decision: return to the stage, or cancel everything?

A second tranche of encore performances is scheduled for the coming weeks, at the theatre fifty metres from Minnie's house.

They weigh up their options, discuss it endlessly, then decide to go ahead with the performances. The show must go on. For Minnie. Theatre was her great passion, after all. She would want it this way, they say. In truth, the decision comes down to the indomitable ambition and narcissism of everyone else involved — theatre people will do anything for the applause of an audience. Perhaps, too, there is a certain curiosity: how will it feel to do this heartbreaking, unnatural thing, to violate all expectations of withdrawal? (Grief as a kind of mortification, or enclosure.)

Thanks to a rapid-fire series of auditions, they find an actress to replace Minnie. She might even be better, a more seasoned performer, but no one is brave enough to say this out loud. The audition process is a kind of ritual, a psychodramatic device. A method of distraction, or torture. Minnie's mother and father are both present for it, as are Minnie's colleagues from the dubbing studio, including, surely, a recent ex-lover or two.

As the first encore performance is in progress, one of the front-of-house staff whispers to me, in the twilight of the theatre.

Crazy, she says, how everything turned out. *Un coup de théâtre.*

She raises a balled-up tissue to her cheekbone — a gesture as affected as her French accent — and repeats: *Un coup de théâtre.*

Only those we leave behind will be able to say who we were, writes Hannah Arendt. As long as we reside among the living, our view of ourselves is distorted, since we can never perceive the fullness of our own form. Our autobiographies are flawed. *Authenticity* is a delusion; the mirror cannot reflect itself. Only after we exit the scene can all our loose ends be tied up, our character arc concluded. Then, and only then, those who were watching can review our performance. A person is a narrative that cannot be owned. We were made to be recomposed, to be retold by others.

Meanwhile, the nature of the spaces in our home has changed.

The positions Minnie used to occupy with her body — sitting, standing, moving between the rooms that grow more and more cramped by the day, filled to bursting with knock-off designer décor — have left imprints, traces. The gestures she made are renewed, more visible than before. Now that they can never be repeated, they fill the space differently, marking a trail into the great beyond, that final mysterious transformation. Our home holds inside it the miracle of her movements, the objects she interacted with, movements and objects that feel now like the relics of a shipwreck. I see Minnie on the white leather of the couch, caressing Rosaspina and León, the latter transfixed by the majestic roundness of her breasts, which she allows him to perch on, as if they were a windowsill. He liked to fall asleep up there. *Wait, don't move, let me take a photo.* The Madonna of the Cats.

The line from person to symbol is a thin thread, one that can unravel reality. I dedicate my thesis (on 'Symbolic Theology in the Work of Edith Stein', that is, on the ways in which perceptible phenomena allude to the unseen) to Minnie. Symbols are the easiest way — for some of us, the only way — to speak about what we might call *the divine.* The unearthly described in earthly terms. Aesthetic empathy: projecting life onto the inanimate.

On the page opposite the title page, I use her actual name and write: *For Viola, my unexpected lesson on the invisible.*

When a person leaves us, they become a total, omnipresent presence. How terrible that the only way to truly occupy the centre of others' lives and thoughts is to die.

February comes to an end, then March.

At first, everyone is crying all the time. As the months pass, we cry less and less.

We start making jokes again, laughing when we thought laughter was impossible, those first peals veiled with estrangement and guilt. People leave birthday wishes on Minnie's Facebook wall, as they will continue to do, year after year.

Always in my thoughts.

Holding you close.

Forever in my heart.

An ex-teacher from Minnie's theatre school is the most fervent online mourner. We nickname her Cloud Diva. She posts something at least once a week: photos from past shows and performances, mostly. Here's Minnie dressed as a nun for Carnevale. Here she is on stage, in the only wedding dress she'll ever wear.

I visit Minnie in the cemetery only once, a few weeks after the funeral. She is resting at the end of a leafy avenue, in a vast lawn dotted with tombstones.

I think how awful it would be if they buried me in Rozzano. Save me a spot — a cremation niche, at the very least — in the Cimitero Monumentale, or a nice Jewish cemetery.

My mother says: You expect us to travel all the way to Milan just to visit your grave?

Melissa says: The Monumentale? On what grounds?

Then, unexpectedly, Saint Minnie blesses me with her grace.

Minnie is my tooth fairy. Only, instead of taking my fallen baby teeth, she fixes my broken adult ones.

A few days after my visit to the graveyard, I learn, through eavesdropped fragments of Pietro's conversations, that one of Minnie's uncles is a dentist. He and his wife have a clinic in a little town not too far from Milan. I decide to take advantage of the bonds created in the wake of Minnie's accident — united in tragedy, we're practically family now — and ask him for a quote, hoping for the best. It pays off: he offers me everything at half-price. After an initial consultation, we arrange a busy schedule of appointments. Each week for a few months, I will take the train to Cadorna, and one by one, he will fix the ten cracked, decayed teeth in my mouth. At least three will need to be completely reconstructed, held together with titanium pins.

Can I pay in instalments? I ask.

Of course, he answers. Just pay me when you can.

This is the opportunity I've been waiting for. Growing up, there was no money to spend on fixing my teeth. My mother did the best she could, sending me to the public dental clinic, where the dentist could only dedicate ten minutes to each consultation. *There's just too many of you.* I remember the yellowed white vinyl of the dentist's chair, torn in places to reveal its foam-and-metal skeleton. The dentist didn't use anaesthesia unless absolutely necessary, and never for check-ups or quick fillings. He scraped, poked, and drilled into nerves without remorse.

Almost done, come on now. What a fuss.

Rather than return for more torture, I'd swallow boxes and boxes of ibuprofen whenever I got a toothache. If the throbbing pain returned, my mother would instruct me to rinse my mouth with baking soda. *It helps, trust me.*

April arrives, and Pietro is no longer sure he wants to continue with the theatre company. Minnie was the main motor behind the company, the antidote to Pietro's pessimism. Where he saw a half-empty glass, Minnie always saw an opportunity to fill it up to overflowing, usually against all odds and common sense. It was Minnie, always Minnie, who injected positivity and optimism into the thoughts of those around her.

And yet, eventually, somehow, a sense of normality returns.

Nothing is the same as it was — a truism, under the

circumstances. But what no one told me is that there can be sadness even in the loss of what was less than good, in the surprising new feeling of spaciousness, in the realisation that the catastrophe has become a historical fact, an event to be spoken about in the past tense.

This is happening. This happened.

Stillness returns. In the spring of 2011, Pietro and Lorenzo resume their full workload. And I take my own leap of faith.

I finally find the courage to tell Pietro the truth.

Corso Como

I am a parasite. My whole life is a lie. I've learnt to deceive the entire world, including myself. I traffic in false emotions, pushing them through the veins of others, trading tenderness for a roof over my head. I can look directly into the eyes of someone who trusts me wholly, without reservation, and lie to them, forcing the truth to the bottom of my throat, strangling it with both hands so it doesn't escape.

What depths would you sink to in order to keep this apartment in the centre of Milan? To keep your place at the centre of the universe?

Typical Gemini, born under the sign of Mercury, that sneaky, fleet-footed little god of trickery. Like him, I have no trouble separating truth from words. Go on, try it: roll them around in your hands a little. That's it. Sophistry is just like juggling. Now hurl them as far as you can — once they're in flight, no one can tell exactly where they came from.

In June, the month of my birth, the Sun in my birth chart returns to its starting position. Pietro and I have another argument — just the foothold I need. From there, I can reach up and tear cleanly through the fragile ceiling separating me from the world

I want to belong to, the world I want to return to. We're sitting on the couch, our two bodies reflected in the glossy doors of the kitchen cabinets Pietro had custom-made, back when things were bearable between us. This scene has played out countless times before. Only this time I don't relent. I'm not even sure why, exactly. Why now?

Are you saying you want to break up?

He's asked me this before. He thinks he's calling my bluff. Usually, he is.

I keep my eyes fixed on the future, on the pulsating promises of the life ahead of me, succulent fruits oozing endorphins. Then, steeling myself for the impact, I say: Yes.

It feels good. It feels like I'm calling things by their name for the first time. Like the reunion of signifier and signified. I half expect legions of angels to gather above me on balconies of clouds, pierced by spears of glorious sunlight, and break into song. My will be done. Today is my personal judgement day. I can feel the cardboard walls of my home-made penitentiary falling away. Beyond them is freedom: luxurious, boundless valleys of love and redemption. The stars in the sky can now realign, the planets can return to their rightful place. This is my Venus–Jupiter conjunction — the sidereal event I've been waiting for my whole life.

I tell him I care about him, but caring isn't enough.

How long have you known? Have you been faking it this whole time?

No. Yes. Why torture ourselves with questions like that? Look to the future; we have our whole lives ahead of us.

Pietro is annihilated, paralysed. He wasn't expecting this. For a whole week, he doesn't get out of bed except to go to the bathroom.

How do we do this? he asks me. How do we get through this? I thought we'd be together forever, I thought you were the one.

The two of us crying, leaking from eyes and noses.

I don't know, I don't know how to do this, but we have to.

It's better this way, I hear myself say. For both of us.

Clichés cushion the blow, form a buffer between us and the truth.

Do you mind if I stay here a while? I ask.

Here?

Yeah. I have to look for a job before I can afford another place.

Exhausted, he replies: I'll have to think about it.

I don't bring it up again. I simply act as if he'd agreed.

From now on, I have to focus on survival.

I'm on my own now.

I'm still receiving three hundred euros in child support from my father each month, but there's no way I can survive on that. Over the past four years, my mother has reorganised everything around her new family. Her real family: mamma, Ivano, and my sister, the three of them bonded by blood. Since I left Rozzano — since the foreign body was expelled — things have settled into an easier, more natural rhythm for them. They moved into a different apartment, and mamma spent ten thousand euros (*ten thousand fucking euros!*) on new furniture. The money was borrowed, she's quick to point out.

I can afford to give you fifty euros a month, she tells me over the phone. Okay, a hundred, but I can't manage more than that.

So that's four hundred a month, in total. Four hundred and fifty, say, if I count the little bits of pocket money I get from my grandparents. Nowhere near enough. My only concern is not being separated from Rosaspina and León. If it weren't for them, I'd give up and go back to Rozzano. Take the easy way out, let that place reabsorb me. But the cats can't live in Rozzano — there are already two dogs in the apartment, and Ivano has a habit of raising his hand against animals as well as women.

My mother's solution: worst-case scenario, Pietro can keep them.

Never, I answer.

And with that, my mind is made up.

My cats go where I go. They are the place where duty and pleasure, love and discipline converge. My first real responsibility, the only one I've ever been willing and able to handle. A psychotherapist will later suggest that I have projected my childhood self onto them. They are like reverse voodoo dolls, intermediary vessels through which to practise the white magic of healing. They are my teachers; they have taught me a lot. It's only for their sake that I learn to stop slipping away from myself, to be present. Pets — any pet will do, even a hamster — allow us to re-enact and reclaim the parental bond, to recreate the love and affection we were denied. A hamster is all it takes to cure the wounds of childhood.

For Rosaspina and León, only the best will do. I buy the most expensive, grain-free, single-protein cat food I can find (none of that poor-quality supermarket-brand shit). They drink bottled spring water, with the lowest mineral content possible (never tap water, which would give them kidney stones and kill them).

I enrol in a class on the theoretical pillars of animal liberation — Regan's *Empty Cages*, Derrida's *The Animal That Therefore I Am* — and by the end of it I'm logically and emotionally convinced by the philosophy of anti-speciesism. When I first stopped eating meat and animal products, it was in an attempt to eliminate impurities from my body. Now my motivation is different. It has something to do with the shared destiny of beasts and humans. Now I have a clear understanding of the industrialised animal holocaust committed, daily, by our society: millions of hot, yearning bodies crammed into trucks, corralled into lines, beaten and kicked, strung up from hooks, bled to death. Stunned with an electric current or a captive bolt to the skull. If you look hard enough, all sentient creatures exhibit personalities, expressions. They all have a face, as Levinas admitted. They are, to borrow Anna Maria Ortese's term, *little people*. My cats usher me into a larger circle of respect — an inductive embrace, reaching from the particular to the universal. My body reverberates with the same emotional rhythm that unites all living creatures, defying taxonomic rank, transcending species.

It's for their sake that I stay in Milan.

If I want to be with my cats, I'll have to figure out how to live independently. For the first time in my life.

My first thought is Piazza Trento, Milan's most famous prostitution hotspot. Let's think. Take a deep breath and work out the details. I'll leave the house in the evenings, around ten, say. I have a tight little yoga body, according to the guys who write to me in the gay chat rooms. The problem is, after doing a bit of research, I learn that Piazza Trento — the version I have in mind, at least — no longer exists. Sex work has moved online.

I've only been to Piazza Trento once, five or six years ago. The first summer after I graduated high school, I started chatting with a guy online. Blond, gorgeous. *Doesn't he look exactly like James Dean?* His profile photo showed him sprawled on a bed, naked torso sinking into a cloud of silk sheets and pink heart-shaped cushions. The insinuation was clear: he was an escort. His bio simply read: *DM for rates.*

I wrote to him: *I don't have any money, but I want to meet you. Please, give me a chance.*

He picked me up at the number 90 tram stop in Piazza Trento. He was decidedly less handsome in real life, and looked around ten years older than in his photos. He was greying, desaturated. James Dean, but in rehab. In the bus on the way to his place — *Where are we going? Not far, two stops* — he told me all about his ex, an eighteen-year-old Brazilian guy who had been on the street since he was fourteen. He tried to quit the prostitution racket, but the kingpin's goons beat him up and kidnapped him and took him to Switzerland. *My poor love. I haven't heard from him in a month.* He also gave me a brief rundown of his neighbourhood, at the head of which sits the Matron: a trans queen bee who runs her own prostitution ring, male and female. *Mess with her and you're a dead man. Every two months, she does this blood detox, haemotherapy, you know like the tv stars do? Trust me, you wanna stay on her good side.*

When we got to his apartment — a tiny studio furnished with a table, two chairs, and a bed — he offered me a drink (vodka, at two thirty in the afternoon) and started recounting more stories with a coke-like freneticism, barely pausing to take a breath. He told me how, in a past life as a door-to-door salesman, he'd learnt how to hypnotise people by twirling a chrome pen between his fingers. Reflections, flashes of light. Infallible techniques. *It's like fucking their nervous system. I can make someone come in the time it takes to smoke a cigarette. Here, sit down.* I reclined on the bed as he lit a Marlboro Red and set it down on the headboard. *I'll be done before this cigarette has burnt out. I can make fifty euros in four minutes. Four.* And he reached into my underwear. We only made out — I was scared he'd make me pay if we did more. As we put our clothes back on, he said: *You wanted a boyfriend, now you've got one.*

Ideas. I need more ideas.

I have no experience in anything. I'm twenty-five years old and I've never held down a job for more than a month. My mind swims back to the self-service restaurant, the blowjob I sold to my grotesque manager. There's only one real option available to me: monetise my yoga practice.

Yoga is fashionable in Milan, particularly among the well-to-do crowd. I freak them out, in class, with my extreme poses, arching my back so far I take hold of my ankles, wrapping both legs around my head in *Yoganidrāsana*, yogic sleep pose. They gush over me: *You're amazing; like a contortionist.*

The most talented yogi in Milan. Take a bow.

My practice is driven, in large part, by my hunger for their praise and attention. My body allows me to briefly transcend my class and social status. The natural flexibility of my flesh is an advantage I can capitalise on.

I decide to pretend to be a yoga teacher. At Virgin Active on Corso Como — the most expensive gym in Milan, frequented by popstars and models and footballers — they're looking for a new instructor to teach evening classes twice a week, plus the odd substitution. The teacher-training business hasn't yet exploded in Milan, but, in a few years, training schools will begin to sprout around the city like mushrooms. Certification will set you back four or five thousand euros. Anyone can enrol, even beginners; the more students they accept, the more money they make. These schools will spit out an army of naïve baby teachers, all repeating their clumsy imitations: America's translation of the Indian tradition, a copy of a copy, an improbable cocktail of Pilates and choreographed breath. Their version of yoga is essentially a fitness class with exotic overtones and the amenities of a wellness centre. These fake teachers will, in turn, train a new army of subpar instructors. A vicious cycle. The situation makes me uncomfortable right from the start.

In order to get the job at Virgin Active, I invent a whole new persona. Extroverted, charismatic. Obviously, there's no contract involved. The manager is a cheerful, distracted Brazilian girl. She doesn't ask to see any diplomas or certificates. Our arrangement is month to month.

Let's see how it goes, she says. This is as much a trial for us as it is for you.

I teach my first class under the effect of sedatives: twenty drops in half a glass of water before I leave the house. I have a stutter — it's better now than it was, but the muscles in my mouth and throat still contract, at times, unexpectedly. I'm scared, but I can't let it show. My first impression must be impeccable, exemplary. I want to impress these affluent Milanese ladies, with their touched-up faces and their expensive activewear.

The class takes place in a windowless basement lit by fluorescent globes. One long wall is entirely covered in mirrors. All eyes — real and reflected — are on me. I don't lift my gaze from the floor. When I feel the urge to gather up my things and run away, I turn my thoughts to the cats, to Milan, to my precarious freedom, which could so easily be snatched from me. There is no growth without change. Certain dysfunctions can only be treated by the threat of death, either real or perceived.

This is my first lesson in disassociation: seeing my own actions from the outside.

Good evening, I'm your new instructor.

And already you hear them whispering. A rising insect hum: *Where did they find this guy? Look at what he's wearing.*

Your faded old cotton shorts and a yellowed tank top don't belong in this room of tight, shiny, coordinated Nike. Two middle-aged women get to their feet, roll up their purple yoga mats, and leave the room, laughing quietly. One woman in the back row, her germophobic feet wrapped in plastic bags, says to her neighbour: The management will be hearing from me after class.

You try to channel the teachers you've had over the years: Anita, Jennifer, Rosella. You summon them one by one and arrange them in a semicircle around you, an invisible altar, a pantheon of guiding deities. You try to reproduce their tone of voice — the result is mellifluous, grotesque — and their elongated vowels, like the mews of a dying cat. Even if you get the Sanskrit words wrong, or mix up the names of the poses, no one will notice.

When they ask you if you trained in India, you lie: Yes.

Where did you get your diploma?

Another lie.

Have you been teaching for long?

You continue lying. You get through the first lesson, then the second and third. One evening at a time. You can get used to anything. An underlying air of suspicion remains, but some students begin to warm to you. One very old woman with long red hair, her skin overcooked from regular visits to a holiday home in Ibiza, tearfully tells you about her husband's recent leg amputation. Another places her hand on her heart and gushes: Your voice is just so relaxing.

Two weeks pass, then a month. Your first pay cheque arrives.

It's not much, three hundred euros, but it's enough to keep you from going back to square one, back to those crumbling public housing towers, an hour and a half by tram from everywhere you'd rather be.

You rolled the dice, and moved forward. You're still in Milan. Your natural place, as Aristotle would put it: the place all bodies seek to return to, due to the elements of which they are composed.

Two months later, I'm still living in the apartment with Pietro. Freeloading. Melissa thinks it's strange I haven't moved out yet. *How long can you go on like this? It's not healthy.*

Pietro tries his luck every now and then: stretched out on the couch, as if nothing had happened, he pulls out his thing and looks at me, or else curls towards me in bed, before I've fallen asleep. *Cut it out*, I say, turning my head. Other times I meet his advances with a cold, humiliating silence.

Pietro thinks our break-up was a brief moment of madness, a rash decision I made and now regret. It takes desire — the reason for everything — to swoop in and clarify everything.

On an afternoon in mid-June, I meet a thirty-eight-year-old actor and director from Bologna. We'd chatted about meeting up thousands of times — *when I finally get my hands on you, you won't be able to stand up for a month* — but now he is passing through Milan, and gets in touch. We arrange to meet at the recently opened Museo del Novecento, in Piazza del Duomo. He looks like Vincent Cassel, but with aquamarine eyes. He runs workshops for the University of Bologna's drama, art, and music studies department. One of his most recent messages, which I still have saved in my inbox, reads: *Your dramaticism turns me on a little.*

Together we walk through the rooms of the Palazzo dell'Arengario, surrounded by colours and the faint electricity particular to first dates. Boccioni, Morandi, Fontana's luminous neon scribbles suspended above our heads; the artworks flow past and around us, but I hardly see them.

He says: Did you know I wrote my thesis on Arte Povera?

He takes a photo on his phone: our reflections, side by side, in one of Pistoletto's mirror paintings. Me in sandals and bermuda shorts, an indigo-blue t-shirt tight against my yoga-toned torso, he in black jeans and a white shirt, taller than me by at least a foot. He posts it on Facebook, and tags me without my knowledge.

Pietro, who is away with his friends in Puglia, sees the photo and realises, maybe for the first time, that I was serious about breaking up.

There's no turning back now.

I warned you, he writes. *You can stay in the apartment as long as you don't bring any guys home.*

He's convinced I've slept with someone in his bed, in our bed, fucked someone else in his apartment — the apartment I still haven't contributed a cent towards. In fact, we didn't even kiss. I would have like to, when we entered the exhibition space on the top floor of the museum, with its intermittently flashing lights — dark, light, dark, light. I would have liked to, but I didn't. I'm only capable of taking the lead from behind a screen: distance as a condition of possibility.

Nothing happened between us, but still it was the final nail in the coffin.

You disgust me, Pietro writes. *I guess I really didn't know you at all.* The bond is finally broken.

July passes, then August. The house empties of words and fills up with foreign gossip magazines, and imported sweets with brand names I've never heard of. I start investigating this behavioural change, via Pietro's browser history and questions directed to our mutual friends. I ask Melissa to ask Christian if he has any idea what's going on. Has Pietro started working at the airport? Is he seeing someone? I'm not jealous, that's not it. I'm afraid. Afraid that from one day to the next I'll be out on the street, with no choice but to go back to where I came from.

It only takes me a few days to figure it out: Pietro is seeing a luxury garden designer from Sydney. He met him when he was away on holiday. An Italian-Australian guy who makes a fortune sculpting bushes into the shapes of animals. Highly sought after — with what he earns, he could easily afford to support the two of them. Talk about a role reversal.

It's not long before Pietro tells me, with little in the way of explanation, on an ordinary weekday evening, as I'm preparing dinner for the two of us out of habit, that he's going to Australia for three months.

Do you want to stay here a little longer? he asks.

My lucky stars are shining bright.

Yes, I say. Of course I do.

Pietro leaves me alone with the apartment and the cats — *I know how much you care about them* — and flies halfway across the world. He's very attached to the cats; he has a deep, paternal affection for them. But there will be absolutely no negotiation when it comes to custody. I'm a fundamentalist in this regard. A sentimental radical. I'd rather blow myself up than be separated from the things I love. Although, when possible, I prefer to detonate smaller explosions in the hearts of others. Sprinkle a little kerosene and set loose a spark, watching my problems be devoured by fiery tongues. The pain of others is acceptable to me when it clears space for my joy.

I'll send photos, I tell him.

Digital copies of our children. *My* children.

Milan and my cats: I delayed my liberation for so long — for years — precisely so that I wouldn't lose this sacred dyad, my universe, my life even before it became my life, the life I wanted and then claimed. Now my reward has been handed to me, debt-free, as though some benevolent, magnanimous aura has been unexpectedly cast over me.

Pietro's three months abroad become six, then a year.

He'll never return to Italy.

He and the designer will get engaged, then married, to make the green-card application a little easier.

Porta Nuova

Each evening, as I'm leaving the gym on Corso Como, I look up. I see flickering lights, cranes bent over the construction site that was once a Luna Park. As a child, any mention of the amusement park made my heart sing. Every so often, my paternal grandparents would take me to Milan to see the iconic Ferris wheel. The park was built on land once occupied by the long-demolished Porta Nuova train station, which mainly ran services to and from Varese, in the Alpine foothills. Since 2009, it has again become a construction site, making way for emerging skyscrapers. Everything is soaring skyward: these new building projects promise to completely reshape the profile of the city, in a slow colonisation of Milan's airspace.

As Milan rises, Rozzano sinks, extending deep into the centre of the Earth. No one knows this — I learnt about it by chance, from an article I saw in a local online newspaper. The secret lies in Via Guido Rossa, a street in Rozzano's most well-to-do neighbourhood, whose privately owned condos we always coveted, as children. There, concealed by trees and bushes, a stairwell opens up into the subsoil: it only exists for those who need it; it is invisible to everyone else. If you follow the stairwell, it leads you down into a hidden city: the realm of the mole people.

A necropolis for the living dead — endless galleries, like catacombs, inhabited by the homeless, immigrants, addicts — lies beneath the place where, on summer evenings, I used to ask my teenaged aunt to take me to see the shimmering frogs leaping in the twilight.

Daylight seeps through the grates and illuminates these subterranean caves that have become bedrooms, kitchens, homes complete with mattresses and wardrobes and bins used as chamber pots. Ten years ago, a company dug out the space in order to build two hundred brand-new underground garages. Then they went bankrupt and abandoned the construction site, leaving it to be claimed by those who needed it.

The author of the article I stumbled upon took care to specify that the garages do, in fact, have electricity. Some 'rooms' even have shutters, which come in handy — even mole people have treasures worth protecting. Entire families live down there, including children: the photos show infants' cots, soft toys, hearts drawn on the walls in chalk. The entire area, they wrote, is the size of a shopping centre. One end is filled with the remains of stolen cars, like stripped carcasses left over from a hunting expedition, rusting in the puddles formed by broken fire hydrants, which, incidentally, serve as the inhabitants' only source of potable water.

How many people live down there? How many are brave enough?

At least forty, maybe fifty, according to the police. Possibly more. Let's round it up to a hundred: a hundred lost people who aren't afraid of the dark. They disappear during the day — it's not safe, the police could raid their hidey-holes, ask them for papers, arrest them.

They only return at night, to their homes under the earth of Rozzano's most respectable neighbourhood. The mole people. Their families. Their children.

Via Lulli

Hey, can you hear me?

A freezing hand on my warm, naked shoulder. My body is motionless, skin dotted with specks of blue rubber, arms and legs splayed wide, forming a kind of soft asterisk. The yoga mat under me has worn out from the friction of a thousand jump backs and sun salutes — two stripes of faded blue mark the place where my feet land. A yellow towel is stretched over me, from neck to thighs, protecting my bare abdomen from the chill.

The cold hand grabs my shoulder and shakes it, trying to bring me back to life. Gently, at first, then harder. It moves to my cheek, then to the shaved dome of my head. My eyelids shudder.

Hey, you okay?

My eyes crack open. I raise my head.

You scared me! Are you feeling alright?

Shit — I come to the slow realisation that I've fallen asleep in *Śavāsana*, there on the floor between the kitchen and the sofa.

I had a yoga class to teach at six thirty. I thought I'd set an alarm, as I always do — I have a tendency to drift into sleep after asana practice. But I must have forgotten, or else I turned the alarm off in my sleep. I stretch out my arm to check the time. It's too late. They're going to fire me for this.

My roommate removes his jacket and hangs it next to the front door, then laughs.

You're exhausted, I've been trying to tell you this for ages.

He's right; this was a long time coming. Between university, work, and my two and a half hours of daily asana practice, I have nothing left. My inguinal hernia has been getting worse for a few months, now. I'm not even sure what caused it initially. Perhaps all the intense diaphragmatic breathing I used to do in my singing lessons. Or maybe it has something to do with the pressure all those insane yoga postures place on my abdomen.

My body is too flexible, too yielding. My internal organs slip out of position easily. The bulge, just above my left testicle, comes and goes depending on the day. Sometimes I try to push it back in manually; other times I take *Śīrsāsana*, headstand pose, in an attempt to reverse the effects of gravity. A year ago, a surgeon told me I should have it surgically removed: if it becomes 'incarcerated', then 'strangulated', it could be fatal.

Sometimes, when I'm teaching yoga, the pain prevents me from moving. It rises in pangs to the pit of my stomach, and I have to stand very still and use only my voice to guide the class.

Some evenings I'm so tired I feel feverish.

The roommate is a necessary evil.

In September, Pietro messages from Australia to say he won't charge me rent, but he needs me to cover the mortgage repayments. Even that is too much. I have no choice but to find someone to sublet the apartment's only bedroom. It shouldn't be hard, in Milan, with rents the way they are. And rising. People are paying four hundred and fifty, five hundred euros for a room.

Demand is forever regenerating, and far exceeds supply. Milan is a city where people still live in share houses in their sixties.

One thing at a time. My first step is to deconstruct the family nest. The huge bed Pietro and I brought with us from the apartment in Via Porpora can literally be taken apart: I dismember it carefully, separating it into two pieces. A practical act more than a symbolic one. I reassemble one half of the bed in a corner of the bedroom, fencing off a small area with a wall of books, most of which I've collected over the past few years. Living with Pietro, I finally felt safe to accumulate possessions, to stack all the novels I'd read in a beautiful pile, a physical display of my intellect.

Voilà: my new bedroom. Three or four square metres of dark, windowless space.

I settle into my corner and rent out the rest of the room. I find a roommate through my university contacts: a naïve first-year literature student from Parma. She's obsessed with gomashio, Japanese sesame salt — she polishes off a packet every three days or so. I overhear her talking to her mother on the phone in the evenings: *I feel so anxious all the time, is it true salt raises your blood pressure?*

After three weeks, she announces her departure.

I'm sorry, she says. I need more privacy.

I don't blame her: this apartment was meant for a couple. It's the home of a couple that never existed. And now I have to fill the void left by its absence.

It's late November when one of my yoga students, Mara, a Chinese Italian woman in her fifties, introduces me to Dylan. Dylan is a graphic designer, an avid weed smoker, and a Michael

Jackson fanatic. He grew up in Corsico, near Rozzano, on the south-western periphery of Milan.

He needs a room, Mara says, and you need a roommate. It's a match made in heaven.

Dylan moves in.

He's forty, I say to Melissa, but he looks ten or fifteen years younger than that.

Do you have a photo?

Let me find one on Facebook.

Wow, you're right.

Dylan must have made some kind of pact with the devil, like Dorian Gray. He is slender, with soft white skin, porcelain skin without a single crease or blemish. What's his secret? Collagen? Acupuncture? His interests are equally youthful: he loves Japanese manga, and collects puppets and figurines of his favourite characters — Tiger Mask, Mazinger, Lupin III, Sailor Moon. He could fill entire rooms with his memorabilia, his fetishes. When he moves in, he brings everything with him. Superheroes, dinosaurs, robots, hundreds of new miniature housemates, whose curious eyes follow me everywhere I go. They live on the highest surfaces of the apartment, where the cats can't reach them.

I soon learn that Dylan isn't his real name. The first of many secrets. My new roommate is actually named Stefano, but his parents — Sicilians who relocated to the North — have always called him by the name of his older brother, who died at birth, as the family were preparing to emigrate to the United States. *I could have been American*. He's a big fan of Madonna, too. He calls her the queen of pop. Jackson was — is — the king. *King and queen.* He refuses to believe the paedophilia accusations.

Wicked allegations, he says, born of envy. *It was a trial by media. They wanted to ruin him. Michael just loved playing with children, he was an innocent soul. Like a sprite.*

We watch a video together, from 1993, in which Jackson speaks directly to the camera, live from Neverland Valley:

I have been forced to submit to a dehumanising and humiliating examination by the Santa Barbara County Sheriff Department and the Los Angeles Police Department earlier this week. They served a search warrant on me which allowed them to view and photograph my body, including my penis, my buttocks, my lower torso, thighs, and any other area that they wanted …

I can't even watch this, Dylan snaps. It makes me so angry.

He plays Jackson's songs and music videos on repeat, but only the most famous ones. I end up memorising them, by osmosis.

On YouTube, he shows me the interview in which Maria Scicolone, Sophia Loren's sister, talks about the day Jackson stayed as a guest in her home:

He knocks on the door and asks if he can ride in the elevator. He goes to the top floor, then comes down again, and keeps going up and down like a madman. My house isn't big, but it has a covered roof terrace. Then he sees my daughters' bedroom and my bedroom and asks if he can jump on the beds. I look over at Sophia and say, 'Who the hell is this guy? He's crazy!' He was like a monkey. He jumped so high he was hitting his head against the ceiling.

When he died, Dylan tells me, I just drove around in my car all night with his music blaring. My life changed forever, that day.

For years, Dylan has worked in an office that edits sewing, knitting, and cross-stitch magazines, but around the same time he moves in, the company starts laying people off. He's one of the unlucky ones. He starts looking into unemployment benefits.

Don't worry, he says, I can still pay the rent. I'll save money on other things.

Like the many expensive creams, serums, and soaps he uses on his skin — each tiny bottle must cost eighty to a hundred euros. He suffers from psoriasis, but it's better now, he tells me.

I used to be covered in it, he says. *Covered* in it! Mostly on my legs. I literally never wore shorts, not even when it was forty degrees.

Patches of itchy red skin with white, flaky scales. According to the internet, the condition is often triggered by a combination of genetic and environmental factors: injuries, stress, trauma.

As well as cutting down on skincare, he can save money by seeing his psychoanalyst less regularly. He's been seeing the same seventy-something-year-old shrink for a decade now, despite having made very little progress in that time.

Just think, he says. Just imagine what kind of shape I'd be in if I'd never started therapy.

The name of his dead brother is only one of many weights he has to bear. His alcoholic father died at some point, I'm not sure when, since he can't bring himself to speak about him (I was under the impression he never had a father). Then there's his gambling-addicted mother, whom he ended up mothering himself, paying the bills and doing the shopping when she couldn't. When he moved to Milan, she was left to look after his cat, Jam, who'd recently had his penis removed because of a tumour. After the operation, Jam started peeing on the sofa, and no veterinarian or pet behaviourist could figure out how to stop him. I hear Dylan repeating the same phone conversation, over and over: *Oh, did it happen again? … I know, I know … I'll figure it out … No, mamma, I'm not having him put to sleep.*

I've tried everything, he tells me, distraught. Then one day he says: Maybe I'll take him to the countryside. I know a lady with a beautiful farmstead who might take him.

Poor cat. I feel for him. I don't approve of him being sent to the farmstead, until an alternative is proposed: Maybe Jam could stay here, with us?

Out of the question — I would never allow anything to disturb Rosaspina and León. The preservation of their space, their privileges, is all that matters to me.

Dylan, I explain, these cats are the reason you found a place to live. They're the reason I needed a roommate. I'm sorry, but your cat can't move in with us.

Then I add: You should have told me about him from the beginning.

Implying: If you'd told me about him from the beginning, I would have found someone else to take the room.

Dylan's presence in the apartment completely reinscribes the space. He transforms what was once a make-believe love nest into a teenager's bedroom. He moves in with his orange loft bed and sits at the desk beneath it, watching anime and science-fiction movies and Nineties music videos on his computer until four in the morning, stoned out of his mind. The weed is another kind of therapy: it helps him feel things less, or feel nothing at all.

I'm worried the cats will become intoxicated by the smoke, or by the bits of marijuana Dylan leaves lying around the house — the THC could damage their nervous systems, or they could get disoriented and escape, or fall from the balcony. I imagine their shattered little bodies, writhing in pain, their little eyes closing, going to sleep.

Please be careful when you go out, I remind him. Always check between your legs before you open the front door.

Of course, he says, are you kidding?

I'm reassured by how much he loves the cats. They sleep on his bed at night; he says he can't get to sleep without them now. But then again, does the fact that we love something necessarily mean we know how to protect it?

Sometimes I go with him to visit his dealer in a part of the city I'm unfamiliar with, somewhere far from the centre. When I ask him where we are, he says he doesn't know.

I only come for this, he says.

He always seems confused. I have to repeat everything I say to him, and break his responses down into simple parts, untangling meanings, reversing double negations. I'm well versed in this kind of translation; I've been practising it with my parents for years.

While he goes to retrieve the weed, I wait on the corner between an abandoned discount supermarket and a bar occupied by old men playing cards. I watch him walk down the deserted avenue and into one of the many imposing grey buildings. We're on Via delle Forze Armate, I'll eventually learn, on the city's western periphery.

Twenty minutes pass; half an hour.

Sorry, he says, returning. I couldn't get away.

As we walk back to the car, he tells me the dealer lives with his girlfriend, and the two of them have a son together.

The kid's got problems, Dylan says. Every time I see him, he's in a corner of the room, screaming. Dirty, drooling, half-naked.

They've got all these toys and stuff for him, but I think they should take him to see a specialist.

Then he adds: I've got a real soft spot for that kid.

Other times, I accompany him to Chinatown, his favourite part of the city. He stocks up on his beloved packaged foods: biscuits, noodles, seaweed crackers, wasabi peanuts, mochi in every flavour — rose, lychee, green tea, blueberry. He has a habit of playing with his food at the table, constructing smiley faces or dinosaurs or igloos on his plate, sometimes even getting his toys involved, composing little scenes with his action figures and photographing them. Later, he'll post the photos on Facebook. A pile of rice becomes a sacred mountain, a dish of broccoli is a trench for toy soldiers.

I gift him a special set of decorated plates, a cryptic message that says: It's okay, Dylan, you're safe to be a child with me.

The two of us form a kind of alliance, out of necessity more than anything. Like a sexless marriage. He claims I'm not his type.

Anyway, he says, friends are strictly off limits.

But he makes plenty of lewd comments when I'm practising yoga at home in my tight boxers, sweaty and shirtless. *Look at that muscly arse. Now that's the body of a real man. So masculine.*

Our interactions are intimate, tender, often unbearable. He asks me to wake him in the mornings, although he detests being roused from sleep — his bed is his safe place. His father was a keen chef, and if I so much as prepare a bowl of pasta for him, he's moved to tears. What if he were to try something? What if he were to slip into my bed one night? He brags about his huge dick: surprisingly big for such a skinny guy, he claims. But nothing happens between us.

Outside us, on the other hand, everything happens.

I'm finally free to go on as many dates as I like, but none of the guys I meet feel like The One.

You're young, Dylan and his friends remind me. *Just have fun. Stop dating anorexic mystics and sad holy men.*

I find myself returning to a theory of concentric circles, or progressive energies: before I met Pietro, I felt that the great love story of my life was approaching gradually, in waves, in a gently intensifying flow. Sometimes I could feel the movement of the waves; other times I couldn't. *There is a plan*, I told myself then, and I tell myself this again now. *There is a grand design at work, but you have to be patient. It's like waiting for the tide to come in; sooner or later, you will be submerged. You just have to have faith.*

While I wait for true love to find me, dozens of more or less forgettable men come and go.

There's L: obsessed with Fellini and Lars von Trier, studying physics at the University of Pisa. He's beautiful, but makes himself ugly on purpose. When we're in the shower together, the water tames his wild curls and I can finally see his face clearly: his beautiful eyes, framed with impossibly long black lashes.

You should cut your hair, I suggest. You'd look better.

L stays over a couple of times, but he's a resolute pessimist. He says the world disgusts him, claims he's incapable of loving anyone. Love is impossible in his world — he'll only make me suffer.

Dylan, observing from the sidelines, comments: Why do all the guys you date smell like old people?

Then there's T, who works at the Vatican, and fucks me with the windows of his attic apartment wide open, so everyone can hear.

And M, who lets me fuck him, at the risk of contracting hepatitis and scabies (to be fair, he was good enough to warn me in advance).

It's stress, he tells me; my immune system is completely shot.

Pasticcini reappears, briefly, and this time it's my turn to ghost him.

Pity, he writes after I've left him on read for a few days. *I thought it might be nice to have some company in this shitty life.*

Then there's A, an old ex of Dylan's. They went out when he was nineteen. Dylan was desperate to be his boyfriend, but the guy was only interested in talking about philosophy — every date was like a private university lecture.

We go out a couple of times, then watch a Jodorowsky film at his place, in Via Padova, and go to bed together. The next morning, he doesn't even offer me breakfast; evidently, I wasn't up to scratch.

Next comes the red-headed cartoonist who wants to be dominated, and asks me to slap him and pull his hair. Then the hairy Freemason I can only bear to see after I've had a couple of drinks, who says he wants to make me come from the inside, without letting me touch myself. Then the tv producer with the huge scar on his chest and the house that stinks of kitty litter.

It sounds like a lot, but my promiscuity pales in comparison to Dylan's. It's not unusual for him to hook up with three different guys in a single day. Not to mention the orgies, for which he'll happily abandon me in the middle of dinner if he gets a last-minute Grindr notification. He's insatiable — often he'll leave one guy's apartment and head straight to the next one, like a sexual carousel. We don't talk about it, but for both of us sex has the potential to become an all-consuming practice, an addiction.

Binge fucking. We'd do anything for the brief embrace of a stranger: lie, deceive, disappoint the people we care about. If anyone dares question us about it, or — god forbid — criticise us for it, we dismiss them as frigid, sexually frustrated, repressed. Within homosexuality, too, there is conformity, resistance to and erasure of otherness, of difference. The closing down of possibilities.

This is the way I am. But I want to be different.

I am well acquainted with the stranglehold of my own libido. Before Pietro — before our relationship curbed my fierce, vile appetite for sex — I'd spend hours, days, entire weekends trawling online chat rooms, neglecting my studies, my hobbies, everything else I needed or wanted to do, in search of excitement or release, winding up alone at the computer, most of the time, or else in the apartment or basement or car of whoever was available. I came to understand these casual hook-ups as a kind of predictable theatre: repetitive, unnatural, contrived. Still, I don't stop. I can't stop. The world of online sex is dark, tinged with violence: sex as debasement, war, rape, domination and submission, the mortification of the flesh — mine, theirs. Then there's the aesthetics of it: the bodies sculpted until they resemble those of porn actors, the hypertrophic penises and bulging muscles and thick beards. The macho ideal. Gay fascism. The important thing is consent; but do you really know what consent is?

In certain communities — ours, certainly, but others, too — resistance to oppression and censorship led to a kind of sexual frenzy. Fucking is good, fucking is freedom; this is beyond dispute. Let's face it: for many of us, sex is our only real ambition in life. But it's ironic to feel free, rebellious even, in the repetition of what are now tired, commonplace tropes. In theory, I'm opposed to anything that impinges on my freedom, but my own sexual urges do just that: they take me away from myself, force me to succumb to the basest, most selfish part of me. Sex is a tyrant.

Now, again, I find myself drawn in by the tide of desire, and everything else is erased. But when I go to bed with someone I really like, someone I want to be with, I feel something different: true connection, a lowering of my defences. Sex becomes something else entirely — it no longer ruins or interrupts things, but rather reinforces them. Romantic orgasms are the only real orgasms; isn't that what women have been saying since forever?

Shortly after Dylan moves in, I enrol in a master's degree (Dylan is convinced this means I'm studying to become a headmaster at a primary school). I go back to San Raffaele — my relationship to that place is a series of abrupt departures and returns — with the help of a new scholarship. Same university, different campus; the philosophy faculty was recently moved to the hospital complex in Via Olgettina, along with medicine and psychology.

A new routine is established. My life takes place less in the places I move between than in the routes to and from them, like the path from Cascina Gobba Metro station to the university, which I usually traverse on foot, past empty fields and landfills and construction sites, in order to avoid the overcrowded bus. There's an automatic train that shuttles between the Metro station and the hospital, but you need a separate ticket to ride it, and I can't justify the extra expense. The National Institute of Statistics should gather data on who can and cannot afford to take that train; I think it would make for an impeccable indicator of socio-economic status.

Since high school, my teachers have been adamant that San Raffaele is *the right place for someone of my capacities*, with its armchairs and crimson carpets and small, pristine classrooms made for civilised groups of twenty-five students. San Raffaele students have direct access to the best teachers in the city, along with everything that entails: prestigious thesis supervisors, research grants, guaranteed careers in their field of choice. Just being there once more, in that space of privilege, I'm filled with the sense that I've made it, that a majestic, smiling future awaits me. But it's not long before I remember why I quit the first time. Provoking the rich kids with my poverty and foul language is easy, but I get nothing out of it. I don't enjoy it.

I look up Roberta De Monticelli, my teacher from the Cesano Maderno campus, whose first-year course introduced me to Hannah Arendt and Max Weber and Czesław Miłosz.

Prof, remember me? I'm back.

I spend two months writing a research paper on the concept of the impersonal in Simone Weil — specifically, in her essay *La personne et le sacré.*

I see a passer-by in the street, Weil writes. *He has long arms, blue eyes, and a mind whose thoughts I do not know, but perhaps they are commonplace. It is neither his person, nor the human personality in him, which is sacred to me. It is he. The whole of him ... At the bottom of the heart of every human being, from the earliest infancy until the tomb, there is something that goes on indomitably expecting, in the teeth of all experience of crimes committed, suffered, and witnessed, that good and not evil will be done to him. It is this above all that is sacred in every human being.*

What is sacred, according to Weil, is the delicate body in us that seeks protection, craves mercy. This could be the starting point — I hypothesise — for a sensational new theory reconciling the personhood of humans and non-human animals. I could dedicate myself to Weil's work, become her official translator. Italy's pre-eminent Weil scholar. I seriously consider taking up French.

But there are too many other things clamouring for my attention. The question still gnaws at me: *Who are you? What do you actually want to do?* Surely success is simply a matter of making a choice and seeing it through. I sometimes wish I could just let myself sink into something — a single idea, a single discipline. Become an expert on something, instead of floating around collecting superficial knowledge on a million different topics. Again, it comes down to the question of consent: I could choose one thing, and dedicate my life to it, but what does it really mean to *choose*?

I finish the research paper in the nick of time. In addition to requesting an electronic copy, the professor asks me to present my essay to the class. I feel like an American university student in a movie: De Monticelli waves me to the front of the classroom and clears her desk, relocating to a chair in the front row, notebook and pen at the ready. I have thirty minutes to impress her, to prove that I deserve to be here, receiving this free world-class education.

Before saying a word, I walk up to the whiteboard and draw a diagram: a human silhouette bisected by a horizontal line. I clear my throat, then begin:

In one of the essays I examined, Simone Weil explores the basic needs of human beings. Our superior and inferior needs. Those that bind and open us up to that which unites us: the impersonal.

The class listens, silently. By way of a kind of psychic osmosis, they seem to have absorbed De Monticelli's apparent respect for my ideas. I'm the oldest student in the class, having wasted three or four years switching schools and courses and campuses. I'm afraid of my classmates, but when I'm speaking about something I love, when I am clothed in words and allowed to dwell completely within them, I feel some of that fear peel away. I feel like I am worth something. Or rather: it's not *me* that is worth something, but the intersection between me and whatever I'm speaking about. The meanings evoked by my words make me more special, more beautiful — like fairies sprinkling magic dust. Sentences pour out of me, in a kind of ecstatic flow. In the company of the word fairies, everything feels possible. They lead me down paths I didn't even know were there.

As time goes on, I see less and less of Melissa.

Melissa is years ahead of me in everything: she's about to finish her second degree, and just started working for the civil service at Castello Sforzesco. Instead of commuting to Via Noto, I now study at home, alone, which is infinitely harder. Without Melissa, I am slow, obsessive, inefficient. I'm almost twenty-seven years old, and the end is still nowhere in sight.

Just be a yoga teacher, Melissa suggests. Who gives a shit. Aren't you sick of studying?

Melissa and Ismene are no longer in touch. Ismene spent her Erasmus year in the south of France — *doing fuck all*, according to Melissa — and the two of them didn't even say goodbye before she left.

Why don't you reach out to her? I ask. It'd be a pity to lose that friendship after so many years.

I'm nostalgic on Melissa's behalf: for the long days spent in the library, the parties, the shopping trips, the gossiping, the shared secrets and outfits and cigarettes, the excitement of passing an exam and the devastation of failing one, the full archive of experiences and memories from which even I, at times, felt excluded.

Melissa shrugs: I have nothing to say to her. If she wants to reach out, she knows where to find me.

It turns out they had a fight, or rather a kind of non-fight. After a minor disagreement, they simply stopped speaking to one another, each abandoning herself to the current of indifference, as so often happens. Melissa disapproved of Ismene's decision to study abroad (did she feel left out? abandoned?) and Ismene relished her new-found independence, free at last from comparisons — she'd always been the dumb one, the weak one, the messy one, with boys, with belongings, with everything.

I want to help them reconcile, heal the rift that has slowly opened up between them, but no olive branches are forthcoming from either side. All I can do is surrender to the way things are, and accept that, sometimes, pride trumps all else.

I don't need her, Melissa says. I get on fine without her.

I say: You've always had a problem with girls.

Me?

Yeah. Every female friendship you've ever had has ended badly.

I reel them off: Paola, Cristina, Arianna, Nicole, Daniela. Need I go on?

Well, I've still got you, don't I?

I laugh; we both laugh, walking across the lawn in front of the Tibaldi library. But she's not wrong: in fact, I feel neither male nor female. I'm certainly not a *man* — the word feels completely alien to me, and unsuitable. I'm willing to accept *guy*, as long as it refers more to a social category than to a gender. But what interests me most is the middle ground, the space where the codes of both sides are freely exchanged and combined — the preadolescent phase, when desires are allowed to mix and collide and everything is still possible. Fertile, open ground, where all spirits, all names, all essences can coexist. I want to remain in that space forever, balanced between things, a living refutation of the idea that a different order is necessarily a *dis*order. (Is what I want to stand still, to never grow up?)

Melissa crushes her cigarette under the sole of her Converse sneaker and heads for the library entrance. I go to follow her, then stop and call out: I forgot to tell you, I got a message from Pietro yesterday.

What did he want?

He's decided to sell the apartment.

I'm sorry, the message said, *you'll have to find somewhere else.*

Seriously? So now what?

Now we're fucked.

At least I'm not alone. When the initial shock of the news wears off, Dylan and I join forces, forming a team with a single, inalienable objective.

If you don't mind, he says one night over dinner, a trace of hesitation in his voice, I'd like us to keep living together.

I agree, of course. I've grown fond of him — more than fond, even.

You don't have to say yes just because, he says. I don't want you to feel obligated.

Dylan is so afraid of rejection that he anticipates it, manifests it, putting words in my mouth that I then have to argue against, inventing reasons where none were needed, defending both of us from his lack of confidence. At some point in his life, probably early on, the universal pact of mutual trust must have been broken, and he had to learn to analyse the words of others for traps, for poisoned apples.

A week or two passes before I suggest posting something on Facebook.

Sure, he says. And I'll ask Mara if she has any leads. She knows a ton of people.

Three weeks become a month, and still nothing. No leads, no replies.

Until, finally, it happens: we find a place. It's bigger, better, more beautiful than Pietro's apartment. We're levelling up. Two bedrooms, a kitchen/dining room, two balconies, high, immaculate ceilings. The building even has a lift, which is lucky, because we're on the top floor. The apartment measures maybe a hundred square metres, right in the heart of the Loreto neighbourhood. Piazza Aspromonte is practically on our doorstep. The rent is nine hundred and fifty euros a month, divided by two. The building is old, from the Twenties or Thirties, and the floors are spectacular: intricate tiles in blue, ochre, sienna. It's like walking on a mosaic. I photograph them and post the images on social media, where they're met with endless cascades of ecstatic comments.

Gorgeous, where is this?

Can you let me know if another apartment in your building becomes available?

Everyone wants to live here. I'm from Rozzano, but now I live in the mostly beautifully tiled apartment in Milan.

Our apartment is in Via Lulli, opposite a row of seedy pay-by-the-hour motels with names like New Milan, Astrid, and Oriente. The neighbourhood is mostly low-rise buildings, leaving wide expanses of Instagrammable sky — the sunrises and sunsets from the balcony are magnificent. Our building even has a surprise sentinel in the form of a stocky middle-aged sex worker, who stands guard all day in her leather jacket and mid-calf boots, hair painted four different shades of orange, waiting for non-existent clients among the parked cars.

How does she make a living? Dylan asks. No one ever seems to pick her up.

He soon befriends her, asking her to keep an eye on the apartment when we're away.

Our new place is large, luminous. Of the two bedrooms, I choose the one with the attic ceiling; it's more intimate. It feels like I'm in a ski lodge. Dylan's bedroom has a balcony, which suits him, because he can smoke out there. We both feel freer, here. In the old apartment, Dylan always felt a bit like a guest, he eventually confesses. Like an imposition. Now, with a bedroom to himself, he introduces a horde of previously unseen toys and puppets. He travels to his mother's place in Corsico to rescue them from her garage, where they have been waiting patiently in storage for months and months. Among the new arrivals is Dylan's pride and joy: a fifty-centimetre-tall action figure of Michael Jackson in his Thriller outfit, meticulously stored in its original packaging, complete with an assortment of accessories including a microphone and Jackson's famous rhinestoned glove.

This should have pride of place, Dylan says.

We set the figurine on a prominent bookshelf in the centre of the house.

Dylan's *horror vacui* is contagious, and I soon embark on my own frantic decoration of the space. I hang a poster of Ganesh, the elephant-headed remover of obstacles, on my bedroom door, and adorn the frame with a rabble of three-dimensional butterfly decals, so it looks like the entrance to a secret grotto. Inside, the entire right-hand wall of my room is taken up by a bookshelf and desk, where I crowd the stacks of books I continue to collect.

This is the first bedroom I've ever had that I can truly call mine.

As a housewarming gift — a dowry, a blessing — my grandmothers give me cotton sheets embroidered with pastel flowers, and thick piles of woollen blankets as heavy as mattresses. I make an impulse purchase from a street vendor: a laundry basket embellished with a poor imitation of Van Gogh's almond blossoms.

Number 1 Via Lulli: my new home.

The place I'm living in when I meet him.

PART TWO

Love is the perception of individuals.
Love is the extremely difficult realisation that
something other than oneself is real.

Iris Murdoch

The Sublime and the Good

Via Simone d'Orsenigo

Through the glass, an endless stream of streets, traffic lights, intersections. Mothers hurry their children — most still wearing school backpacks, some fitted tight and high, others dangling lackadaisically from one shoulder, although several hours have passed since the school day ended — home from dance or karate or catechism classes, rushing towards the dinner tables and tv screens that await them, as I watch silently from the other side of a tram window, hoping he won't write.

Inhale, *I love you.*

Exhale, *I don't love you anymore.*

I stand up and change seats, telling myself maybe it's just a matter of perspective. Move the body, move the mind; perhaps physical motion will dislodge whatever is stuck inside me. It doesn't help. As I inch towards the back doors of the tram, the thought remains like a stone in my heart, questioning everything, predicting the worst. *It's over*, the thought says, repeats, as people wash around me, muttering curse words under their breath. *It has to end here.*

I cross my legs, then widen them, stretching out the hips. I squeeze them together, kneecap to kneecap, bones cracking — I wish they would explode into a million pieces, and rain their splinters down on everything with a terrible noise loud enough to drown out the one in my head. I keep trying out my body, looking for an anatomical key that might unlock something: I tilt my torso forward, squeezing the sponges of my lungs, the bronchi and alveoli, then straighten, inhaling, feeling the breath as it opens wide the bones of the rib cage. But the extra space doesn't change anything. I've lost whatever it was that I had before.

There's no rewinding, no reset button. The tram moves, stops. Moves again, stops again. It's December 2013. On this hopeless, impenetrable evening, I inhale again and hold the breath inside me as I disembark and walk the last few blocks to the dance school, where my students are waiting for me. I'm not sure how I'm going to get through the class; I'm not sure I can keep the mask from slipping. I keep inhaling and exhaling, the resentment mounting for this technique that, it turns out, is completely useless — so much for *Pranayama*, the taming of the mind via the energies of the body. The whole thing is a sham, a miserable lie perpetuated by a series of charlatans. The more I focus on my breath, the less I recognise myself, and it scares me.

Crossing the street, I pass the organic bistro I've been wanting to take him to for months. Through the windows I glimpse wicker baskets cascading with greenery, and beyond them the smiling faces of friends and couples passing dishes and raising shining glasses to their lips.

Long live life, and death to love!

I lower my eyes to the ground, concentrate on placing one foot in front of the other. For the next hour and a quarter, I have to pretend everything is fine.

Piazza Oberdan

His face is a triangle, pointing downwards. It is somehow both an old face and the face of a child. The forehead is unusually wide. He looks like a balding child with facial hair, I think. The moustache is slightly longer than the rest of his beard, and twisted at the ends, in the hipster fashion. His eyes are large and clear, a guileful blend between sage green and hazelnut brown, and the corners slant down slightly. His eyebrows are light and neatly arched, architectural, and his nose is long, the nose of a boxer or a lion, the septum embellished with a large ring that dangles between his round nostrils, illuminating everything around it. His mouth is asymmetrical, the lower lip fleshier and poutier than the top. On the pink of its interior, I'll discover later, is a tattoo of the word *liar*, done at the age of sixteen by the boyfriend of a classmate. His protruding ears are perfection.

Why him?

My original reasons for choosing him vanish when I try to grasp them; anyway, it would be useless to try and analyse the almost cosmic attraction I feel to him. Because he's beautiful, that's why. Let's make beauty my a posteriori justification. To me, he is beautiful: the way in which his cells are arranged, the way his DNA was formed at the moment of his creation, is exactly what I have been waiting for my whole life. The real question is: why me? Why did *he* choose *me*? What could he possibly see in this nothing of a person, this nothing of a body that has been rejected by so many, by everyone?

What made him stay — what makes him stay — when everyone else left?

April 2013.

His username is MapioGoldfish.

The awful, low-res photos on his GayRomeo profile show him crouching, in briefs and combat boots, in what looks like an old house, with blue doors and cheap furniture. He's giving Berghain vibes. Sperm, nicotine, bottles of beer, party drugs. I write him a private message, with little hope of a reply. One of many half-hearted cries sent out into the digital void. *He won't respond* — my years of online experience have granted me the ability to foresee the future. My intuition is infallible.

Anyway, he's too young. Eight years my junior. He'll just be looking for sex. And I can't do that, not with guys I actually like. When I sleep with someone I'm attracted to, the next day I find it impossible to act as if nothing happened. I need to dissolve myself in them, slipping from the boundaries of my skin and forgetting the way back into my own body. Because of this, I've ended up associating casual sex with violence, with self-harm. I seek out men I'm not attracted to: repulsive faces, pockmarked skin, dentures. Men older than my father. Desolate, ugly old men. Disgust as safety mechanism. The further I am from my aesthetic ideal, the safer I'll be: this is my subconscious philosophy, and practising it keeps my heart almost completely undisturbed.

Over the years, the subconscious has become conscious. A few weeks ago, I left the apartment late at night to attend a threesome, without telling Dylan. I made my way to Viale Gran Sasso, in Piola, to the apartment of a slimy, misshapen sixty-year-old I'd visited a few times before. He hadn't told me anything about the third member of our ménage à trois, except to reassure me that he was 'chill', and that I'd like him. The moment I stepped into the apartment, I saw him: he was sitting on a couch at the back of the room, still dressed. His face was lovely, too lovely, his sad eyes framed by a sweet mop of hair and a short beard. Exactly my type.

A few years ago, I would have been too embarrassed to turn around and leave, but now, on the cusp of twenty-seven, I'm shameless. I make an excuse, say I'm not feeling well. Our host is already in his underwear, cutting neat lines of coke on the nice wooden coffee table, where two vials of poppers are also at the ready. The tv shows a tangle of light and dark bodies, an interracial orgy with the volume turned down low.

What do you mean? Won't you at least stay and watch?

I'm sorry, I can't.

I'm sorry, I repeat, my foot already out the door.

The next day, I track down the beautiful stranger and send him a message: *Hey, sorry about last night. Wanna grab a coffee?* My mind is already floating into the future: we'll wind up in a bar, or at a gallery, taking our time, soaking up each other's presence, slowly setting the foundations for a relationship that exists only in my imagination. We met under strange circumstances, it's true, but when destiny calls, there is no obstacle we cannot surmount.

He responds right away, his status blinking to *online*, the green circle next to his name a karmic gift.

I'm looking for older guys sorry.

The circle turns grey: user unavailable.

As predicted, MapioGoldfish gives no sign of life.

The message I sent him gradually slips deeper into my inbox, and is soon lost in a sea of similar messages, desperate lures cast into a dark ocean, only a handful of which will ever see a bite.

I abandon the computer and move to the kitchen. I tip some kibble into the cats' bowl and start preparing lunch. I strip and chop an onion, a few zucchinis. I make a mental note to buy more rice as water hisses to a boil on the stove. Later, back in my room, I stick my head out the door and yell: Hey Dylan, want to go out tomorrow night?

Then, out of nowhere, it happens: the trill of a notification from the dating site, a fairy-like jingling of bells that usually only heralds the arrival of a dick pic. Not this time, though. There, sitting in my inbox, is a message from MapioGoldfish.

It's a comment on my profile picture: *Nice cats, what breed are they?*

Mapio. Marius. Mario, to his Italian friends.

I add him on Facebook, where I find more photos, both his own and ones he's been tagged in. Here he is surrounded by fluorescent palm trees, now crystals, unicorns, metallic beetles, Versace logos, blurred-out penises. Here he is behind superimposed text that yells, in all caps: HORNY, FUCK, HARDER, TOTAL BLISS. Neo-surrealist collages in which Mapio/Marius is transfigured into the version of himself he would like us — his spectators, his audience — to see. A few of the photos he's tagged in are promo snaps from nightclubs across

Milan: Popstarz, Rocket, Glitter, Plastic. He appears adorned in leopard-print, in lilac furs, in Bollywood garb, in shining metal necklaces with rings on every bright-nailed finger.

I could never belong in that world. I've barely set foot in a nightclub, and I know nothing about fashion. My dress sense is random, chaotic in a daggy way — Dylan says I look like I've stepped out of a Seventies cartoon. But this only makes me like Marius more. Looking at his glittering collection of photos, I feel like a small celestial body from the outer reaches of space slowly advancing towards the centre of the universe; a tiny, miraculous meteorite, suddenly struck by the heat of a glorious Sun.

I show the photos to Melissa: Isn't he gorgeous?

Sure, yeah, he's cute.

Dylan approves without reservation: Finally, someone decent-looking.

We don't exchange many messages. Marius is a man of few words, a fact confirmed by the limits he places on our modes of contact: he agrees to chat via webcam, but refuses to turn his microphone on. *I don't love my voice*, he writes, by way of explanation. He's timid, then. But assertive: he makes the rules, that much is clear.

He suggests we meet up: *You free for a walk in the next few days?*

I reply: *Does Friday work for you?*

We arrange to meet at four thirty in Piazza Oberdan. I wait for him on the corner of Viale Piave, at an intersection scarred with disused tram tracks that die, half-buried, against the footpath. He arrives late, closer to five o'clock. I spot him from about a hundred metres away, stepping off the tram.

Sorry, he says as he approaches. I had bad luck with the public transport.

His photos gave me the impression that he was short, but in fact he's taller than I am: I estimate around 183, 185 centimetres. I've often found that people's faces give an inaccurate sense of their height — maybe what I'm sensing is in fact the stature of their personality.

He walks beside me, lighting a cigarette. Plaid shirt unbuttoned over a ratty t-shirt that looks at least ten years old. Jeans ripped off at the knee, chunky black and white leather sneakers, terry socks. I sense almost nothing of the attitude exuded by his online presence. His appearance suggests it, but it's completely absent from his expressions, gestures, movements. I try to abandon the fantasy version of him that exists in my mind and recalibrate my expectations. I try to exist in the present, open myself up to the possibilities of him.

We enter the Porta Venezia gardens via the gate next to the Rasini palace and tower. We pass the miniature train ride, the legions of joggers, and sit at one of the many park benches. At our backs is the large sloping lawn that serves, in the summertime, as a favourite meeting place for couples and groups of friends, most of whom come laden with books and dogs and sunscreen. Facing each other on the dark-green metal of the bench, we talk for I don't know how long — two hours, at least — under a slowly contracting, slowly darkening sky.

So you study fashion?

Yeah, at the New Academy of Fine Arts, near Romolo. I'm only in my first year.

That's a private university, right?

Yeah, but I have a scholarship that covers, like, sixty per cent of my tuition. I could never afford it otherwise.

And your name?

It's Romanian. I was born there.

I wouldn't have guessed. I mean, you don't have an accent. You speak perfect Italian.

I found out that he came to Italy when he was very young. His father, an ex-soldier, worked as a bricklayer, and his mother as an in-home nurse.

I grew up in Marsciano, he says, near Perugia. Do you know it? My father came over first, just him on his own, after they executed Ceaușescu, but we stayed in Focșani. He lived in Rome for a while, my father. Did a bunch of different jobs: painter, gardener, parking attendant. In the evenings, he'd walk around and note down all the poorly maintained shop shutters, then the next day he'd approach the shopkeepers and offer to repair them. When he worked as an attendant in a parking lot, one of those underground ones, he'd always send us photos of all the fancy cars he saw: Ferraris, Porsches, Lamborghinis. My brother used to show our friends and tell them they were ours, that our father lived in Italy and collected fancy cars.

While he remained in Romania, Marius saw very little of his father. He only visited home once or twice a year.

But he was always sending us gifts, Marius tells me. Typical toys for boys.

One birthday, he remembers receiving a remote-controlled police car with the Italian flag printed on the front doors. It would screech to a halt, and two cops would shout something in Italian through the windows.

I memorised the sounds they made, Marius says, so that when I finally made it to Italy I'd know how to stop thieves in their tracks.

His laughter dissipates any tension between us, and everything becomes easy.

His father, he continues, would also send him clothes and packaged cakes from Italy.

My god, the cakes.

Didn't you have them back home?

We had cakes, and packaged desserts, but not the pre-portioned, individually wrapped ones you get here. I was obsessed with the little cardboard bases they sit on, I'd collect them and make characters out of them: queens and princesses with giant ruffled skirts, like mountains. Everyone at school was so jealous of my Italian croissants. I imagined Italy as this beautiful paradise, an enormous garden with flowers everywhere. My father also sent us pictures of Rome, and I remember seeing photos of avenues all lined with oleander. In Romania, the streets were lined with flower beds and little, low-growing shrubs. I thought my father must be rich in Italy, and that when we joined him, we'd be rich, too, and eat millions of individually wrapped cakes every day. I made the ones he sent me last as long as possible, for fear I'd run out.

Marius was six when he came to Italy.

The first thing he remembers, the very first thing, is the smell of Marseille soap on the terracotta floor of their house in Marsciano.

His most vivid memory from Romania is a pear tree in his grandmother's garden, which he used to climb. He was the smallest and lightest in the family, so he got all the pears to himself.

My grandmother is a witch, you know, he says out of nowhere.

Down in the cellar she had all these little jars of green and yellow liquids, extracts, herbal infusions, which she used for massaging people. Sometimes she even used petroleum. She could also remove curses, the evil eye. People who were unwell would come to our house, and my grandmother would put her hand on their forehead and draw a cross with her thumb, and whisper something over and over, and they'd recover. Or she'd use a knife, the biggest knife in the kitchen, a meat knife, and leave light marks on their skin with the blade, without drawing blood. Whenever I made the sign of the cross, she'd warn me to keep my fingers closed tight: *the devil's tail can slip through the smallest of spaces*, she'd say.

According to local legend, Marius's grandmother resuscitated a dead baby when she was a young girl. Newborns are the most susceptible to the evil eye, Marius tells me. It's considered dangerous to give young children compliments, especially before they've been baptised.

Eventually, Marius, his mother, and brother joined their father in Umbria: Italy's green lungs, the land of saints. (No, he says when I ask him, I've never been to Assisi.) The bus ride from Focșani to Perugia took thirty hours.

We arrived late at night, he says. When I first laid eyes on this new place that was about to become my home, it looked so strange. There weren't as many flowers as I'd imagined. Our house was in a narrow laneway in the historic centre — are you familiar with Umbrian villages? Everything is made of stone, I felt like I was in a movie, one with knights and princesses. There was even a medieval tower near our house.

He laughs, he laughs constantly, his face wide open and eyes drooping beautifully. He tells me more stories about his family, their immigration to Italy in search of a better life, as he struggles to keep his long thin legs crossed on the park bench, like mine, which have the unfair advantage of unusually compliant joints.

Six months ago, in October, he moved to Milan from the provinces of Perugia. It had been his dream since he was fourteen: to live in Milan and study fashion design.

I knew nothing about Milan, he says. I just knew I wanted to come here.

His parents send him five hundred euros a month. Half of that goes to renting the room he shares with an economics student who also works as a DJ in a couple of local dive bars. The other half he spends on groceries, public transport, nightclubs. When the money runs out, he skips meals, or steals packets of crackers from his housemates. Anyway, alcohol has calories in it, and most of the time that's free. Aside from the DJ, two other guys share his apartment — all three are straight, and he hates them. Especially one of them, a metalhead from Turin.

Why, what did he do?

Last month, for example, I was in the kitchen talking to a friend of mine, Beatrice, and suddenly he swoops in from the other room and holds a fork to my neck. He'd heard me using a swear word. I mean, in Umbria everyone swears all the time. *Next time*, he told me, *this'll be a knife*.

So, typical metalhead then.

Anyway, what about you? What do you do?

I study philosophy, and teach yoga at a few places.

Sounds serious.

Well, that depends.

Do you live alone?

I have a roommate, I've lived with him for a year and a half.

Before that, I was living with my ex, but now he's in Sydney.

Wow, you made him leave the country?

More or less.

The words travel lightly between us, autonomous corpuscles, until the rain that has been threatening to fall does, forcing us to get up and return to our meeting place. It's almost eight o'clock. Corso Buenos Aires stretches ahead of us, the ramparts of Porta Venezia stand at our backs. I don't want to, but I've learnt to bridle my urges — managing an addiction is an art. The idea is to get burnt without letting yourself catch fire, to find the perfect balance between withdrawal and overdose.

Which part of town are you in?

Loreto. You?

Ripamonti, the far end.

Oh yeah, I have friends who study out that way.

How shitty is this rain, I hate it — and he runs a hand over his fine, gold, glorious damp hair.

I don't want you to get wet. We'll be in touch?

He agrees, nodding in the sea of passers-by, nodding with his head and with his eyes, and while it looks convincing, I know by now that this nod means nothing. A kind of confusion often takes place after first dates, an automatic attraction born from the excitement and novelty of human contact, but later the feeling fades.

He walks away, in the direction of the tram stop.

Two strangers briefly united, now divided once more.

Piazza Argentina. Water and exaltation descend from the sky. Via Pecchio, Piazza Aspromonte. My body against the wind. Intercom — *it's just me* — then lift. Crossing the threshold of the front door, I'm assaulted by a wave of laughter, the sounds of plates and cutlery. Dylan is there, in shorts and a Captain America t-shirt, about to eat dinner with his friend Pia, a photographer. She's young, only twenty-one, and always in a hurry; she's new to Milan, but already has more work than she can handle, constantly rushing between fashion shoots and ad agencies. She's beautiful or plain, depending on the day, with a memorable nose and teeth, reminiscent of Lady Gaga (*Oh yeah, I get that all the time*, she says). Her father, who lives in Emilia-Romagna, sends her as much money as she needs. This makes all the difference — in this city, a financial safety net is essential if you want to establish a career as a creative. With her material needs covered, Pia has no need to enter the deadly cycle of unpaid internships and exploitative work-for-exposure arrangements.

Hey, ciao.

Well good evening.

Dylan and Pia are setting the kitchen table, their movements swift and coordinated. Aluminium trays are removed from plastic bags, releasing the sweet smell of Chinese takeaway.

You should have told me you'd be home, Dylan says. I would have ordered you some.

No, don't be silly. I'll heat up some of that pasta from last night.

How did it go?

I think it went well.

Aw, come on! Are you going to meet up again?

Who knows.

Standing before the open fridge, he asks: Want a beer?

Dylan loves dark, potent beers, the kind that quickly ease the mind into a cosy fug, letting everything else — disappointment, negative thoughts — fade gently away.

I say yes.

Later, as I slip into bed, abandoning my body to the coolness of the sheets, I feel a drifting sense of hope, which insists despite my best attempts to repress it. *Who knows.* The last thing I do, before letting my mind slide beyond the veil of consciousness, is glance at my phone, a gesture I'll repeat first thing in the morning, the moment I wake up.

A whole day passes, a full, endless, insufferable day of silence. I resist the urge to message Marius. Fine, I guess this is how it goes. I begin to turn my thoughts away from this new failure, the latest in a long line of missed opportunities, towards more mundane affairs, like the study proposal I have to submit to the university secretariat.

Dylan, I call, want to get breakfast at the bar downstairs?

Wholemeal brioche, almond butter, oat-milk cappuccino.

It would have been nice to see him again, I admit. I would have liked that.

The whole affair was like the rebirth and sudden death of a star.

It's late in the evening when the screen of my old Samsung phone lights up with a single sentence, all in lower case:

you still haven't introduced me to your cats

It means nothing — I know this. It's just a text message. Still, it sends my synapses into bloom, blossoming into an almond of light, a cerebral solstice.

I like him; maybe he likes me, too.

Then a second thought: *Don't get ahead of yourself.*

We'll have to fix that, I text back.

Two hours later, a photo of a strange feline appears on my Facebook wall: it looks a bit like a jaguar, but with a more intricate coat. The cat is staring directly into the camera with large, kohl-rimmed eyes, pink nose shocking against the fur mask with its vivid black markings, like lines drawn in charcoal by some ancient shamanic finger.

I get the feeling you're a bit of an ocelot, Marius writes underneath the photo.

Google informs me that the ocelot — its Nahuatl name — is also known as the painted leopard. Ocelots are particularly docile when young, purring like kittens, but can become quite aggressive as adults. The Aztecs believed their flesh and blood possessed magical healing properties, and these still fetch high prices on the black market.

I pick up my phone, barely pausing to think.

Want to come over tomorrow afternoon?

Porta Ticinese

Marius is a cataclysm from which I don't want to be saved.

A real boyfriend. A new altar at which to worship. Falling in love fills me with a strength and energy I've never felt, coupled with the constant fear of imminent collapse. It's like having the most exquisite harmonies playing inside my head, day and night, but at any moment the tune might turn to one of total anguish: I'll worry I've said the wrong thing, or think I catch a glimpse of displeasure in his gestures, his expression, an unmistakable sign that he's having second thoughts. The song in my head is by turns gorgeous and excruciating.

To fall in love is always to crack open a shell, to expose the pulpy interior and offer it up like the flesh of Prometheus. We're like naïve invertebrates, molluscs desperate to lose our shells, then trembling at our sudden vulnerability.

I'm always on alert, ready to interpret my destiny from every offhand comment. I see spectres of disaster in every disappointment: every fading smile, every half-hearted answer, a kiss that falls a little short of passionate.

It's a Sunday afternoon, forty-eight hours after the park bench in Porta Venezia, when Marius comes over for the first time. The intercom announces his arrival innocently, ungratefully, with the same dull sound it makes for everyone.

Hi — fifth floor, first door on your left.

The next seventy or eighty seconds are breathless, a herd of beasts in my chest.

I open the front door as the lift is ascending; it jerks to a halt with its usual clangour. It's colder today than it has been the past few days. Or am I imagining it? As he closes the interior doors of the lift, I take in the sight of him: small round sunglasses, long dark-grey coat, under which I glimpse a black t-shirt with two yellow eyes peering out — merch from the musical *Cats*. He removes his earbuds as he comes towards me.

You like it? he asks, tapping his chest. I got it at the flea market in Piazzale Cuoco. I can take you one day, if you want.

He has the effortless look of a New York party monster. I could never pull off his style, not even after several days of vintage shopping and fussing in mirrors. He's different from me. Better. Falling in love is like an ethnographic journey into a superior culture; I want to learn from him.

Did you find the address okay?

Yesss. I did have to ask a girl for directions at one point, but it's super close to the Metro station. Where can I put this?

He gestures at his coat.

Give it to me, I'll hang it up.

There they are! — the cats have come dashing down the corridor to check out the intruder, León leading the way, as usual. He's always been more extroverted than his sister, greedier for human touch. Rosaspina prefers to keep her distance, remaining watchful.

They just woke up, I say.

My god, they're so beautiful.

A lot of people find them disturbing, actually. The other morning, one of them escaped and ran upstairs, and I could hear a woman screaming: *What in god's name is that?* She thought he'd crawled out of the garbage or something.

Poor thing, he laughs, stroking León's head.

Come in, I say.

We shut ourselves in my bedroom and sit on pillows on the floor, removing our shoes first. Later, we recline, his head on my belly, and I admire the top of his head from close up: his impossibly fine hair, the eyebrows tracing the contours of his eye sockets, the glimmer of his septum piercing. The late April sun grows weaker through the skylight, casting perfect, gentle shadows.

Wait, let me take this out. He reaches into his nostrils and removes the piercing — it's fake, a cheap ring from Zara or H&M.

You just have to cut out a little piece with some pliers, he explains. They fit great.

We talk until our words start to seek each other, grasping at each other, forming a chain of breath between our lips. His mouth is incredible. His little moustache doesn't bother me at all, nor do his crooked teeth — when I have the money, he told me, I want to have them all pulled out and replaced with ceramic implants.

We kiss for an hour, two hours. Then we dance, on the most coveted floor in Milan, embracing each other, swaying as one. Without music — we don't need music. My feet on top of this, then his on top of mine; our bodies merging, occupying a single point. We are redesigning the laws of physics.

He's a little taller than me.

How much taller? I ask. Three centimetres?

He jokes that he doesn't usually date guys shorter than him, but he's willing to make an exception for me.

How magnanimous of you, I say.

We continue swaying. We have the apartment to ourselves; Dylan generously offered to go to the movies with his photographer friend.

I'll be back after dinner, he assured me. Take your time.

When we make love, the first time and the many times that follow, it will always be this way: I can't help but search for his eyes, our pupils aligning, and everything I feel shows plainly on my face, the muscles and cheekbones lifting, exploding into smiles. I am defenceless.

Do I make you laugh? he asks. Well, you make me laugh, too.

We are both uninhibited, each utterly free from the fear of ridicule.

Our lovemaking is continuous, ebbing and flowing for hours in my small bed crammed against the slope of the attic roof. I find his face again and smile, and — yes — even laugh, joy spilling out of me. Everything is devotional: his saliva, mine, the mingling of the two. Here, between us, the obscene is holy. The coils of hair on his chest, his pubis, the circles of his nipples. They deserve to be kept in glass display cabinets, preserved for posterity, protected from the ravages of time. Everyone must know that this, all of this, existed. This cock, this sacred orifice that I kiss and open and suck and fill. His spit and cum is my Eucharist. I use every trick I've ever learnt, everything that has ever given me pleasure; finally, this meaningless repertoire has found its true purpose. I'll do whatever you want: fuck you, let you fuck me, let you consume me, tear me apart and offer me up in sacrifice to your homophobic Orthodox god. I imagine the two of us entwined in mutual penetration, him inside me, me inside him, two halves re-forming, like Plato's mythical soulmates, into some perfect original being.

I feel good before, during, and after we make love. I still feel good if I come too soon, or if I don't come at all. The breath passes between our sealed lips — we are a single, autonomous organism, a closed system. Poison me with your carbon dioxide. There is squeezing, biting. We leave private runes on each other's skin. The possession is total, yet it is never enough, because when you fall in love, the other is always in some sense a hypothesis, a creature of potential, always promised but never completely there. Unquantifiable, ungraspable. Some ultra-corporeal essence always overflows from the physical presence beside you. Still, I don't stop trying. I'll never stop trying. I attempt to capture his form in portraits: thin, but with thick extremities, large hands and feet. I draw him over and over again, on sketchpads and notepads and spare bits of cardboard, whatever I have at hand. I take photos, too. The morning after he first spends the night, I frame him in the kitchen, wearing my black-and-white-striped shirt underneath his own, open denim shirt.

Stay there, don't move.

One of the cats is perched on his shoulder, like a monkey — the cats are already obsessed with him, crawling all over his body.

I can't bring myself to ask if he'll text me, if I'll see him again.

You know, he'll tell me one day, in that easy manner of his, these cats are the only reason I replied to that first message you sent. I was curious to see what they were like in the flesh.

Did you hear that, you two? You made quite the impression.

Let's be honest: who would be enticed by a photo of me?

I'm not appealing on my own, but I'm good at surrounding myself with appealing things.

The second time we meet, I take another photo: he has my red wool scarf around his neck, the one I've never worn, a gift from some relative or another, standing in front of the bathroom door, on which Dylan has hung a large poster of a mermaid immersed in aquatic spirals and vortices. Framing him in the rectangle of my phone, I'm aware that the impulse is one of documentation: I need evidence that this was real, that all of this actually happened.

Another photo immortalises our first time on public transport together: the Metro to Duomo, then the number 14 tram towards Ticinese. *Everyone look, witness us.* The brilliant green of the tram seats never looked so vibrant.

I'm accompanying him to the post office out by the Columns of San Lorenzo. The building is hot, packed full of people fanning themselves with documents and snorting like impatient farm animals.

Wait for me outside, he insists.

He's trying to track down a parcel from his parents that never arrived. He's in the post office for an hour and a half, abandoning the queue every now and then to visit me outside, and kiss me. The warmth of the April air helps fix the memory on my skin: the euphoria of those early days of love.

The next weekend, like a rat behind the pied piper, I follow him to one of his fashion meccas: the Piazzale Cuoco flea market. It's raining. The market is in a part of Milan I've never been to before, and I feel out of place. He says you can find super cool things here for two or three euros: Lee jeans, sheepskin coats, designer clothes from brands like Valentino and Yves Saint Laurent. He never shops at H&M, he tells me: too expensive. Although sometimes he and his friends go there to steal. They use pliers to remove the security tags, or scissors to cut out the fabric around them. Some of the tags spill coloured liquid on the clothes, but that's okay — you just have to remember to tuck the spoiled bit of fabric into your jeans, or cover it up with something.

Piazzale Cuoco is a large, dusty field filled with stalls, the best placed of which are fronted by fierce, chatty saleswomen putting on their weekly show, flanked by headless mannequins whose shapely bodies remind me of Diana Prince — plastic, incognito Wonder Women.

Don't go to them, he warns me. They're all thieves.

He only buys from North African stallholders, whom we find surrounded by mountains of clothing, kilos and kilos of fabric that, for Marius at least, hold untold treasures. To me, it looks like a fungal infection waiting to happen. It all reminds me too much of the market in Rozzano, the cheap clothes I hated. I put the difference down to our eight-year age gap. Fashion demarcates the different worlds we grew up in, worlds that are consecutive but separate. I can barely bring myself to touch some of the garments he picks up, thinking they're the definition of cool. Still, I enjoy myself. I enjoy being in his company.

Finally, he relents: Okay, I'm done. We can go if you want.

His only purchase was a pair of pants he's not in love with — at best, he says, I can unstitch them and turn them into a backpack or something.

We take the number 90 tram towards a yoga studio I recently began teaching at: Shanti Urban Yoga, in Carrobbio. It's one of the trendiest studios in the city, frequented by young creative types. The owner is having photos taken for the new website: individual shots of all the teachers, then a group shot, like one big endorphin-fuelled family.

Please come with me, I'd begged Marius. I hate this stuff.

The owner, a former producer for an advertising company, is obsessed with promotions and special offers: BRING A FRIEND, GET ONE WEEK FREE, that kind of thing. His goal is expansion — first within Milan, then beyond. He wants to make Shanti Urban Yoga a chain, a franchise, staffed by an army of hastily trained instructors, leaving him free to trot the globe on a fat passive income. *I'm a free spirit*, he repeats constantly. *A free spirit at heart*. After each of my classes, he checks at the front desk to see how many students attended. The number is often low: most students, especially the gay ones, come to the studio for him. They hope to be gently adjusted by his freckled, tattooed hands, or sneak a glimpse of his balls as he transitions between poses (he doesn't wear underwear when he teaches). When my class numbers are too low, his voice turns careful and eloquent, and I know I'll have a few less shifts on next week's roster.

Ever since yoga became the way I earn my living, it has lost some of its allure. I've grown disillusioned by what I've seen: the petty feuds between yoga schools, the teachers who cheat on their wives with their protégés, the overwrought, dull language of it all, the fake enlightened smiles. The honeymoon period is over — now all I see is fitness with a false conscience.

The tram slides ahead, then stops.

Here, this is us.

Our relationship moves quickly, a procession of milestones. The evening after the photo shoot at the yoga studio, I introduce

Marius to my friends. Melissa and the art historians meet us for an aperitif in Porta Genova, followed by a gelato in Via Torino. Our first public exhibition. Look: here is the supernatural parasite I have let inside my body, inside my heart, so he might colonise it. Look how beautiful he is — my boyfriend. Like an emissary of Venus. All the angst of the past few years has been transfigured into this handsome form, his stylish exterior. First, I exploited love to get out of Rozzano; now, I use it to borrow the light of an angel.

Are you coming to university with me tomorrow? I ask him when we're in bed, naked, cradling the bottle of prosecco we brought with us.

Are you sure I can get in? Won't security make a fuss?

Of course you can. Even if they check, it's fine. I can get away with anything.

He sits with me through a class on contemporary ethics, two long hours I can barely make sense of: deontology, formalism, act versus rule utilitarianism. But at the beginning of a love story, there is no such thing as boredom. The usual categories we use to orient our interests are inverted; everything is a north star.

At San Raffaele, we attract attention, sitting together in the small classroom on the second floor of the glass-clad university building, surrounded by greenery. There are only about fifteen students in the room, all wearing Lacoste shirts and business jackets, and we stand out in our black and silver nail polish, our trinkets adorned with Egyptian symbols. Already, I've started borrowing his clothes. It's more than just mimesis, or emulation: through him, I am able to fully embody myself, to bring to life parts of me that were unattainable before. Love finally legitimises me, ushers me into the world of genre and gender play: he, she, they, gutter punk, Spice Girl. I can be anything and everything, my image is an open construction site, a warehouse filled with every possible shape and model. (For my birthday party, one month after my first visit to Piazzale Cuoco, I will dress as Madonna in the music video for *Frozen*: hooded black cape, hands embellished with henna, an extravagant dragon-shaped medallion around my neck. Forty euros from Zara. My friends think I look ridiculous; we pity them, still in their twenties and already so conservative.)

Come here, I want to show you something, I say, leading him by the hand as he's finishing a cigarette in front of the university I will never think of as mine.

I take him to see the caged animals kept between the two wings of the hospital. The area was originally conceived in the Eighties as a kind of 'oasis', in line with the utterly Berlusconian spirit of the building. These days, it's a ruin. In one cage, soft, sad crowds of exotic birds — swans, giant parrots, macaws — roost above tiles splashed with fallen fruit and excrement.

Do they use them for experiments? he asks.

Who knows. It's terrible.

It's the two of us now, united against all the evil of the world.

Follow me, I say, revealing a small path between the hospital wings, like a secret clearing in the woods. Let's get out of here.

Our love feels like a kind of cosmic emergence.

April 2013: we've known each other for three weeks now, and already we have formed a new element, an indivisible particle with a life of its own. It feels like they should be writing about us in the newspapers, talking about us on the tv. I protect this glowing thing between us, this incipient blaze, with every inch and milligram of my body. Nothing else exists; this is everything. I struggle to remember what it was that filled my life before — the commitments, the people I used to busy myself with. Our ecstasy is a radiant force that destroys all life around it. I think it was Hannah Arendt who wrote: *Love has no world, love is the absence of world.* It's impossible, when you are falling in love, to keep the shape of your past life intact. If anything, the past is a threat to the new order of things, a distraction to be avoided by any means possible, lest it lead to even the briefest of separations. When the past does intrude, we take pains to evoke the magic of our union across space and time, casting digital spells in the form of emoji: endless strings of pink hearts, shining or dancing or pierced with Cupid's arrow. *You have islands in your eyes*, sings Tiziano Ferro, and to me this might as well be Our Song.

Wyd? he texts, checking in, and I feel a tide of relief swelling in me.

I miss you, he adds, catching me by surprise.

I miss you more, I answer.

Can I come over later? Or are you busy?

He only just left my apartment on the number 24 tram. We've been apart all of five minutes.

I was about to invite you. Of course you can.

You can. You must. We must. There is no possible moderation, no restraint or control at this stage. To fall in love is to become incomprehensible, ridiculous, undignified in the eyes of everyone who exists outside the temple of Venus.

He starts sleeping at the Via Lulli apartment almost every night. Every so often he'll head home for a few hours, long enough to change his clothes, then come straight back. My place is quieter, after all, more pleasant. A niggling suspicion creeps in, but I dare not give voice to it: what if he's only doing this for the space, the square metres, the peace and quiet?

How to exist, now, on the other side of love?

I can't get enough of Marius. To me, he is like Willy Wonka's everlasting gobstopper. Others wonder aloud if we aren't *taking things too fast*. To hell with their timelines — we burn through the stages of commitment like there's no tomorrow. Three weeks in, we're already practically living together. I don't ask Dylan for permission, I simply stop informing him that Marius will be staying over for the trillionth night in a row. It just happens. It's not up for discussion. It's not even up to me. I want to say: *Dylan, listen to me, I AM Marius! He is always on my mind, always, always — not like a happy thought, but like my own self, the way I inhabit my own mind, the way my consciousness inhabits my body. So there's no longer any point talking about separation. Separation is impossible.*

I let Marius smoke inside — in the bathroom, in the kitchen, everywhere — when I've always asked Dylan not to. If I have classes, Marius stays in the apartment without me, alone. He's not shy about occupying space, chilling out on the couch in his underwear. He acts as if the apartment were his home. And it could be. It is. It will be.

Dylan and I have our routines, our customs around breakfast, lunch, dinner, coffee, aperitifs. Now all that is over — how jealous are you, on a scale from one to ten? When Marius and I are about to eat, we close the kitchen door: a not-so-subtle signal that this is just for us, a private event. This is *our* lunch, *our* dinner. You don't get a look-in anymore. If you're hungry, you can just wait your turn.

Even so, Dylan likes Marius. They have a lot of things in common. They talk about music, American popstars, viral Vines and YouTube videos. In fact, Dylan has more in common with Marius than I do. He'll often call him into his bedroom to show him something on the computer: Beyoncé's latest concert, a new Katy Perry music video, a Facebook Live by Rihanna. Dylan loves pointing out the traces of past trends, motifs from the Eighties and Nineties, that he finds scattered throughout modern pop culture. Everything comes back, he says. Everything that is new has already happened.

Marius! he calls. For the love of god, get in here! Your philosopher boyfriend understands absolutely nothing about aesthetics.

Three minutes in Dylan's room become five, then ten; I'm not suspicious, obviously, but why have they suddenly gone quiet?

I move soundlessly to the edge of the hallway, silencing even my breath, listening. I imagine catching them in the act, the hands of one in the pants of the other. I shudder at the image, a wave of blood rising to my brain.

At the first opportunity, when Marius isn't there, I confront Dylan. His arms are full of washing freshly fished from the machine. Socks, underpants, the vanilla scent of fabric softener. Magic Angel Creamy Mami watches me from the poster he hung from the wall between our bedrooms.

My mouth fills with cruelties: He comes here to see me, you know. Not you. He talks to you because he's kind, because he feels obligated. But he's not your friend.

I have to stop myself from adding: He told me he feels sorry for you.

Marius is the first to text *I love you*. I've never said it to anyone before. I've imagined saying it, hundreds of times, whispering it into the ear of The One, practising kisses against the bathroom mirror.

I love you too, I text back. And a voice inside me answers: *Are you sure?*

It's terrifying, placing those three words next to each other in a line for the first time. But once the threshold has been crossed, I repeat them over and over, saying them with my mouth and typing them with my fingers, proclaiming them with my body. *I love you.* So this is how it feels to want someone who wants you back. This is the dream: to have your feelings reciprocated, to see your own devotion reflected in another. To be desired, exclusively, by the one you desire. To be chosen.

I open Facebook and update my status: *Those of you who aren't in love, how do you get out of bed in the morning?*

The comments collect below:

What a shitty thing to write.

It's not like I want to be alone.

Yeah, you could have kept this one to yourself.

Easy to say now, get back to me in three months.

The material world suddenly has a spiritual quality to it. For lovers, even food takes on a transcendental quality. Each breakfast we share is holy, an unrepeatable celebration. No more hasty lunches or frugal, improvised dinners. Meals are more than just sustenance now — they are a way to express the immensity of what is happening inside and between us. We never repeat dishes, instead devising unusual new recipes with expensive ingredients. I'm working more, earning seven or eight hundred euros a month, so I can even afford to take him out for dinner. The nights I teach, Marius waits for me in Piazza Argentina, and before heading home we stop at a trattoria, a pizza place, somewhere cheap and cheerful. Each outing in the city has the quality of an overseas jaunt, each visit to the supermarket is imbued with an intoxicating new domesticity. Everything feels alive, its meaning restored. Just being here, anywhere, with him, in this moment, is enough. He is my Messiah, my anointed one, the one I've been waiting for. It's not pure hyperbole: aren't religions born, after all, from this kind of infatuation? Cult leaders know how to exploit this feeling, its almost psychotropic effect. The conviction that *this is it, this is everything, this is all I need.* There is comfort in the knowledge that I'm not alone in my delirium — there are two of us here, each of us as mad as the other.

My lovesickness persists even when, after eating, we browse the closed shop windows on our way home — clothes shops, paint shops, bakeries — and he talks nonstop, half to himself, loosing a nonsense stream of phrases (*Okay then! Love! Oh wow! I'm dead!*) punctuated by exaggerated gestures, strange faces, spontaneous laughter. I want to say: *I'm so tired, can you please shut up?* Or: *What are you laughing at?* But there's no need. Just looking at him, my irritation evaporates. It must. It has no choice but to vanish.

In the end, we are one person. Our bodies fused, welded. When we walk down the street, day or night, we hold hands. If we encounter an obstacle, like a pole or a lamp post, he refuses to let go: we move aside as one, our fingers still tightly interwound. A fist, a small nest of flesh, a symbol of his intention to stay — forever? — but also his will to fight, knowing that nobody stays together by chance. Or: pure superstition. He is the grandson of a witch, after all.

We hold hands in the Cloister of the Frogs, at Santa Maria delle Grazie church, where we end up one day, almost by accident, and are enchanted by the mild fountain with its four oversized bronze frogs spitting streams of water. We hold hands inside the church itself, defiantly, imagining the disapproval of the priests and sextons. Our hands stay joined even as we pass through threatening groups of heterosexual men, our natural predators. I'm ready to retaliate, almost daring them to say something.

His full name is Marius Mădălin, the masculine, Romanian form of Mary Magdalene. The redeemed whore. Redeemed by us, by our love. José, one of Marius's friends from university — half Abruzzese, half Bolivian — likes to humiliate me with allusions to the past: *You can take the girl off the streets, but you can't take the streets out of the girl.* Or: *Do you have any idea how many dicks this one used to catch in her day?*

José is seething with jealousy. He slanders Marius because he's lonely, the last piece of fruit left rotting at the bottom of the bowl. He's desperate, pitiful, reduced to posting photos of his naked arse on Facebook. Still, his comments have an effect on me. I start digging deeper through Marius's old photos on Facebook. I want to know how many guys there have been, who they were, what they looked like. Then I stop myself — on second thoughts, maybe I don't want to know.

Should we both delete our Grindr profiles? I ask one day, innocently.

The outside world doesn't interest us anymore. Now there is only us. The past is in the past.

You know, before we met there were days when I'd just lie in bed and cry, Marius reveals.

Then he adds: Knowing I could kill myself kept me going. The thought that, if things got unbearable, there was always a way out.

There it is: proof, confirmation that we were meant to be together. We saved one another. He was waiting for me, just as

I was waiting for him. Or maybe, like me, he was just unlovable. Unwanted. Maybe we're both just rejects, feeding on scraps.

Immediately before we met, he was seeing someone. A tall, older guy — taller than me? Marius really liked him, and things were starting to get serious when the guy backed off. I'm the first one who has ever stayed, he tells me. The only one who has ever wanted to spend more than a few hours in his company.

Then, one afternoon, my fingers won't stop scratching. It must be my jeans.

Marius notices: What is it, what's wrong?

Look at this — does that look like a mole? Here's another one. Come here, under the light.

With the blade of my fingernail, I remove the mole-like thing from the base of my pubic hair and place it on the edge of the bathroom sink. It looks like a small crust of skin, until tiny legs unfold from its curled body. The thing can walk.

Crabs. Who had them first? It doesn't matter. What matters is that there are microscopic creatures living on us, sucking our blood and laying eggs in our nether regions.

It says here they can't be transferred to head hair.

What about facial hair?

It's okay — every problem has a solution. It must. Nothing good comes without sacrifice; all sacred spaces demand ablutions. I will cleanse myself of all traces of past evils, his and mine.

I go straight to the pharmacy on Via Pecchio.

You stay here, I insist. I'll take care of it.

On the way, I google the most effective treatments and take note of the brand names. I practise saying them aloud to myself, gaining confidence so I won't have to ask the pharmacist for advice. I'll just walk straight up to the counter and ask for what I need, the way I always do: *One bottle of this and one packet of that, please.* For all they know, my little brother could have caught head lice at school.

I'm in and out of the pharmacy quickly, and return with everything we need.

It takes two or three consecutive treatments to rid our bodies of the parasites. We hole up in the bathroom and lather ourselves with the insecticide, clouds of soap enclosing our bodies like foaming dresses — wait, rinse, repeat — carefully following the instruction leaflet that unfolds on the floor to the size of a bedsheet. We spend almost two hours in the bathroom, committing our diligent genocide.

Shh, shut up for a second …

Footsteps in the hallway, the doorhandle turning.

Dylan walks in without knocking: Oh fuck, sorry.

Then, as he's closing the door, he adds: I should just brush my teeth quickly.

This is his house, too. He has the right to take a piss in his own bathroom.

Later, he takes me aside: Look, I get it. I'm not saying he shouldn't stay over. I like the guy. But seriously — crabs? For god's sake, man.

Viale Alemagna

The tram staggers to a stop. The old doors swing open noisily. There are so many of them. Four — no, six. A herd, a gang, all wearing black, a tangle of bare skin and chiffon.

Behind us, the nocturnal gloom of Parco Sempione extends like a haunted forest. A few steps from us is the snake pit, an important archaeological site in queer Milan: a strip of greenery between the Triennale design museum and the Cadorna railway line, historically known as a gay cruising area.

The six jump and squeal as they descend the tram, all glitter and greasepaint, grinding and twerking on the poles and benches of the tram stop, mouths and bodies sprawling.

He's cuter in real life, they say, referring to me.

They've been drinking, and it shows. They had 'pre-drinks', Marius explains, which is a practice that involves intensive alcohol consumption — mainly of cheap spirits — immediately before going out to a club, in order to save money. Marius's friends are young, like him, all born between 1993 and 1995. Vania, Gemma (known as Gem), Filo, Samuele, Mia, and Leo. I'm almost ten years their senior, but already I can sense that they've lived many things I haven't. I feel they might have things to teach me. Tonight, they're letting me into their world. This is the acid test.

Δ

Until tonight, I'd only heard their names mentioned in Marius's brief summaries of our days apart: yesterday, after class, he and Leo went for a McDonald's thickshake; tomorrow, they're all going to Filo's place to finish a design assignment. This is my first time meeting them.

An hour earlier, Marius and I met at Cadorna station after I finished teaching yoga. The plan was to have a drink before meeting up with the others.

Ciao, he said, kissing me hello. Then he retreated a little, his gaze wandering up and down, not fixed on my body, exactly, but taking in the fullness of its surroundings, as though to verify what he was seeing.

Is that what you're wearing?

In his voice I sensed dismay, disgust.

He'd been looking forward to this evening. The plan was to head to Old Fashion, one of Milan's hottest clubs — *oh yeah*, I'd said, nodding, although I'd never heard of it — for a popular weekly event hosted by Maria del Gasoline. Clearly, my yoga outfit was not going to cut it: an old, pilled tracksuit, the bottoms once black but now sun-faded, the top a mismatching grey. I still had my yoga mat slung over my shoulder.

I mean, obviously I was going to change, I said. But I don't know, I didn't know — what should I wear?

Ah okay, he answered, and his relief was palpable.

These nights out are serious business. They are the stage on which Marius and his peers — fashion and makeup students from all over Italy, and even beyond, who have made the ultimate pilgrimage to Milan on their parents' dime — present themselves to the world. They spend days preparing outfits, faces, hairstyles. Looks must never be repeated. The unspoken objective of the evening is to catch the eye of the event photographer, who each week immortalises a select few of the most beautiful, the most special attendees, arousing the envy of the masses.

Similar evenings are scattered across the calendar, three or four a week, and showing up to them is the most serious commitment these young fashionistas have ever made. Often they'll stay up all night, then head straight to class in the morning — with the help of coffee, Red Bull, amphetamines? They share a specific verbal and visual language, mediated by social media, and worship the same idols, the most cherished of whom are the wayward rich kids of Noughties America: Lindsay Lohan, Nicole Richie, Paris Hilton, the Olsen twins. The aesthetic is pop whore, party drugs, sex toys, eating disorders, all rendered in the fanzine graphics of teenagerhood. *Slut* is a compliment of the highest order. Sexual misadventures are recounted like mythological sagas.

Let's stop by the apartment quickly, I said. There's plenty of time.

We descended to the platform and boarded a train. The few other passengers were weary, caving into themselves after a long workday. We got off at Loreto and made the brief walk to Via Lulli. Standing at my wardrobe, Marius curated an outfit for me, selecting only worthy garments that promised not to embarrass him. When he was satisfied, we headed back out and made our way towards Viale Alemagna.

The others are taking the number 5, Marius said as we passed the entrance of Parco Sempione. Let's wait for them at the tram stop.

△

When the tram doors open, his friends explode into the street like firecrackers.

Ciaoooo, ciaoooo, so nice to meeeet you!

We need to get a move on — it's already past midnight, and after twelve thirty you have to pay to get in. But first: a pit stop. We sit on the steps of the Triennale, and the girls open their voluminous designer bags to reveal a pair of two-litre plastic Coke bottles with the labels removed. One contains vodka and lemonade, the other they can't remember. We pass them around until they're empty.

Who would have thought, Marius's friends say, turning to him. We all figured you'd be the last of us to get hitched.

I know, he answers. I hardly recognise myself.

My job is just to nod, to elicit smiles.

Fuck, someone says, it's twenty-eight past midnight.

We run down the hill and through the trees towards the club. There isn't much of a queue. We make it past the bouncers, and my boyfriend's friends lead me through the misty false twilight past the doors. Turning a corner, we enter a large, humid room crowded with young people. They all seem to know each other, addressing everyone as *babe* and *love*, even — I'll discover later — their mortal enemies. The room is a rainbow of lurex shorts, mesh shirts, pink hair, blue hair, braids. A girl with dirty green locks is busy with knobs and mixers behind the DJ deck, sipping intermittently from a glass someone has placed next to her. Three more girls are standing on a raised platform in the middle of the room, waving something phosphorescent that sends luminous trails curling around their bodies.

We down two, three, four cocktails each. I'd lose count if I weren't the one paying for them. Marius loves to dance. He's an incredible dancer, emitting rays of charisma that draw people to him. He studied dance for years, he tells me, but had to stop when he moved to Milan. Like the rest of his generation, he copies his moves from Black culture — all the straight men want to be rappers, and all the gay men want to be African American women.

Everything moves through a gloam of fake smoke and fuchsia lights. The baseline of *We Found Love* keeps me on my feet, despite my exhaustion. I'm bone tired. But here, now, everything seems possible. I am one of *them.* A being who moves to the rhythms of Azealia Banks, Die Antwoord, Charli XCX, Missy Elliot. Every couple of songs, we drag our bodies from the writhing crowd to smoke a cigarette, or three, or ten, by the fence separating the club from the dark park. I had quit smoking, but that's over now. True love is worth risking lung cancer for.

I drink, too. From my glass, from his, from any receptacle I cross paths with.

One of Marius's friends, Leo — mildly goth, dressed in a black crop top with tulle sleeves — collapses on a couch after about an hour, crying and vomiting, his head between his legs.

Leave him, they say. He always does this.

Another friend, Gem, finds two straight guys to fuck her behind the bushes in the park, away from the streetlights. Both married, she reports gleefully upon her return.

The objective of these nights out, I come to understand, is total liberation from the boundaries of the self. To become invisible, or enormous; to evaporate. What remains when you drive out the conscious mind? Only vibration, gentle or devastating, a tremor or an earthquake that brings everything crashing together:

words, fears, desires. *We don't owe anyone anything*. We — a single, pulsating impulse, shared by all of us, passing through each of us, a symbiotic network that wipes every slate clean and leads us all back to some original, primal belonging. This is where we end up. This is where, tonight, we start again.

I can't bring myself to surrender completely to this annihilation of the self. I find myself holding back, isolating myself. I keep watch over Marius — this, I decide, is my mission, my purpose. If someone tries to approach him, I force my way between them using elbows and knees: *Stay away*. I am a sentinel, his bodyguard. The later it gets, the more bodies crowd into the room, growing closer and sweatier, coupling on the dance floor, or, better yet, peeling off into the bathrooms for some privacy, where they consume one another behind the too-short toilet doors. Gays with girls, friends with friends — there are no rules in here.

I know Marius has fucked in this club, several times. José told me all about it.

This one time, he said, *it was three of us in this guy's car out the front. Me, your boyfriend, and this rando we both wanted to rail.*

He also told me that Gem, the manipulative bitch, used to encourage Marius to fuck guys in exchange for drinks or a lift home.

But everything is different now, right? I'm here now. To protect you, protect us, from the euphoria, from our own libidos. From these so-called friends of yours, carnivorous plants each and every one of them, who would sell your body for a shot of vodka.

If it came to it — I find myself playing out the scenario in my head, imagining every detail — I would smash a glass and hold its jagged edge to a man's throat, or reach across the bar for a bottle of spirits and use it to beat his skull to a pulp. But there's no need: Marius looks over at me and smiles, leans in to kiss me.

Relax. All is well.

What exists between us remains as hard and unchanged as a diamond, even when everything is swirling and burning around us, a thousand tiny fires.

We dance until three or four in the morning. Without realising it, I collapse on one of the white leather couches, now filthy with footprints and sticky with spilt drinks.

A voice I don't recognise laughs, says: He's fallen asleep, the old man. Like my nonno after lunch.

A bouncer in a white shirt shakes me awake. I have no idea how long I've been out.

No sleeping in here, he says.

I stand up, my head a hellscape, neck muscles screaming after their crumpled nap. I find myself outside with Marius and the others, standing among the flowerbeds and stone-lined paths of the park.

Hey, a voice says. Has anyone seen Gem?

I'll call her, says another.

She'll have gone home with someone.

Has she ever told you about the time she woke up in hospital? She was fine, she'd just fallen asleep on the footpath. Someone must have picked her up and dropped her at the ED.

Are you guys getting a taxi or what?

I think we're walking.

I have no idea how long it takes us to get home on foot — it could be twenty minutes or three hours. Marius makes fun of me because I keep nodding off as I walk. My feet move as if of their own accord, but my chin keeps crumpling into my neck, my eyelids closing momentarily.

Like a horse, he says, laughing.

Δ

Three days later, we go out again. It's *Akeem of Zamunda* night, another of Marius's favourites (the name comes from Eddie Murphy's character in the movie *Coming to America*) at a club called Rocket. This time the music is all hip-hop and R'n'B.

Let's have dinner at my place first, Marius suggests.

Wow, really?

Rocket's not far from mine. We can walk there.

I take the tram to his apartment, or what was his apartment, since he practically lives at my place now. It's in Via Ada Negri, in Vigentino: a neighbourhood of ex–public housing buildings, now run-down private dwellings inhabited by students and immigrants. A shithole, as Marius puts it. But that doesn't stop him coming and going at all hours in flamboyant outfits. His fabulous walks of shame. Nothing can stop him now that he's made it to Milan.

He leads me up the stairwell to his apartment, and through the front door. This way: first room on the right. Are the other rooms occupied? Is there anyone else home? I wonder how it must be to live like this, crammed in like sardines, one bathroom shared between four people — six, when girlfriends sleep over.

This is my first time visiting his apartment, his bedroom. It's small, the two single beds closely set, separated only by a narrow bedside table. In the mornings, Marius says, he wakes to the sound of his housemate working out: sit-ups, push-ups. *Does that turn you on?* The thoughts come to me, unstoppable. *Do you want to fuck him?* The old fear that our love won't be enough for him, can never be enough.

One wall of the room, the right-hand one, is all his: a wall of ex-votos. There's a giant Chanel bag he found in the garbage, hung like a painting. A photo of Kate Moss. A long pendant of blonde hair, which turns out to be a necklace from H&M's Maison Margiela collection. A small yellow-frocked doll he found in the street, with curly red hair and a half-burnt face. A shiny silver skull holding a collection of cigarette lighters.

His sewing machine and fashion magazines sit on a small desk. The floor is littered with fabric scraps and clothes, some clean, others used.

Look, he says, handing me a thick brochure. The cover shows a woman with the head of a frog, wearing an unusual headdress. Her limbs are made of twigs, and she is standing in the middle of the desert. The heels on her shoes are enormous, half the length of her leg.

It's my final dissertation, he explains. Instead of the usual boring format, I thought I'd present it like this. Like a brochure.

I open it and read: *Marius Mădălin Musat, Class 5B, 2011/2012.*

The columns of text below summarise his education history: he graduated from an art institute in Deruta, near Perugia, and for his final thesis he chose to examine the history of high heels, finding that in periods of socio-economic hardship, heels got higher — a symbolic lifting out of misery — and when things were going well, they shrank back down.

Still reading, I sit at the vintage barstool beside the desk, and Marius straddles me.

Woah, are your housemates home?

I don't care.

He kisses me and starts unbuttoning his jeans. I sit up enough to unbutton my own and lower them, kissing his nipples until they come alive like taut little animals. I bring my hand to my mouth, taking saliva, and sigh all the air from my body as I sink into him. He is warm, hot, and I dig my nails into my thighs, secretly pinching the hairs above my knee to delay the pleasure. In this tiny, miserable bedroom, we feel revolutionary. I close his lips, quieting him as the sensations radiate from us. Despite the nails and the pinched hairs, I don't last long. We continue anyway. I could do this for hours, my body completely at his disposal, devoted to his pleasure. Love has turned me into a Tantric god. *Tell me when you're ready* — and I come again, both of us wide-mouthed and gasping, our bodies melting and trembling into one another, then closing into an embrace, not an atom of empty space between us, the universe having shifted on its axis.

I'll just take a quick shower, he says, dancing out of the room, pants still down, shirt lifted. I'll be right back.

While I wait, I try on his jewellery — earrings, necklaces, he has so many accessories, things I've never owned but that feel so *me* — and take a series of selfies. In one, I'm lying in his bed balancing a blue plastic prism on my forehead. I choose a filter — cool, subaquatic tones — and post the photo to Instagram. I caption it: *Crystal therapy.*

Hey, he says, re-emerging from the doorway, one towel around his waist and another over his shoulders.

Done already?

Let's eat, we're running late.

In the small, narrow kitchen — petrol green, with a fold-down bench serving as a rickety dining table — he has prepared a candlelit dinner. In the middle of the makeshift table sits a single omelette (he must have forgotten I'm vegan, but I don't say anything) and a single red votive candle.

I found it in the cupboard, he admits. I have no idea where it came from.

As we sit down, he realises there's no bread.

Damn it, he says, annoyed with himself. I should have made a side dish. Are you very hungry?

His housemates come and go from the kitchen, tense-faced, and I half expect a fight to break out.

How can you stand to live here? I ask when we're alone.

How do you mean? This was the best place I could find, I looked at six or seven.

I can't imagine what the others must have been like.

Anyway, I'm pretty much always out.

Out in search of something, I think. *What makes you think he'll stop looking now?*

We clear the table, and he washes the two plates and the worn-out frying pan. I can't wait to get out of here.

Before leaving, we assemble my outfit under his close supervision. This time, we have his wardrobe to play with. It's like another world has been opened up.

He fishes something from a pile of denim: Here, try this on.

I slip into a pair of very tight pants, and he approves.

You should definitely be going slimmer in the legs, he says, nodding.

He completes the look with a thread of black eyeliner and a Celtic-knot necklace.

We head downstairs and wait for the bus. The club is in Via Pezzotti, a stone's throw from the tram line that leads to Rozzano (six years ago, I was robbed at the Via Volvinio tram stop, just a few hundred metres away). Before going inside, we stop at the cheap Chinese-run bar next door: one euro for a shot of vodka. My shout, Marius says.

Checking my phone, I announce: Pia and Bart might be joining us.

Bart is a friend who works at the gay bar next to Central Station, an exclusive club for male homosexuals where, two or three times a year, they hold an international fisting convention.

What about Dylan?

I don't know, and I don't care.

As we're smoking on the footpath opposite the Church of the Four Evangelists, a short girl with aubergine lipstick asks us for a light.

Are you guys brothers? she asks, releasing a mouthful of smoke.

I'm flattered, of course. Marius not so much. The first sign, perhaps, that our talents are not so evenly distributed. Or that he cares more about the truth than I do.

Inside, the club is tiny. We can barely move. When the music volume lowers below ear-splitting for a rare, brief moment, I say: Tomorrow we'll both knuckle down and study, promise?

I feel the need to close the gap between our two dimensions, to hold his desires and mine together, to intertwine them.

In three days — *fuck, only three* — he has to present his final dissertation, and I'm way behind on my summer exam prep. His deadlines loom as large as mine in my mind, now. We both have scholarships to hold on to, after all. My job, I decide, is to introduce some discipline in the wake of this sudden symbiosis that has done away with our previous, autonomous lives. My job is to keep things under control.

Via Lario

The day after Rocket, hung over at my kitchen table, now *our* kitchen table, Marius tells me all about his studies at the New Academy of Fine Arts. It all sounds so foreign to me: research, mood boards, collage. In touch class — *touch* class? Yes, he says, like the sense, one of the five senses — they were asked to build a loom. In textile-culture class, they learnt all the different symbols you can put on care labels: *cold wash, wool blend, dry clean only.* They do a lot of practical tasks, in groups. To me, it sounds like an extremely overpriced primary school. An academy for rich children. The students who can't keep up with the workload simply buy their dissertations from students who have already passed. Complete projects, designs and all, printed and ready to go; all they have to do is change the title page. If you have enough money, you can get through an entire degree this way.

Our study session doesn't last long.

Marius closes his book and says: What a beautiful day! Look at this sunshine! Should we go outside and study in the park?

Soon we're sprawled in the grass of the same gardens where we first met. I'm reading through my lecture notes on public ethics — John Rawls, moral conflict, civil disobedience — without taking much in, highlighting lines almost at random. Marius is ostensibly studying for his oral exam on 'fashion anthropology', which will be administered by world-famous ex-supermodel and fervent feminist Benedetta Barzini. Now in her sixties, Barzini wears her hair in a grey chignon and her face clean of makeup, the dense nests of wrinkles a political statement, an anti-fashion accessory. She doesn't ask her students to memorise concepts or theories; rather, her aim is to educate a new generation of anti-misogynist designers and stylists by having them analyse the pervasive effects of patriarchy and consumerism as perpetuated by the fashion industry. In other words, she wants them to notice — and help destroy — the beauty norms society would have them replicate, time and time again, in order to control people's behaviour and bodies.

Help, Marius says, what should I say?

Exhuming some memories from an old course on aesthetics, I find the edges of an idea. I love this process: assembling a path, drawing connections, seeing everything fall into place.

Okay, how about this: in my first year of university, I read an essay on fashion by Georg Simmel, a German sociologist. It was written in the early twentieth century, and basically it argued that fashion expresses the paradoxical tension between our desire to imitate and belong to a group, on the one hand, and on the other hand our desire to differentiate ourselves, to be unique. You could present something on that — what do you think? You could also talk about Leopardi's *Dialogue Between Fashion and Death*, in which he posits the two as sisters, because they're both constantly changing and renewing the world.

Okay, cool. Are they long?

No, I don't think so.

Like, do they have CliffsNotes or something? I'm not a massive reader.

You could google it and find out, I answer.

Whenever I'd imagined my future boyfriend, he'd always been a book-lover. A philosopher, a critic, maybe a journalist. I based him on celebrities like Andrea Pezzi, Massimo Coppola, Matteo Bordone: dreamboat intellectuals from the television, Milanese posers dressed in trench coats and desert boots.

Hey, Marius says, shall we take a break?

Another one?

You know what we could do? Romanian lessons. I'll teach you. That way, we can talk about people in front of them and they won't understand what we're saying.

Language comes easily to him, the bilingual child with the plastic brain. He's used to slipping effortlessly between one language and the other. He taught himself English watching YouTube videos and American tv. He speaks it better than me — I studied it for ten years, but still freeze up when it comes to having a simple conversation.

Okay, here we go. The verb *to be*, the numbers from *one* to *ten*.

Eu sunt. Tu ești.

Unu, doi, trei, patru, cinci …

Marius can't remember how to spell certain words. He never learnt Romanian formally, since he came to Italy before starting primary school. In part, I suspect he wants to teach me his mother tongue as a way of repeating it to himself, of making sure it's still there.

The first phrases I learn are insults and curses.

Hai la mama la semințe: Go and get some seeds from your mother. (Poor Romanian women made their living selling sunflower seeds on the street.)

Mânca-ți-aș ochii: I will eat your eyes.

Băga-ți-aș sârmă-n nas: I will stick a wire through your nose. (Like they do to pigs, he clarifies.)

Together, we translate the text of O-Zone's *Dragostea Din Teï*, Romania's chief contribution to contemporary pop culture. Then we compose a little self-introduction speech that I practise, out loud, until I've learnt it by heart: *Am douăzeci și șapte de ani, sunt un învățător de yoga, studiez Filozofie, m-am născut la Rozzano dar trăiesc la Milano cu două pisici*. I'm twenty-seven years old, I work as a yoga teacher, I study philosophy, I was born in Rozzano but I live in Milan with two cats.

I was hesitant at first, but now I'm elated — my foreign lover has opened my mind. I will be a polyglot, and together we will live happily ever after in the impenetrable land of Balkan syntax.

Little by little, I pick up this language of thieves and nurses. It would be more practical if he helped me with my English. As if to justify the Romanian lessons, I daydream about specialising in Eastern European philosophy; maybe I'll discover some hitherto unknown Romanian genius, become the pre-eminent scholar of their work. I start researching the work of Emil Cioran, Romania's famed aphorist and nihilist, despite the fact that his philosophical pessimism couldn't be further from the work of the authors I'm most passionate about. A glacial disappointment descends when I learn that Cioran wrote in French.

Let's learn something serious, I suggest. How do you say *love*?

Love is *iubire*. Or, with the definite article, *iuberea*.

What about *I love you*?

Te iubesc.

I'll call you *Iubesc*, then. Or *Iuby*. Let's call each other *Iuby*.

Did you know we have two words for *kiss*? *Pupic*, which is like this — his lips pressed against mine, a chaste stamp — and *sărut*, which is like this — his wet tongue inside my mouth.

In order to imitate certain words, I have to bring my chin forward, opening my throat. Romanian has sounds we don't have in Italian, harder, more guttural sounds. When Marius speaks to his parents on the phone, his voice transforms completely. It's almost an octave lower, a man's voice. I wonder if he does it consciously, or if happens automatically. He hasn't told his parents he's gay.

I'm mostly scared of how my dad will react, he says. I know he'll blame mamma.

Mothers are always to blame. They are the ones who introduce defects, flaws, obscene deformities, their sinful bodies spoiling the father's perfect genetic material, diluting the precious elixir of his testosterone.

So Marius stays silent, waiting, pretending. When they FaceTime, he removes his earrings, necklaces, septum piercing. He accepts the restrictions imposed on him by a world that demands perpetual confirmation of its own supremacy. Watching his performance, I imagine the tattoo inside his mouth shining with all its force. *Liar.* Lying lets him be both what he is and what they need him to be. He shatters himself into pieces and hands each person the shard they want to see.

I'll have to go to Umbria soon, he announces after one of these familial phone calls. They want me to come down for my cousin's wedding.

Our first separation — will we survive it? How long will you leave me alone?

Such a pain in the arse, he adds. If I go I'll have to cut my hair and shave my beard. According to my family, only Satanists and drug addicts have long beards. I'd invite you but I don't know where you'd stay. You know what? Let's get a tent and camp at

Lake Trasimeno for a few days.

We research everything online: the lake, the islands, it's going to be amazing. We learn about the animals that live there and imagine ourselves surrounded by olive groves, just us and the shrews and hedgehogs, immersed in the landscape of the mystics, our own little Eden, swimming in a mirror of freshwater, embracing under a night sky brimming with constellations: Pegasus, Cygnus, the creamy Milky Way.

Two days later, the dream is over.

Sorry, he says. My parents won't let me go to the lake.

That's okay, I lie. I wasn't sure I could make it work anyway. I'm sure the week will go quickly. Anyway, it's still a while away.

In the meantime, we celebrate our first monthiversary.

We mark it by spending a few days in Genoa, thanks to a Groupon the art historians gave me as an early birthday present. I must have manifested it with a Facebook status I posted a week ago: *I haven't seen the sea in six years. Take me to the sea.*

Pietro and I never once took a holiday together. Even if we had, his poor body image would have meant the beach was strictly off limits.

In fact, Marius and I don't make it to the beach, either. We wander the narrow *caruggi* of the historical city centre, visit the aquarium, dip hot oily focaccia into our cappuccinos like locals. We spend an entire afternoon in the Museum of Oriental Art, perched on a hill at the heart of a botanical garden, looking at war masks and samurai armour. We employ that magic power lovers have to find beauty in every little thing, dowsing for fairytales everywhere we go. We return from Genoa into the arms of a Milan summer, finding relief in the electric-blue water of the Ponzio — the outdoor swimming pool near Piola Metro station — somersaulting alongside the other chlorine-scented have-nots (summer in this city is a kind of sieve, leaving only the coarse, unrefined stock behind).

As we're drying off from a dip, an aeroplane glides overhead, lifting our gaze.

You know, I've never been in one of those, he says.

Never been on a plane. Never even been to another country. Except for Romania.

I make a promise — to him, to myself — that we will remedy that as soon as possible. We'll take a map, or a globe if we can find one, and close our eyes and point to a place, somewhere far away from here. As soon as we have money, we'll spend it all on travel, on long-haul flights. We'll cover the world with celebratory flags.

It's impossible to study and be in love at the same time. I end up sitting only two of my five exams. Marius sits two of six. It's not enough, not by a long shot, but we try to look on the bright side: two is better than none.

To celebrate, Marius suggests we go out for gelato. He blames astrology for his sweet tooth, which he claims is typical of those born under the influence of Venus (in fact, he's a Capricorn, but his Moon and Mars are in Cancer). He devours Romanian *cozonac* and Umbrian *ciaramicola* with equal passion, and loves even the most unsophisticated of sweets: sugared almonds, fruit jelly, bright-pink frosting. He takes five or six sugars in his tea, spreads half a jar of Nutella on a single slice of bread. I want to ask if he was allowed to eat like this at home — back in Rozzano, my mother used to ration our sweets, forcing on us the frugal elegance of self-denial.

Gelato is Marius's absolute favourite food, so when he suggests it, I agree: Yes, let's go. I'll take you to the best gelato place in Milan.

We eat outside, sitting at one of the cracked plastic tables. He finishes his extra-large cup and proposes seconds. *Your wish is my command.*

As he's polishing off his second cup, he says: Oh, what's the time?

He looks at his phone, answering his own question.

I have to buy fabric for my design-methodology class, he says. There's a textiles outlet near here, between Garibaldi and Zara, will you come with me?

The outlet is on Via Lario. We wander the endless aisles stacked high with rolls of fabric in every imaginable pattern and texture, and he examines them for quality and tone, looking for the best he can afford. I stop, enchanted, in front of the remnants bin, suddenly plunged into the fantasies of my childhood: violet chenille, tiger-print satin, blue fur, shantung silk, iridescent lamé. I drape them over myself, one by one.

Look, I say, calling him over. Take a photo!

Here's me in a pink fur turban. In a blue leopard-print shawl. Here's me as a countess, as a white witch.

The register is a paradise of buttons, ribbons, ornate trims.

Have you got enough? I ask as he bundles his selection onto the cashier's desk. Is there anything else you need?

All good, he says. My allowance just came through.

He pays in cash: eighty-six euros, a third of his monthly budget. The money his parents give him is nowhere near enough to cover the expensive materials he needs for his studies. *What happens at the end of the month?* I think, but I keep my mouth shut.

We leave the outlet and head in the direction of Loreto. There's no need to discuss whether or not he's coming back to mine.

We catch a bus, then the Metro.

I feel like pizza, he says.

So pizza it is.

After pizza, we get more gelato, followed by a drink at Mono, our favourite bar in Via Lecco. By the time we get back to the apartment, it's almost midnight. The lights are off in the hallway and kitchen, which means Dylan must be out.

One cat, León, comes to greet us.

Hey there, little monster. Where's your sister?

I check my room, then Dylan's. I try my usual, unfailing trick: calling *pappa, pappa,* as I shake the tin containing their quail and pomegranate kibble (or their tuna, barley, and papaya kibble, depending on the week). I check the wardrobe, between the couch cushions, under the dining chairs.

Where is she hiding, Iuby? Can you see if she's in the bathroom?

I search the lounge room and kitchen again, opening and closing doors like a manic cuckoo clock, my heart rate accelerating. I strip the beds — Rosaspina is so small she could be confused for a fold in a bedsheet — and throw all the cushions on the floor, leaving no crevice unprobed.

She's gone. She has vanished into thin air.

I go out to the balcony and peer into the darkness, scanning the spaces between the garbage bins, between the glossy metal bonnets of the parked cars. Deep down, I already know what has happened. *That piece of shit.*

Iuby, wait here, I yell. I'm going downstairs. I've got my phone. If you find her, call me straightaway.

Piazza Aspromonte

I fly down the stairs, all five flights of them, an unstemmable tide of stairs. I know where she is, I just need confirmation, but I'm panicking, and the panic is what drives me down and down and then through the wood door of the entrance, a thick medieval door, practically immovable, it takes both hands to push it open and thrust my body through to the other side, into the placid indifference of the warm street. A couple walks past wearing t-shirts. Cars roll by with their windows down.

She's not on the footpath — could they already have removed her crushed body? I want to cry thinking about that tiny body, the one I protected for four years from hunger, thirst, poison, flames, balconies. From loneliness, from separation. Now mashed beneath the black tyres of a car, all two and a half kilos of her annihilated in a split second. Or else lost, confused, and disoriented among the weeds and manholes and nocturnal creatures of Piazza Aspromonte. Already a stray, scratched and violated by males on heat, infected with feline leukaemia virus. Or perhaps found, saved, warm, and safe with her new family. My mind races through every possible scenario. Whatever happened, there's nothing I can do but resign myself to her loss. Accept that I failed her, failed to defend her from the world. The sooner

I remove this harpoon from my chest, the better. There's always a way out of pain — all it takes is a refusal to feel, a dull fall into the arms of numbness.

And yet, I find myself walking towards the intersection. First Via Vallazze, then Via Andrea Costa. The search is random, pointless. What's the use of looking if I have no leads to follow, no clue as to where she might be? I head home and walk back up the five flights of stairs, calling her name at each landing, a pathetic litany, a dirge, a rosary.

Marius's head appears above me, peering down: Did you find her?

No.

No — no — the last sound I want to hear coming out of my mouth, but the only one there is. No, she's not found. No, she's not here. My cat is gone.

I can't bring myself to give up the search. I walk up and down the stairs, hundreds of times it seems, until the steps merge into one continuous puzzle, like an Escher painting. I'm certain it was him: Dylan. He was jealous, so he took it out on her. He made her disappear. The spiteful, passive-aggressive little worm. I was out all day; he had plenty of time to enact his evil plan. His revenge. This is my punishment for letting a stranger into our house, for shattering our rules, our routines, our friendship. But then, were we ever really friends? Since I fell in love, Dylan has counted for nothing. Less than nothing. But he didn't have to take it out on Spina. It was my fault, not hers.

I decide he must have sold her. He couldn't possibly have killed her. He must have sold her.

At each landing, I stop and tune in to the silence of the building, listening. My despair takes on the qualities of a ritual:

at the top of each stairwell, I pause, listen, then call her name. It's all I can do. If she's still here, I tell myself, if she's still alive and in this building, she will hear me, and she will come to me.

Ground floor, first floor, second, third, fourth, fifth. Then the reverse: fifth, fourth, third. If he'd never come into my life, if I'd never met Marius, this would never have happened. Love giveth and love taketh away. There is only so much room in a person's life: each new blessing takes the place of an old one; each arrival necessitates a painful goodbye.

I call her name again, and again I'm met with nothing but the echo of my own lament, returned to me by the high old walls of the landing. My pace slows, until finally I stop. That's it; I give up. I need sleep. As if I could sleep in this condition. I need to come to terms with reality, make do with what's left: her brother. Her less beautiful brother, who will forever remind me of her, of this June evening thick with fear and guilt and remorse.

One last lap, I decide, then I'll quit.

Call it god, call it destiny, call it intuition, but something urged me to try again, just one more time.

I call her name more loudly now, more desperately. I don't care if I wake everyone in the building. In fact, I hope I wake them. Let them come out here and help me. Let them bring their torches and ropes and ladders and search the rooftops, the elevator shaft, the grates and gutters and sewers, a pyjamaed army of neighbours hunting for my heart outside my body.

I call and call, and then it happens.

A muffled cry, dampened by walls and furniture and curtains and more walls, almost an auditory hallucination, like the meowing of a ghost. It's coming from the second floor, or maybe the third. It sounds like she's buried alive, suffocating. The sound of her grows louder, and I knock on the door she seems to be behind, stabbing furiously at the doorbell, but there's no answer. Her kidnappers must be sleeping, or else they're pretending they're not home. I crouch next to the door that separates us and say, *I'm here, I'm here*, repeating the words like a mantra. How long has she been stuck in there, without food or water? Wilting, unable to walk, dragging her dehydrated body across the floor to the door to meow weakly, using her last ounce of strength to call out to me. I take my phone from my pocket.

Iuby, she's here, I found her. Come downstairs.

Where?

Here, just come downstairs, I don't know what floor I'm on.

I'm coming, I'm coming.

Then I hear his sandals flapping against the marble steps.

It's almost one in the morning, but we knock on the door of the apartment across the landing. There's no answer. We try the other door — there are three apartments on each floor. Nothing.

Then, five or ten minutes later, we hear: *Sì?* A woman's voice, hoarse with sleep.

Signora, good evening, my cat is locked in the apartment next door, would you happen to know who lives there?

The woman doesn't answer, but through the unopened door I hear her body moving away, retreating.

Signora, please, I say, but in my head I'm saying: *I hope you die, you old bitch.*

Most of the residents of this building are in their seventies — it's practically an old folk's home. It's late, she must be afraid. The Cat Scam. There's no way she's ever going to open the door.

I try the other door again, bashing loudly, hoping to rouse

whoever's in there from their slumber.

Hello? Is there anyone home?

Fifteen minutes pass, then half an hour, then an hour.

I'm calling the police, I tell Marius. What's the number again?

So this is what it's come to: calling the authorities.

Good evening, I say to the voice that answers the phone. My cat went missing earlier tonight, and I just realised she's here in the building, my building, locked inside someone's apartment.

That doesn't fall within our remit, the voice says. Call the fire brigade.

I call the fire brigade: Good evening. My cat, she went missing, please help me, my cat, she's being imprisoned in someone's apartment.

The man on the other end asks: How do you know it's your cat?

Then he adds: I'm sorry, but if it's on private property, there's nothing we can do.

Really?

Call back tomorrow. Or even better, after the weekend.

A column of steam rises in my throat and throws my jaws wide, and I scream, while Rosaspina cries behind the door, and curses start pouring down the stairwell from the floors above: *Disgraceful! People are trying to sleep here!*

I curl up on the stairs, prepared to stay there all night if I have to. An hour later, two officers arrive. I don't know if they're policemen, they look more like traffic wardens. They try knocking on the doors of the two neighbouring apartments, to no avail. Then, suddenly, both doors open almost at once, revealing two very old women, one grey-haired in pyjamas, eyes squinting against the light, the other wearing a bathrobe, her head a tangle of sparse, straw-coloured hair. They both deny knowing anything about anything, then one of them adds: That apartment is empty, no one lives there. You're wasting your time.

How long has it been empty?

Years.

So are you suggesting my cat can walk through walls?

Signora, the officers insist, do you know the owners?

She shakes her head, lips pursed. No, not at all.

They can sense she's lying.

Signora, are you sure?

Well, okay, this afternoon I went in there very briefly to drop off a few things, she confesses. *Very briefly*, she says. Occasionally I use it as storage for boxes, packages, things like that.

So you don't know the owners, but you use their apartment as a storage facility?

Signora, one of the officers says, do you have the keys to this apartment?

No, no, she answers, directing her eyes to the floor.

Then help me understand: how did you get in without the keys?

I don't know, she says. Maybe I'm misremembering.

She looks at the officers, then at the door that hasn't stopped meowing, and adds: Maybe I do have the keys. Let me check.

She turns, disappears, then returns holding the bundle of tinkling metal. The officer is unimpressed.

Signora, he says, please open the door and we can all go back to bed.

It must have happened like this: Dylan left the house in a hurry, either this morning or this afternoon, high, as usual, and

Rosaspina slipped between his legs without him noticing. She must have snuck into the other apartment — it's in the exact same position as ours, just a few floors below — when the old woman was dropping off her boxes. There was no evil plot, no vendetta. Just a series of accidents.

Marius has already given notice to his housemates in Via Ada Negri, and is about to move in with me — with us — definitively. My room is filled with his belongings, piles of suitcases sitting there like security deposits. Dylan and I haven't spoken in weeks, and I know his friends have been putting all sorts of ideas into his head. *Don't let them push you around. There are two of them, they should pay more. If they refuse, kick them out.* But I can't afford to pay any more rent, and Marius is practically destitute. What are we supposed to do?

Our daily routines — once synchronised, superimposed, resting gently against one another — now diverge completely. We stop greeting each other when we get home. He starts inviting new friends over without introducing them, turning up unannounced in the company of people I've never seen before in my life, entrusting them with the keys to the apartment. An eye for an eye. Some of the guys he brings home are practically boys, some look younger than eighteen. Imagining them together in his bedroom — his hands on them, removing their underwear — brings up memories of my own adolescence, all the vile thirty- and forty-somethings who hounded me online, cajoling, wanting my young flesh for a night, and to whom I delivered it, naïvely, thinking sex had value, thinking I'd at least get something in return, as if coitus were a contract signed in bodily fluids.

He starts offering our apartment to friends of friends, people in need of a couch to crash on, foreign students looking for accommodation. Our home becomes a youth hostel, strangers come and go at all hours. Finally, Marius and I give in. We have no choice: we have to move out.

Farewell, Loreto. Farewell, abundant Metro lines. Farewell, mosaic floors — the most beautiful floors in the city.

The sooner we leave, the better, I decide. Things are getting ugly. As soon as summer is over, we're out of here. I have no idea how we're going to afford it. But we have no choice.

In the meantime, I grit my teeth and bear it all. I daydream about making Dylan pay, driving a sharp blade into his soft flesh, into the tenderest parts of him. Instead, I empty his shelves of dolls and playthings into a black garbage bag. *How do you like that?* Then: the ultimate revenge. My pièce de résistance.

The decapitation of Michael Jackson.

Via Carlo Darwin

It's dark. Crowded.

Are they going to start or what? Someone tell them to get a move on.

Then, all of a sudden, lights fire above the cheering crowd, illuminating the empty runway. A disembodied voice purrs: *Welcome to the ballroom.* The pulse of synthesisers swells like a wave.

Marius's house is the first to come out: *All Black Androgyny*. Marius stays hidden in the wings while a small army of ink-black silhouettes advances down the catwalk with long, solemn strides, tall and graceful in stilettos and platform heels. The floor is vibrating with bass, magnificently. Now it's time for *her* to emerge: the main event. The room explodes into thunderous applause, an arena full of people screaming, stamping for their queen, for my enormous, tiny queen — no longer mine but *ours*, the sovereign of the world.

The crowd is euphoric tonight. This is the grand finale, the battle that will decide who takes home the prize, after months and months of preparation.

She turns, sending her black cape gaping; beneath, she wears a neoprene bodysuit, reassembled, as per the professor's guidelines, from recycled fabric. *To create is to regenerate, kids.* She is the star of the show, heading up the procession of shadowy beings that now fan out behind her for a final lap of the runway.

My boyfriend — my girlfriend — the drag queen, resplendent in black-and-white greasepaint. Voguer extraordinaire, collapsing the male-female binary, spinning like a Sufi mystic before her adoring fans. She looks incredible. Divine. Is that really him?

Marius! Marius!

His house, *All Black Androgyny*, comprises him and three of his classmates: Vania, Filo, and Mia. Every house, or family, has a soloist, and Marius has been elected theirs. The decision was unanimous: he is far and away the best performer of the four.

The voguing battles take place on the university campus, in Via Carlo Darwin. In its true form, voguing is more a subculture than a style of dance. Born in New York in the late Eighties, as an evolution of the Harlem ballroom scene, it belongs primarily to the Latinx and African American queer communities. Stylistically, it draws inspiration from the poses struck by models in fashion magazines — hence the name — as well as Egyptian hieroglyphs. Each swift, angular movement imitates a high-fashion photograph, a freeze frame. It's all in the hands, Marius explains. And the wrists.

Think, like, the Madonna film clip.

In the Eighties, voguers were outcasts, kids kicked out of home in the midst of a raging AIDS epidemic, boys and young men who dreamt of gracing the covers of forbidden fashion magazines. The families and houses they created were, above all, a form of refuge — a sanctuary, a lifeline. Here in Milan, at this school for rich kids, all that remains of that original spirit is the aesthetic.

Tonight, Marius's house has chosen to embody the theme of *androgyny*: gender-neutral aliens sewn into skin-tight black costumes, marching to the electric rhythms of a song borrowed from one of Gareth Pugh's recent runway shows. The other houses have chosen more bizarre themes: pregnant women, Teletubbies. There's no contest. It's clear who has talent and who doesn't.

The first phase is a group battle, after which the finalists send their house soloists to face off in the grand finale. It's Marius versus some poor blond kid dressed like George Michael in his Wham! era. They perform dramatic spins and dips, mimicking the choreography of *RuPaul's Drag Race* — arms out, backs to the floor, *shablam*, death drop, duckwalk, catwalk, bodies dripping with disdain, throwing buckets of shade.

In preparation for this evening's battle, Marius removed all the hair from his body. It took three tubes of depilatory cream: beard, chest, arms, legs.

I'd love to do drag, he confessed as he was dressing.

Oh for god's sake, I replied — a kneejerk reaction.

I'm sorry, why not?

I have no real answer for him. My response comes from a place of hostility, of fear, and I'm almost surprised to hear myself say, with a nervous laugh: I don't want to be with a girl.

But it's just a performance.

But what if you decide you like it?

If I were lucid, I would see exactly what was rising in me: the universal inclination to repress, to deny others the freedom we seek for ourselves. No mind is immune; we all waste energy hating perfectly harmless crimes, hunting ghosts and holograms. My real enemies are the fears I've always held but barely acknowledged:

alcohol, the night, the loss of control, the lowering of inhibitions. I should be following Marius wherever he wants to go, but I'm afraid that the night will take him from me, that the darkness holds untold temptations: exciting, anonymous bodies pushing and rubbing and grabbing at him. The reality is, fearing the night won't make those temptations disappear.

This morning, sitting on the bed, Marius said: I'm leaving tomorrow, remember?

Already?

I told you. It was either tomorrow or the day after, but tomorrow is better.

I thought maybe it was still up in the air. Do you know what time?

I'll have to look up the bus timetable. I hope there are still tickets.

Can't you take the train?

The train costs three times as much.

Do you need —

There are still tickets, he says before I can finish, bringing up the FlixBus booking page. I can leave tomorrow at eight.

In the morning?

Yesss. Will you come with me?

Of course.

What will you do while I'm gone?

I need to pack up all the house stuff.

Good boy. Now can I have a kiss?

We're still in the phase of our relationship when everything can be resolved with a kiss.

That was this morning, just this morning, in my bedroom,

although it won't be mine much longer. Now it's evening, and we are here in this hot packed room, waiting for the MC to announce the winning house.

They've turned the music down low.

And the winners are …

Marius's house wins, as expected. A roar rises from the crowd, joyful streams of silver confetti dance from the ceiling as people kiss and hug and shake hands.

You were amazing, my love. Amazing.

I'll just get changed, he yells back, costume already partially removed, sleeves wagging like black tails as the crowd begins to flow towards the exit.

Outside the air is still, the stars hidden behind a veil of streetlights. The orange sky of our last night together.

Via Tito Vignoli

In the bare rooms, bright with July sunlight, my mother and sister move like strangers. The walls are ultra-white, the cheap floor tiles a glazed grey, and dust spins in the beams of light pouring through the windows. They look around the empty apartment in awe; the only buildings they've ever lived in are public housing towers.

My mother cools her face with the fan she stole from a Chinese restaurant, boats against a gold sunset — *Jesus it's hot* — and my sister mimics the motion using the manga paperback she was reading on the tram. I only invited them so I wouldn't have to inspect the place alone.

What do you think, does it look okay? I ask when we're out of earshot of the owner, a seventy-year-old man, and his daughter, who looks to be about my age. An old high-school friend passed me their details after I put out a call on Facebook.

My mother takes note of things to keep an eye on: peeling plaster, the hot-water boiler, window fixtures, radiators. For years, after my father left, she had to be both the man and woman of the house, so she knows what to look out for.

It looks like they did it up recently, she says.

My mother is forty-eight years old. She still lives in Rozzano, although she constantly talks about leaving. Ever since she was a little girl, growing up in Cassino Scanasio — the part of Rozzano that overlooks the canal — she's dreamt of living in the countryside. After a life spent working gruelling jobs in a jungle of government-supplied concrete, she craves flowers, baby goats, the redemptive embrace of nature. Her body is falling apart: herniated discs, carpal tunnel syndrome, premature osteoarthritis, her bones crumbling like dry bread. Not to mention the uterine fibroids and polyps. Not everyone can afford to match their work to their constitution.

My mother has always dreamt of leaving Rozzano, but she's still there. No longer in the same Via Giacinti apartment, at least; now she's in Viale Lazio, where the public housing towers are more severe, more imposing, looming nine or ten storeys tall. To me, they recall the architecture of the Soviet Union.

My mother was born in Rozzano. All her major life events have occurred in Rozzano. I wonder if, at this point, she is incapable of imagining herself outside that place, that land of pariahs and deprivation.

Then there's my sister: no longer the beautiful baby I washed and cuddled and dressed in stolen accessories from Fiordaliso, but a girl on the brink of adulthood, almost fourteen years old.

Her nerves are shot, my mother confided in me a few weeks ago. Her anxiety manifests physically: *Every morning, before school, your sister gets up and runs to the bathroom to spew her poor little guts up*. Small white spots have started emerging on the skin of her eyelids, and in the creases of her elbows. Depigmentation: they suspect it's vitiligo. There's no treatment for it; all she can do is hope it doesn't get much worse.

Each member of our family invents their own code, their own language, expressed through the organs and tissues of the body, so as not to remain completely silent. A poetics of minor bodies.

I don't know what to do, my mother said. *Should I take her to see a psychologist? Do you know someone cheap?*

Because my mother stayed in Rozzano, my sister, like me, had no choice but to grow up there. Middle school was hell: girls waiting for her after class, threatening violence. In Rozzano, weak links are quickly identified, and the girls fight like boys. They're used to giving and receiving beatings. My sister isn't like them, so they target her. She keeps it all to herself, crying in secret, pretending nothing is wrong.

And at home? What was happening at home in those years after I left? Surely things aren't as bad now as they used to be, when I was growing up.

Years later, my sister will tell me that the violence never left. One time, her father lifted our mother up by the throat — my sister saw it all unfold — and my mother had a kind of seizure, losing consciousness, collapsing to the floor as if all the bones in her body had suddenly disintegrated, eyes rolling back into her head. No one called an ambulance. When our mother came to, she made light of it: *I'm fine, I'm fine. Shall we order pizza for dinner?*

My sister's body kept the score, and raised its voice: *Look*, it said, *here is the proof that nothing has changed. Don't believe them when they tell you the worst is over.*

If our mother were to admit she is in danger, then she would have to do something about it. Her word is not to be trusted. She will never stop diminishing, omitting, minimising Ivano's violence until it is small enough to live with, rendering the daily humiliations negligible, years and years of tiny, forgettable mistakes.

After I left home, and washed my hands of it all, everything stayed exactly as it was. Variations on a theme. I saved myself, like a rat leaping from a sinking ship. I wasn't the big brother I should have been: the one who guides, who protects. But now I have a second chance, an opportunity to redeem myself. Middle school is over — a relief, a crucial step — and my sister has decided to enrol in a technical high school that trains kids to be hotel and hospitality workers. The same school my aunt's daughter goes to, in Pavia. Role models are important at that age, but hers is too close, too comfortable. Does she really want to be a cook? A waitress? To spend a lifetime in the service of others? *Better than cleaning toilets*, my mother interjects, *like I did for twenty years.*

I can see the charms of a trade, especially when you're fourteen and hating school. But I won't accept that for her. She should go to a real high school. A linguistic or artistic high school, if she prefers — somewhere that will give her options, open up her future instead of closing it down. It's too little too late, I know, but at least now I have an opportunity to intervene, to influence the direction of her life with what little wisdom I've acquired, channelling some of Milan's light into Rozzano's gloomy dead ends.

I won't let her end up in a technical school.

Then again — who says I even get a say?

High school is too hard, my sister says. *High school isn't for people like us.*

What makes me think I can just turn up and start making decisions on her behalf, like she's a character in The Sims?

Let's face it: where have all my life choices and grand ambitions got me? To the big city, sure, but with no idea where I'm headed. With a stopgap job that I've turned into a lifestyle, a fake identity. Crawling my way through an endless series of truncated university degrees. Who's at a dead end, again?

Even if I do eventually make it through my master's, what happens then? I've always found comfort in the idea of a PhD, the panacea of every perpetual student. But everyone knows that the only doctorates worth having are found outside Italy: in the universities of France, the Netherlands, Germany, Britain, or, better yet, the United States of America. I can't study abroad; I can barely afford my rent. It's not like I can count on my family to support me. The familiar alibi, an easy excuse for my lack of motivation. My lack of talent. Take languages, for example: I can barely speak English. If I wanted a career in academia, I should have made the effort to learn it properly. All the leaps and bounds I've made, running from the legacy of my illiterate grandparents, have only been for show.

But now there's Marius. We're about to move in together. No more housemates, no more nights apart. Four months together, and already we'll have a home of our own. This is enough to chase everything else away, all my failures and shortcomings. This is the jewel at the centre of it all, my hidden treasure finally unearthed. Him and me, the two of us, and nothing in between.

Whatever comes next will be the right thing. Life finally meeting itself.

I take a dozen photos of the apartment and send them to Marius on WhatsApp. He's in Umbria, at his parents' place, and won't be back until next week. *This could be ours*, I think. This hallway, this small bathroom, this bedroom with the tiny closet. What else do we need?

The place is completely empty, bare except for the essentials: a stove, an oven, some kitchen cabinets. *A blank slate*, as the owner put it. The building is fairly charmless — classic Seventies Milan, the foyer decked out in fake plants and bad art, a far cry from the marbled atriums and crystal chandeliers of the city centre — but we don't have to live here forever. The apartment is on Via Tito Vignola, past Piazza Napoli, not far from the historical social housing precinct of Giambellino. *For you are from the fringes, and to the fringes you shall return.* But it doesn't pay to be judgemental: just around the corner is the Reform synagogue where, years ago, I met the rabbi who advised me on converting to Judaism. When you're used to being in places that aren't quite where you want to be, you learn to look for silver linings. A single detail can completely transform a place, if you need it to.

Because the apartment is unfurnished, it's more affordable: six hundred euros a month, excluding bills. And since they're not renting it out through an agent, we don't need a guarantor, or even proof of income. All they want is a month's rent upfront. Combining Marius's allowance with the money I earn from teaching, we can make it work. Less a calculation than a decision.

Our will, our intention, is more powerful than our limitations.

We thank the owner of the apartment — owner of the entire building, it turns out, along with several other buildings across Milan — and walk in the direction of the number 14 tram stop.

So, what do you think? I ask.

It's nice, my mother says, but what will you do for furniture?

I notice she avoids offering to help.

We'll figure it out, I answer.

If you say so. Nora, do you have a cigarette? I forgot mine.

Mamma quit smoking years ago, but as soon as she learnt my sister had started, she resumed the habit.

So, when do I get to meet this Marcus?

Marius. You'll meet him when he gets back to Milan. I'm writing to him now. He likes the photos, I think I'll call the owner tomorrow and confirm it.

And have you heard from your father at all?

Pff. I haven't seen him in, what, six months?

Is he still with that woman?

I think so.

That woman is Noemi. She and my father met in the gourmet food shop where she works, next door to the police headquarters, selling buffalo mozzarella and Amalfi lemons and Black Casertano Pig salami. She had a boyfriend at the time, but my father convinced her to leave him.

Poor thing, my mother says. Someone tell her it's not too late to get away.

The stories of my father's women have always followed the same script, ever since my mother. At first he treats them like princesses, or queens, but then the arguments start, followed by the cheating, then the insults. He doesn't hit them, as far as I know — like me, he uses words as his weapons. His preferred form of abuse is systematic humiliation, a slow degrading of their self-esteem. Eventually, he dumps them and starts all over again, setting off in search of fresh meat, young pussy, new notches for his bedpost. Pathological narcissists rarely end up in therapy.

On the few occasions I've spent time with my father over the past few years, all I've felt is estrangement and embarrassment. Nothing else is left of our relationship. We have nothing to say to each other. To me, he's just the man who got my mother pregnant twenty-eight years ago. Genetics count for nothing, they can't put words in our mouths. Language evades the laws of the cellular body. My whole life, society has insisted that we persist with one another. The usual broken record: *He's still your father. He'll always be your son.* But it's like trying to light a fire with wet wood.

The last time he called was to ask me to cancel the formal child-support payments he's being paying — late — for the past twenty years. *Just your signature, that's all I need.* I refused. I need that money, I pay my rent with that money.

You don't trust me, he said.

Then, in the next breath: *Fine, but don't think I'll forget this.*

The man who fathered me can boast one, enormous talent: he is capable of absolutely anything. Not just in the negative sense. He is powerfully reckless, an archer firing arrows of desire into the heart of the sun. In the grand scheme of things, perhaps it's unfair to think of his lack of paternal instinct as a personality flaw. All he did was fertilise an egg; he never signed a contract, never assumed any duty of care. He was only twenty-one when he got my mother pregnant. Jobless, directionless. But his family insisted they have the baby, because all children are gifts from God, even the ones who end up wasting their lives in a purgatory of books and pointless university studies.

We board the tram. I ride with my mother and sister for a few stops, then we part ways.

Ciao, kisses, talk soon. Are you coming to lunch next week?

I continue my journey on foot: Via Torino, San Babila, then my favourite, Corso Venezia. Every time I walk down this street, I'm swept up on a wave of enthusiasm, and a strange lightness comes over me. It feels as if I'm tuning in to the city's past lives, caught up in some mysterious cycle of metempsychosis. Corso Venezia used to be called Corso di Porta Orientale, the Avenue of the Eastern Gate, and in the late eighteenth century it was lined with the mansions and palazzi of old aristocratic families: Palazzo Servelloni, Palazzo Saporiti, Palazzo Castiglioni, Casa Rasini, Casa Fontana-Silvestri, Palazzo della società Buonarroti-Carpaccio-Giotto. This avenue hosted the nightly *passeggiate* of the Milanese nobility, among other, even more illustrious residents: Napoleon Bonaparte, Stendhal, Filippo Tommaso Marinetti. In March 1848, it was the scene of the Five Days of Milan, the Milanese insurrection against the Austrian Empire. A century and a half later, on the morning of 27 March 1995, it witnessed the murder of Maurizio Gucci. The assassin was Benedetto Ceraulo, an unemployed bricklayer, hired for the hit by the victim's ex-wife: Patrizia Reggiani. Lady Gucci. The daughter of a poor single mother. After her divorce, faced with the prospect of Gucci's remarriage and the subsequent halving of her alimony, she was afraid of falling back into poverty.

Corso Venezia's triumphant neoclassical architecture recalls Europe's proudest capitals: Vienna, Paris. I walk in the shadow of nine divine sentinels — Janus, Ceres, Bacchus, Diana, Apollo, Jupiter, Juno, Venus, Mercury — who grace the façade of Palazzo Saporiti, their temperaments changing with the sky and weather. I knew none of this when I first fell in love with Corso Venezia; the attraction was purely atmospheric. When it comes to the objects of our fascination, intuition exceeds the bounds of conscious knowledge. Perhaps we know more than we think. *The lover*, Max Scheler wrote, *must always precede the connoisseur.*

It's as if I'm watching my own life unfold, observing myself from the outside.

I will live here, one day. Corso Venezia, Palestro. One day

soon, this will be my home. Less a promise than a prophecy.

But not yet.

For now, I need to focus on arranging this next move. Recruiting friends to help — friends with cars, ideally. If no one can help, then we'll do it all ourselves, on foot, hauling our worldly belongings in reusable supermarket bags. If we don't have enough supermarket bags, we'll use garbage bags. The same black garbage bags we sealed our bedsheets in, all those months ago, to quarantine the crabs and kill their microscopic eggs. The ritual mass murder with which we first blessed our union.

On the Metro, with our suitcases, people take us for evictees, or immigrants. Here, now, our only goal is to stay together.

The first thing we do when we move into the new apartment is write our surnames next to the doorbell, in permanent marker. The two of us, chained together; an anchor.

This is how magical thinking operates: we make an association, articulate a desire, and wager that our tiny ceremony will be honoured by the universe.

I leave Dylan with three months of unpaid rent and bills.

He texts politely: *Hi, sorry, just in case you weren't aware …*

I reply a few weeks later. He should be grateful that I deigned to respond at all.

This is what you get, I write, *for behaving the way you did. For all the harm you caused.*

Before he can reply, I block his number.

Via Valpetrosa

If you're not studying anymore, why don't you just come home?

I catch only fragments of the conversation, rapid-fire sentences in a language I don't know, but in a tone I think I understand. Soon the meaning of the words will be translated for me, paralysing me.

Forty-eight hours after we move to the new apartment, Marius learns he hasn't earnt enough credits to continue with his studies. He missed one too many exams. *It is with great regret that we inform you that your scholarship will not be renewed for the coming academic year.* If he wants to stay enrolled, he'll have to pay the standard tuition: ten, fifteen thousand euros.

Can't you try talking to the school secretary? I ask, desperate. Maybe they can come to a compromise. You could try emailing Benedetta Barzini …

I should have kept a closer eye on him, I should have made sure he wasn't failing. It's my fault. I'm to blame as much as he is.

Marius is silent for half an hour after the phone call. He's a classic head-in-the-sand type; I'm only just beginning to learn this about him. When things go wrong, he freezes, like a deer in the headlights, and pretends nothing is wrong. As though, if he doesn't react, he can avoid the problem altogether. In reality, all that is removed is his fear of the problem, all anticipation and anxiety around it. I wonder how it must feel to be free from the fear of pain.

Even if they wanted to, his parents could never afford the tuition fees. And they don't want to. Their reaction is immediate, simple: *Come home.* Be reabsorbed into the family — the family that, after all, supports you, and has the right to decide when to extend or withdraw that support. Marius is simply an offshoot of a larger body, which can choose to reclaim him at any time. Our relationship was just a short interlude, a brief moment of bliss. I suppose that's what I get for falling in love with someone who hasn't yet graduated from adolescence: a *dependant*, someone else's property.

His father's voice: *You're coming home. To your family. Either you make your own way down here or we'll come up and get you.*

Something bristles in me, and I feel a protective fence rising. If there's one thing in the world that will never come to pass, it is this.

I'll take care of it. From now on, I'm responsible.

Tell them you're not going anywhere, I say. Tell them you don't need their money. Or don't say anything — maintain a proud silence. Don't answer the phone when they call, hang up on them. Can you block their numbers?

I have to uproot him, untether him. My deracinated love. He must have no past and no future. One by one, I will sever the suffocating threads that would draw him away from me.

I'll work more. I ask for more hours at all the gyms and yoga studios I teach in. I'll substitute for other instructors: dance, Pilates, seniors' aerobics, whatever they need.

One gym owner, in his office of wall-to-wall black lacquered wood, asks: *Can I put you down for Zumba?*

Absolutely — that's what YouTube tutorials are for.

I say yes to every job that comes my way. I teach styles and disciplines I've never practised before in my life, risking the bodies of my students in the process, since I know nothing about anatomy. Incorrect, improvised movements cause injuries, trigger bad knees: *Don't worry, signora. Discomfort is just a symptom of your body changing, getting stronger. Welcome the pain. Exhale deeply — that's it.*

You need to start looking for work, I say to Marius.

My mother's voice coming out of my mouth: maturity as ventriloquism.

He's never worked before in his life.

What kind of work? he asks. He sounds scared.

Whatever. Waiting tables, babysitting. As a sales assistant at H&M. In the cloak room at a club. Unloading crates of fruit at the market. Anything.

Shitty jobs I've never done myself, would never do.

I hate teaching in gyms, but the pay is good: thirty or forty euros an hour. If I were smarter about it, better at selling myself, I could find private work, too. I know of former models, all women, who earn a hundred and fifty euros an hour teaching private lessons in some of Milan's most luxurious apartments — the lofts and penthouses of Via Brera, Corso Garibaldi, Isola. Downward-facing nymphs, the goddesses of Milan yoga, dressed head-to-toe in designer activewear. There's a market for private male teachers, too, albeit a much smaller one. One time, a fifty-something-year-old student of mine messaged me, back when I was still living with Dylan: *Do you also do massage?* Without waiting for a reply, he sent his address, followed by a photo of his erection straining against the once-white fabric of his boxer briefs. I didn't accept the invitation, and no similar offers have arrived since.

When I tell Marius he has to look for work, what I don't say is: *It's not my fault you didn't fight hard enough for your dream.*

The dream is fashion: he wants to be a famous fashion designer. The name of his label will be MMM — he already has the logo designed, ready to be stamped on tags and belt buckles and the letterheads of press releases. He's been feeding this dream since he was a kid in Umbria, following his favourite designers on social media, studying their collections until he knows them by heart, season by season.

His one big life ambition, and he let it slip away.

The least I can do is help him write a CV.

What shall we put in it?

Italian citizenship? No. All these years and he never bothered to get it — how is that possible?

Previous experience? None. We google the names and addresses of some clothes stores in Umbria, shaping a respectable career. Who's going to check?

We do have one stroke of good luck, in this period: Esselunga supermarket introduces self-service checkouts. Stealing groceries becomes a breeze — I just have to shop at the busiest time of day, and slip the occasional item into my shopping bag without scanning it. I pay about a third of what I should, a sixty-euro shop reduced to twenty. I don't think of it as a crime so much as a necessity. Stealing from the rich to make ends meet.

Then, in one of the yoga studios where I teach, I stop registering the students who pay for their classes in cash, slipping the euro notes directly into my wallet instead of into the enamelled metal safe behind the front desk. I already have my defence ready, in case the owner accuses me: *What are you saying? You think I'm that desperate?*

At least we have a roof over our heads. For now. Without Marius's monthly allowance from his parents, we won't be able to cover the rent. We have no choice but to set aside our dream of an apartment to ourselves, furnished to our taste — Marius imagined everything white, minimalist, like a stark Berlin loft — and sublet a room.

Luckily, the apartment technically has two bedrooms. Tiny, but indisputable. The better of the two looks onto the street, with a view of the San Vito al Giambellino church. It's a little more spacious, and much more photogenic. The lease agreement strictly prohibits subletting, and there's a risk one of the other residents in the building — mostly elderly relatives of the owner — might snitch on us. But it's a risk worth taking. The lesser of two evils.

Okay, who should we look for? Guy or girl? Girls are quieter, cleaner (a stereotype friends quickly disabuse me of, by way of anecdotal evidence). Eighty per cent of straight men are terrifying, but another gay in the house would be too dangerous (what if he and Marius like each other?). We decide to look for a woman. The gender binary exists when we need it to; it can be convenient, even comforting.

We spread the word through our respective networks. Responses quickly start pouring in, mostly from university contacts: fellow students, friends of classmates. We set up a schedule of interviews, resigned now to our fate.

We settle on Melina, a San Raffaele philosophy graduate and talented pianist. She's twenty-seven, originally from Lake Como, and nervous, with reddish curls and a face full of tics. She's obsessed with Desigual, the Spanish fast-fashion label. *So stylish*, she repeats, euphoric. *Don't you love it?* Marius changes the subject.

The rent is six hundred a month, and we charge her four hundred. Actually, let's make it four fifty. She can afford it, you can tell. Her parents help her with the move. When it's done, hers is the only furnished room in the apartment. Bed, bedside table, desk, wardrobe, upright piano against one wall. A beautiful little bedroom.

The rest of the house is barren. Our *blank slate* has become a gaping void. The best we can do is procure some pots and kitchen utensils from the Chinese-run variety store down the street: a few bowls, a dish rack, some poor-quality knives. *Do you think this plastic is carcinogenic?* We steal some folding chairs from the terrace of a tourist bar on Foro Buonaparte. We fashion the rest of our furniture from cardboard boxes: a coffee table, a chest of drawers. Like a home-made doll's house. We flatten more boxes to place underneath the mattress we can't afford — I had no idea how expensive even terrible, spine-deforming mattresses are. For now, we lay some of my nonnas' blankets over the insulating layer of cardboard. It almost resembles a futon. We make do with this for a month, until one of the art historians lends us an inflatable mattress, which the cats manage to puncture within a week. Even though we patch up the holes with masking tape, the poor mattress requires nightly examination and resuscitation. Like an endless game of Operation. We put off buying a new one, holding out for better times.

Δ

September arrives, then October. Temperatures fall, and I spend more and more nights alone on our beached life raft of a bed as Marius resumes his clubbing habit. After a brief period of reluctant abstention, his passion for Milan's nightlife is greater than ever. But what once struck me as inspiring now seems dangerous, threatening.

He goes out without me, not because he wants to but because I can't go with him. *I* have obligations. *I* have a day job. We fall in love with a person's imperfections, imagining that they can be remedied, but eventually we learn that the perfect whole we imagined will never exist. There's a reason those puzzle pieces were missing in the first place, or were purposefully removed.

His friends are the real problem. Completely ignorant of our circumstances, they are relentless, inviting him out night after night, cajoling him into joining them even when, on certain rare occasions, he hesitates, or even declines, influenced by my lack of enthusiasm. I hate them: spoilt clowns whose parents unwittingly subsidise their outrageous lifestyles, convinced their precious progeny are pouring their hearts and souls into their studies when in reality they're barely passing, too busy jumping from cock to cock. They are wayward children without ambition — have they ever even opened a book? Future hairdressers and window dressers and Zara shop assistants. *You're not like them*, I want to tell him. *You're not like them anymore.* I want to reproach him, put him in his place: *I'm supporting you now.* These words never leave my imagination; I could never say these things to him. I place all the blame on his friends: his wicked, vandalising friends, who would usurp me if given half a chance. I want them gone. I want to scorch the earth around him and start afresh. The only love I've ever known is conditional.

My first fight is with Samuele, an eighteen-year-old from Puglia (after pretty much failing high school, Samuele came to Milan 'to have a look around', as he puts it). I've been waiting up for Marius for hours, simmering in one of my increasingly frequent nocturnal rages. It's past 3.00 am, and there's still no sign of him. He's not coming home, I think. In order to release some of the building anguish, I go out onto the balcony: the disc of the moon veiling and unveiling herself in clouds, a climactic wind, the skeletal trees bending almost to breaking point. I won't let this happen; I can't let this happen. I feel my body overflowing with amorous, murderous fury. I want to smash my fists through the window, breaking glass and skin, raising sleeves of blood to the vault of the sky. Instead, I pick up my phone and start typing, my heart a drum.

If you ever do this again I'll rip your face off.

Samuele's reply is instant: *What?*

You know what. This is your first and last warning.

My mind runs wild with fantasies of punishment. I want to make an example of him. Grab that stupid tuft of strawberry blond hair and rip at it until it comes out in fistfuls, then smash his head against the footpath, scrape his pretty photogenic face against the asphalt, my opponent transfigured into Francis Bacon's *Portrait of Pope Innocent X.*

Act two unfolds a few days later, in the form of a fight with Gem outside California Bakery. We've just had brunch, courtesy of the money I pocketed from three yoga classes. As we're walking back towards the tram stop, Gem brings up Samuele — evidently, he told her about what happened the other night.

You went overboard, she proclaims. There's nothing wrong with having some fun every now and then.

Her tone is smug, authoritative, like she thinks she's some kind of life coach. I listen in silence. The reservoir of my patience is large, deep, but as I listen I feel myself beginning to swell like a balloon.

Anyway, she adds, you can't blame Marius for wanting to hang out with people his own age.

She has drawn her pistol — this is now a duel. The most pathetic Western of all time.

What would you do if your boyfriend went clubbing without you and didn't come home? I say. How would you feel? Then again, I guess you've never had a relationship that lasted more than two hours.

What does that have to do with anyth—

And I guess it's different when you've got fuck-all to do the next day.

What are you trying to say?

That you're a fucking loser.

Wow, and you're a fucking piece of sh—

Things are heated enough between us now to spark a physical fight: I want to spit in her face, bring her to the ground. I imagine her raising her arms to protect her head against my blows. But the fantasy doesn't have time to be fulfilled.

Hey, that's enough, Marius screams, pulling me away from her.

A clash of wills — my beloved's autonomy is a thorn in my side, an obstacle. I wish I could absorb him completely. Love as Pac-Man: the only way to survive is to devour every other creature in sight. Or to amputate the object of your desire, limb by limb, like in that movie *Boxing Helena.* Reduce them to a piece of furniture. My bonsai boyfriend, sitting beautifully on a glass tabletop.

We continue along Via Torino, then Marius ducks suddenly into a side street. He gasps for air outside a Hare Krishna restaurant, eyes bulging out of his head.

Hey, what the fuck is happening?

He doesn't answer. His mouth is a tiny hole between his lips, gaze fixed on the dark-red wall in front of him. He's wheezing, leaning forward with his hands on his hips.

It might be my heart, he manages.

Just breathe, everybody keep breathing.

Should I call someone?

It'll pass, he says.

How do you know?

It happens sometimes. It's just a bit of tachycardia.

Corso San Gottardo

Liceo delle scienze umane. Human sciences high school. If I could go back in time, that's where I'd study. Without a doubt.

I've been telling myself this for years now, fantasising about remaking the past. Now I project those regrets onto my little sister, accessorising her — the Skipper to my Barbie — with my old dreams, in the doll's house of my imagination. I try gently pushing her in the right direction: towards psychology, anthropology, sociology, all the most fascinating parts of being human. Imagine learning at fourteen the things I only started studying at twenty-two, twenty-five. Not to mention the things I'll never get the chance to study.

In the end, she chooses a socio-pedagogical high school: an all-girls school that will prepare her to become a teacher. Better than a training institute for waitstaff, at least. She will get a solid, basic education. She will study theory, Italian, even Latin — which I never learnt, and wished I had, once I got to university and noticed the yawning gap in my knowledge.

I introduced Marius to my mother and sister at the beginning of August, when we all went together to enrol Nora at her new high school. Marius and Nora hit it off straightaway — there are only six years between them, after all. When they spoke, I felt a subtle generational divide opening up, and I found myself on the wrong side of it.

I should have written: when we *tried* to enrol Nora at her new high school.

When we got there, it turned out August enrolments had already closed.

You're too late, said the woman who met us at reception. You'll have to wait until December.

Let me talk to her, I said, superseding my mother. Sorry, good morning. What's your role here? Janitor?

Education assistant.

Do you realise that a young girl's future is at stake here?

No can do. Enrolments are closed.

I actually wanted to enrol her in a different school, one closer to Milan — the city air would do her good; I know from experience how purifying it can be, has been — but time and distance constraints meant we were forced to make do with this one, Liceo Agnesi, a high school with the same name as a pasta manufacturer, at the southern tip of the city. There's no getting away from the south.

Listen, the education assistant continued, the best I can do is put you on a waitlist. If someone drops out, we'll give you a call.

That was August. In October, my sister finally enrols. Crisis averted.

So, how's school going? I ask when I next see her. Do you like it?

It's okay. So so.

I want to snap at her: *Sorry, what? Say that again?* But then I think better of it.

Try to transcend this moment of frustration, I tell myself. There is no salvation without persistence. Give her time to persist.

Now when I go to Rozzano for lunch on weekends, Marius comes with me. A love story without secrets, without blind spots. True love accepts no compromises. True love wants to be flaunted, to take up space. Up to a point — I constantly have to remind Marius that, where we're going, it's safest not to be the fullest versions of ourselves. *Don't wear anything too flashy*, I say. Or simply: *You should go change.* Our personal preferences must be moderated, muted, for the sake of our safety. *We don't want to provoke the locals.*

So, like, is this too much? Marius asks, showing me a pair of sneakers with a two-inch-thick sole.

We never hold hands in Rozzano, never kiss in public. On the tram, our bodies already begin to separate, pulling apart as we approach Via dei Missaglia, or even sooner. In the place where I grew up, Marius and I must pass as friends, or brothers, or colleagues. The magnetic field of the looming Telecom tower neutralises all anomalies, zapping them like mosquitoes in a bug trap.

I bring Marius along to lunch at my mother's place first, then later to my nonna's. A Romanian among Neapolitans. I take photos and post them on Facebook and Instagram, my small act of celebration. Our relationship only exists if everyone else witnesses it. Mine is a generation that lives vicariously through the visual records of others.

When Marius and my sister are chatting in the other room, leaving me and my mother alone, mamma asks: So, has he found something yet? The tone of her voice is careful.

Not yet, I answer. We've been dropping his CV around.

And his parents aren't giving him anything?

They gave him a hundred euros this month.

Is that all?

It's deliberate. They want him to come home.

And what exactly do they expect him to do down there in the countryside? Milk cows?

When faced with the concerns and inquisitions of others, I protect Marius by omitting certain details. I don't say, for example, that he spends his days scrolling YouTube and Tumblr while I traipse all over the city teaching class after class. He lacks motivation — worse than that, he has zero motivation. I protect him by not revealing how aimless he is, how adrift, rarely stirring from our half-deflated mattress until his friends coax him into yet another night out: openings, parties, Fashion Week events. *Are you sure you don't want to come?*

When I accuse him of being idle, he takes his sewing machine out of the box and starts feeding it scraps of cloth, remnants of fabric collected in the wake of various university projects. Shirts and bags and palazzo pants emerge: *See, I'm not completely useless.*

Why don't you try selling them online? I propose.

There's so much wasted talent in this house. Sometimes it feels like we came together only to bring each other down. A mutual burial.

The money his parents send him is quickly spent on cigarettes. No matter how dire things get, quitting is off the cards. I encourage him to at least cut down, but that, too, seems impossible. When the money and the cigarettes run out, he asks me to lend him five euros. I always give him at least twenty — what kind of monster hands a five-euro note to the person they love?

In an attempt to pull him out of his funk, I prepare a kind of road map, a plan for action drawn up on butcher's paper, with different colours designating different objectives. There's a list of places to deliver his CV to in person, another of emails to be sent. We attach the enormous sheet of paper to our bedroom wall, next to the window. If he looks at it enough, even by accident, it's bound to stimulate some kind of response.

We can't continue like this much longer, I say after the road map goes up. Are you sure you want to stay here in Milan? Do you want to stay with me? Or is this apathy and lack of initiative your way of breaking up with me?

Please, the voice inside adds, *please don't break up with me.*

The notion is dismissed with a handful of syllables: Of course not. Just tell me what to do and I'll do it.

Each time I bring it up, he dismisses me, then falls right back into the same rut.

If I were in his situation, I can't say it would be any different.

While this is going on, the house ceases to be ours. The romantic utopia we imagined when we first arrived is shattered by the arrival of our subletter.

The moment Melina moves in, her energy unsettles things: boots stomping, doors slamming, heavy hands and feet echoing through the house like threats.

She's crazy, right? I whisper to Marius as we listen to her crashing through the apartment. Maybe she should go for a run or something. Or a swim in the canal.

It's the door slamming, above all, that racks my nerves. She's paranoid about the cats getting into her room.

Not trying to offend you or anything, she says, but living with animals isn't very hygienic.

Her bedroom is like a monastic cell. On her bedside table I spy *The Confessions of Saint Augustine*, *Siddhartha*, several novels by Paulo Coelho. She has three separate fragrance diffusers filled with white musk oil. She is sanctimonious, but holds all her anger inside — Hippocrates would examine her liver, expecting to find it swollen with yellow bile. We nickname her The Devil. She tortures us with tedious piano scales in preparation for mediocre performances, to which she invites us, cruelly. The constant trills and arpeggios make it impossible to study. I read the same texts over and over for three months, unable to concentrate.

All I want to do is be with Marius; the only life I want is a life with him. A life at once doubled and halved. The activity of the mind is stubbornly singular. All my *me* time is *us* time. Gradually, my solo interests slip away, and all that remains are the things we can do together. We are a team, our home reduced to a single room: our bedroom, the only Melina-free environment. Our lives completely entangled, osmotic.

The scales and arpeggios continue, and I rap my knuckles against the wall, wanting to scream: *I rented you a bedroom, not a rehearsal space!*

I'm so sorry, she says, like a little saint forced to descend from her mountaintop. Her face is a mask of submission. Then she resumes her stamping and door slamming, closing herself in the kitchen for hours, silently boiling vegetables, turning carrots and zucchini into tasteless sponges, or else preparing vile tuna and parmesan loaves, which, swaddled in aluminium foil and tea towels, she gifts to her friends, with all the ceremony of the Magi.

After a month that feels like a year, we decide we need to get rid of her. Together, we decide on an elaborate lie: we pretend we're being evicted. We print off a fake email from the landlord, feigning regret and despair. We give her two weeks to find somewhere else to live.

In the meantime, we start looking for a replacement, since leaving the room unoccupied isn't an option. Someone we know, this time. Someone we have something in common with. Marius suggests a friend of one of his exes. More of an acquaintance, really.

What's she like? I ask.

She's Venezuelan. I think she's studying at the same university as me.

Fashion?

I think so.

Have you met her?

I'm not sure. Maybe. I think I know her face.

Invite her over, I say. Do you think she could come tomorrow?

Her name is Milagros, but everyone calls her Vee, for Venezuela. She's about twenty-two, barely out of adolescence, but already she has the air of a middle-aged woman. A cheerful, curious, Latin American woman.

You know who she reminds me of? I say to Marius. My nonna Bina.

She has small hands and feet, wears organza blouses, and decorates her fingernails with black-cherry stickers. Polka-dotted headscarves spill ropes of her thick black hair.

She's perfect. Spirited, but sweet.

Her parents are both finance lawyers in Caracas, so she comes from a wealthy family. That explains how she came to be studying at a private university in Italy. Given the circumstances, we raise the rent a little: five hundred euros a month, we decide, to be paid in three-monthly instalments.

Seeing her in person jogs Marius's memory: he met her a few times, before we met, before he became close with Gem and Samuele and the rest.

I remember seeing her at a couple of birthday parties, he says. She would always bring cake, like a crazy cheesecake or something.

Cake Girl.

And she'd always be the one to help clean up before leaving, he recalls.

Like a jolly mother: cooking, laughing, dancing. The kind of person it's easy to feel safe with. Become friends with. More than friends, even — family.

The afternoon she comes to our apartment for the first time, Vee spends all of five minutes looking around. The apartment is small, and anyway, she's not the kind of person to linger over details.

At the moment, she says in her joyful accent, her mouth full of sunshine, I'm living in a two-bedroom place with seven other people. The sooner I can move, the better.

Five minutes and everything is decided. As she's leaving, she pauses in the hallway, between the doors to our respective bedrooms. She raises her porcelain-white shoulders, red lips hinting at a smile, and asks, her voice like a flute:

Escuse me, but is it okay to fuck in this house?

Piazza del Duomo

She should have just asked.

Shut in our bedroom, fuming, we can only repeat this to ourselves like a mantra.

Morning, afternoon, evening, sun rising and falling outside the window, bringing feeble autumn light, or leaving darkness.

If she'd at least asked.

Let's be reasonable, let's restore some common sense here. When a normal person takes a room in a share house, no one is going to begrudge them the occasional visitor: friends, family, lovers. Everyone has the right to invite others into their home. But I think we can all agree that there is a limit to this, and for the sake of the harmony of the house it's important to strike a balance. More than that: it's important to define the terms of the agreement. For example: what constitutes a visitor?

The speed with which it all transpires makes it clear that this was all decided in advance. A surreptitious plan. A conspiracy.

A few days after Vee moves in, her mother arrives. They haven't seen each other in years, she says. It's more likely Vee was looking for a place to host both her and her mother. If this is how it starts, I think, how much longer until her whole family is living here?

The mother promises she won't stay long. Two days become two weeks, then three, then a month. A month of sharing forty square metres with the two of them. *How long is she going to stay? Why doesn't she get a hotel?*

With her being a woman of a certain age, a woman in her fifties with a respectable career, we'd at least hoped she might bring some order to the place, keep her daughter's slovenly behaviour in check. But they're as bad as each other. The bathroom floor and fixtures are soon adorned with their dirty underwear, the lace panties of the daughter artfully arranged beside the cotton knickers of the mother. On the wall next to the toilet, we discover globs of snot, extracted from one or both noses and smeared there like graffiti. Used sanitary pads are left next to the basin taps, wrapped up like little gifts — in response, we buy a wastebasket from the variety store down the street, hoping they'll understand what it's for. We consider leaving a note, then decide against it.

They return from the supermarket laden with bags and fill the fridge with meat, which they leave marinating (rotting) in various trays and bowls. *Our* trays, *our* bowls, now grotesque aquariums of putrefying flesh. They cook huge quantities of food, enough for a family of eight, all meat and butter and corn, and the little space left in the fridge is crammed with their leftovers. The smell is nauseating. *Where should we put our food?* I want to ask, feeling like a guest in my own home.

They rarely leave the house, occasionally making sporadic outings to tourist destinations, from which they return sporting tacky souvenirs: a plastic miniature of the Duomo, an I LOVE ITALY apron. They wear sunglasses and straw hats in November. *My Italian Holiday.* The rest of the time they're in the apartment.

Our tiny apartment. Tinier, now, than ever.

It's all the more unbearable for their general lack of courtesy. Some mornings, Vee knocks on our bedroom door and flings it open without waiting for a response: *Holiiiii, I made pancakes, want some?* Whenever she crosses paths with Spina or León, she hops and laughs in feigned astonishment, crying: *Marica, gato pelado, gato pelado!* Every second exclamation, in fact, is *marica* or *maricón*, homophobic slurs tossed around without a second thought.

If Marius is friendly with them — of the two of us, he is the more tolerant, the more naïve — I reprimand him later on: *Ignore them, we have to act as if they don't exist.* I want the house to frost over. I want to freeze them out.

Lacking the confidence to ask the mother directly how much longer she plans to stay, I start eavesdropping. I listen behind the kitchen door while they're preparing and devouring their feasts of charred animal flesh, and finally the information is revealed: three more days.

Thank god. We're saved. Only half a week to go. My heart is a handful of feathers. I am overwhelmed with joy. Five days later, though, there are still no signs of imminent departure. I must have misunderstood — I don't speak Spanish, after all.

Six days pass, then seven. Suddenly, unexpectedly, it happens: suitcases appear in the hallway, a taxi is called, mother and daughter share a tearful farewell.

Now that our torture is over, we can recover some semblance of lucidity. This first month and a half was a hiccup, a bump in the road, but let's not allow a simple misunderstanding to spoil the rest of our time together.

The truth is, we can't risk kicking Vee out. Sooner or later, one of our neighbours will notice the revolving door of tenants, the parade of new faces, the makeshift furniture of our subletters migrating up and down the stairs. Besides, we'll never find a replacement willing to pay the kind of money we're asking of Vee.

December arrives, and with it a much-needed break. A necessary one, it turns out, since a professor at San Raffaele has asked me to do a new Italian translation of Mary Wollstonecraft's *A Vindication of the Rights of Woman*, which she plans to publish. (Practically all the professors at San Raffaele work for publishing houses in their spare time, directing academic imprints, publishing edition after edition of their own work — as Melissa likes to put it, they've all got their snouts in the trough.) It's an incredible opportunity, a potential turning point in my studies, a path out of my current stagnation. I look up the existing Italian translation, reading passages at random, already anticipating the acclaim that awaits me: the articles I'll write, the interviews I'll give, the invitations to prestigious conferences, where I'll wax lyrical on lexical choices, on departures from the earlier translation, on the merits of the text and its enduring cultural significance. An intellectual is born. The mere thought of it reignites something in me. Newly motivated, I drag myself from the quagmire of procrastination that has trapped me for so long. Despite still being behind in my exams, I turn my thoughts to my master's thesis. *Look to the future.*

My thesis proposal applies a Husserlian framework to the question of gender, giving rise to a phenomenology of sexual difference. I present the proposal to Francesca De Vecchi, an ex-assistant of De Monticelli and a professor of social ontology —

the ideal person to supervise this kind of research. She's young, savvy, and understands what is at stake. Success, in academic terms, demands a keen awareness of the current intellectual marketplace, its trends and indices. De Vecchi is interested, enthusiastic even, her eyes lively behind her round Gandhi spectacles. It feels like a meeting of kindred spirits, mine and hers.

Very little research has been done in this space, she confirms, before suggesting a small clutch of indispensable texts: Federica Giardini's *Relazioni*, Sara Ahmed's *Queer Phenomenology*. Yours certainly won't be the kind of thesis that leans heavily on existing literature, she adds.

That's exactly what I was hoping to hear. I want to be brilliant. I want to reinvigorate academia, rewrite the rules of engagement.

As the holy mountain of research takes shape before me, I see a path forming. A way up. It's December 2013, and I feel like I'm returning to myself. Finally, a sense of purpose.

The surge of motivation doesn't last long.

Even now that I know what I need to do, I find myself incapable of doing it. Something feels wrong; something has felt wrong for a few days now (if pressed, I would describe the feeling as *foreboding*).

I find a million reasons to put off beginning the translation. I don't even pick up the original text, or re-read the existing translation. The thesis project stagnates, too, untouched inside the perfect shell of the ideal. I tell myself I'm just tired. That I've felt this way before. I hold up the past as a kind of shield, like a lawyer finding comfort in precedent. Looking back in order to deny what lies ahead.

It's impossible to read or write. The pages I look at are mute, impenetrable. I open and close books without taking a single word from them, leaving them scattered in different places across the bedroom, or else returning them to the dark boxes from which they emerged, stacked like poorly wielded Tetris blocks, reconsigning them to oblivion. It takes all my willpower just to drag my body to and from yoga classes — an obligation more than a decision, our only source of income. A veil of confusion descends, obscuring everything.

When the thought first begins to form, I avoid it. It's an unthinkable thought. But it's insistent, insinuating itself into the space between my bones, into the mucous membranes within my skull. Timidly, at first, innocuously, as if this is all just a game the mind is playing with itself.

What if — come on, say it.

Repeat after me.

It's a mid-December evening, at the tram stop on Via Orefici, en route to a dance school in Viale Campania, when the thought finally makes itself heard.

I have to leave him.

PART THREE

Love is not love
Which alters when it alteration finds
William Shakespeare
Sonnet 116

The pathological extensions of love not only touch upon but overlap with normal experience, and it is not always easy to accept that one of our most valued experiences may merge into psychopathology.
Paul E. Mullen & Michele Pathé

Via Orefici

Inhale, *Do I love you?*

Exhale, *I don't love you anymore.*

Don't speak, just smile, as the decision settles into your bones. Keep smiling, don't stop.

Christmas is upon us already. Marius is beside you, waiting with you for the tram at the intersection of Via Torino and Via Orefici: lights, shop signs, chapped lips, last-minute shoppers. Down jackets, fur collars, roast chestnuts. Hands clutching phones, mouths releasing tiny clouds of breath. Breathless conversations, peals of laughter.

Merry Christmas, signora. And if we don't see you, Happy New Year.

The sounds and colours swell and flow like mist around you, peripheral, barely perceived. In the midst of the festive chaos, your attention is tuned to one thing: the thin voice that has suddenly risen in you, risen from you.

It's over. You have to leave him.

When? Now? Tomorrow?

Better to wait until tomorrow.

How much time do we have left?

None. There is no more time. You have to put an end to it.

The world disappears, then comes back into focus. What has been thought cannot be unthought. The egg cannot be uncracked. And certain thoughts, once they emerge from their shells, proceed to crack open everything around them. This should have been the best winter of your life, and instead here you are, at ten to seven in the evening, feeling a cavern open up beneath you, a deep gorge widening in the earth.

You have to teach a dance class in less than an hour, at a school in Viale Campania. The school is run by two women. One is an ex-dancer (with the dancer part in inverted commas), the other hasn't danced a day in her life.

You're running late. The tram approaches, and you kiss Marius goodbye.

See you at home. What do you want for dinner?

Time to unveil that smile again: a tranquil, tranquilising smile.

You hear yourself answer: Whatever you want.

I'll make you a surprise, then.

Meanwhile: the tram. You board, then disembark after a number of stops you know by heart. Life on autopilot. You arrive at the dance school, exchange obligatory sentences with the receptionist — a sad woman in her forties who always dreamt of being a singer, and once enjoyed fifteen minutes of fame as a celebrity impersonator in a shopping centre. Upstairs, as you change in the locker room, steeped in the lingering scent of warm, sweaty, post-hip-hop-class teenagers, you feel the urge to take your phone from your backpack and text him on WhatsApp. Something like: *Can we talk later.* Or: *Something feels wrong.*

The cliché, in times like this, is to liken the mind to a

whirlwind: *Everything was spinning. I felt dizzy.* But that's not how it is for you at all. On the contrary, nothing moves you. You feel still, clear. You start to imagine the chain of events you're about to initiate, like the trailer for a film that hasn't been made yet. You type a sentence into your phone, knowing once it's sent there's no turning back. Then you erase it. You send nothing.

A sudden wave of chills forces you to sit, shivering, on the bench against the locker room wall. A patina of sweat forms on your skin. It's time to start over. Go back to the beginning. Your thoughts ignite one another like a chain of Molotov cocktails.

Inhale, *Do I love you?*

Exhale, *I don't love you anymore.*

How to tell you I'm leaving you?

Ekam, dve, treeni, chatvaari — I count in Sanskrit, trying to set a tone. Each week, there are fewer and fewer students in my class, unsurprisingly. Tonight, I'm distracted, trying to locate the origins of this sudden voice that has come to announce the end of everything. I don't bother correcting the students' bad posture, their collapsing shoulders and misaligned pelvises. It's their own fault. They should have gone to a real dance school, with qualified teachers, not imposters like me.

Something is happening to me and I don't know what it is. All I can think about is going home, being with him, holding him, leaving him. The task calls me to it with a strange urgency. It feels inevitable, as though I've entered a sealed passage with only one exit. All I can do is execute the voice's command.

My head is full of the conversation to come: me telling him it's over, him asking how long I've known, me saying an hour, that I only realised an hour ago. There can be no compromising

— I've never believed in *taking a little break.*

And then what? Where will these new cracks in the earth take us? What sound does a diamond make when it shatters?

I imagine him packing his suitcases, saying: *I'll go back to Umbria for a while. Can I call you, every now and then?*

Each word, each gesture I anticipate takes hold of an organ and rips it from my body, until I am hollow, nothing but space, a paper-thin vessel where all that resonates is the low bell of my decision. I am both victim and aggressor — for the first time, I understand that two completely opposite roles can play out in a single mind. The wonders of psychopathology: what multitudes do I contain, what army of protagonists and antagonists resides inside me, like a set of sinister matryoshka dolls?

I make it through the seventy-five-minute class — not a second longer — and leave the dance school as quickly as I can.

I board the tram home, but sitting still is impossible, so I disembark early. I end up lost in streets whose names I don't recognise: Fogazzaro, Spartaco, Anfossi, streets I've only ever glimpsed through the glass of the tram window. I feel like I'm heading in the wrong direction, away from the apartment.

I text Marius: *Missed the tram, I'll be a bit late home.*

Okay, I'll hold off on dinner.

His care, his tenderness, wounds me, because I am about to murder it. A monster is about to burst forth from my body, all clawed feet and raging fangs, and rip everything to shreds. I am the monster. The monster is me. I imagine him pottering in the kitchen, oblivious, preparing our dinner, setting our nightly altar, two hearts around a tablecloth. The paper towel and cutlery we will use to eat, before or after we break up. Because this is the only question remaining: do I tell him before or after dinner? Is it even possible to eat when you no longer have a soul? Does digestion require a beating heart?

When I eventually make it back up to the apartment, I avoid making eye contact with him. I never want to look him in the eyes again.

Stay away from me, I think. *Please, don't follow me.* But then I turn, and embrace him. I want to feel something, but there is nothing left. I need space — I walk into our bedroom and pretend to busy myself with the contents of my backpack. I put away my change of clothes, although in truth there is no putting things away in this makeshift, furniture-less bedroom, so the clothes end up on the floor, or draped over the radiator, or thrown into a cardboard box. Back in the kitchen, I wind my arms around his abdomen, feeling the heat of his skin, the scent of it. *And now? Do you feel something now?* His skin is sweet, like a foreign fruit.

I'm going to take a shower, I announce, looking for an escape route.

The bathroom's occupied, he answers. Vee's been in there for a while, she's going out tonight.

In that case, I think I'll have a quick lie-down, I improvise. I've got a bit of a headache. Tonight was exhausting.

I need time, space. I need to place something between me and the unbearable normality of things.

Lying on the mattress I feel my body start to vibrate, tremble, a real or imaginary tremor. My stomach tenses, hardens, threatens to empty itself on the floor, all over the walls. I scan the room for a bag, a bucket, a jar, a hat, anything — is it possible to vomit in silence?

Standing up helps. Pacing the sullen, dusty bedroom. Let's face it: we're living in our own filth. This room is a hive of mites and bacteria, boxes overflowing with disembowelled books, piles of dirty laundry — how long has it been since anyone vacuumed in here? My linear pacing turns circular, first clockwise, then anticlockwise. *You spend all day in this shitty room, couldn't you at least clean it once in a while?* I realise I'm standing in Pietro's shoes. So this is how love works: a doubling, a karmic mirroring. A constant and endless repetition.

I try to breathe more deeply, extending the exhalation as long as possible, activating the parasympathetic nervous system. There, it's passing. The feeling is passing. I can smell potatoes sizzling in a pan, soy cutlets. I hear the fridge opening and closing. Maybe I'm just hungry. Maybe there is no connection between the voice in my head and this feeling in my body.

A head pokes through the door, his head.

Dinner's ready. You can take a shower later.

Coming, I answer, in the calmest voice I can summon.

In the tiny, domestic collisions of dinner — fork against plate, glass against table — I hear the voice again, repeating itself: *You don't love him anymore. If you do, prove it.* If only there were silence, if only the objects around me would be still. The knives, frying pan, door, chairs, dish towel, bottle, ladle, flame, paper towels: I wish they would all just give me a moment's peace.

As we eat, I keep my eyes on the plate. I want to face-plant into my recently defrosted dinner. Thankfully, we're not alone; Vee appears in the doorway, all dressed up in a short leather miniskirt and a fur coat that appears to be crafted from gently swaying tufts of white and purple hair. Her own hair is oiled and gathered into a pompom on top of her head, like the tail of a bunny, and two saucer-sized shells hang heavily from her earlobes. Where is she off to at eleven in the evening, dressed like that? It's unusual for her. She must have a date. She'll freeze out there, in that miniskirt.

Holiii, see you later, she says, before tripping down the hallway and out the front door, leaving a trail of fruity perfume in her wake.

I chew and swallow the tasteless mush in front of me. As recently as yesterday I would have praised his cooking, thanked him for the delicious meal, but now I can barely keep each mouthful down. I pray I don't start gagging in front of him. He mustn't notice anything is wrong, not until I understand exactly what is going on. He mustn't suspect a thing. My body is a room with moving walls — I can feel them closing in. One wall is a question, the other is dissimulation, and in the middle of the walls is me. No matter how closely I scrutinise this shrinking compartment, I can't figure out how to stop it closing around me like a trap. It's over, but I don't want it to be over. I don't love him anymore, but I want to love him again.

Iuby, he says, let me wash the dishes tonight. You must be tired.

I wish he wouldn't call me that. I can't bear the sound of that word anymore: a relic, a linguistic artifact of a love that no longer exists, of an enchanted time that has passed. *Please*, I think, *don't be so kind. Not when I'm about to be so unkind.*

But all I say is: Okay, thanks.

And I leave him alone in the kitchen.

Vee reappears and slips quietly into her bedroom. She must have been gone all of ten minutes.

I lock myself in the bathroom and undress. My nakedness brings no relief. I separate my clothes into cleanish and dirty, placing the latter in the laundry basket and the former on the closed lid of the toilet. I wish I could establish this kind of easy order elsewhere, where it's needed. In the shower, I bury my face under a stream of too-hot water, wanting to disappear down the drain along with it. If only I could shapeshift, evaporate into clouds of steam, or crystallise to the point of invincibility. If only I could change the structure of my molecules and become liquid, so I could simply flow elsewhere, become river, ocean, sea floor. If only I were anywhere but here. I scrub my skin long after the foaming soap has washed away, my gestures frenetic, fearful.

Movement slows thought: I figured this out on my own at some point in my life, I'm not sure when. Moving the body helps the mind not to think, physical activity interfering with mental activity. I spread my fingers over my hips like rays of sunlight, then against my thighs, my groin, my lower back. Little suns attached to rotating wrists. I dig my nails into my scalp. Then I get out of the shower and into the purple IKEA bathrobe Pietro gave me. A towel passes over my face, then wraps around my head like a turban, the way my mother always used to do.

I steel myself to leave the bathroom. The mirror shows me the same face it always does, a face that's neither ugly nor beautiful, but now seems to me almost wicked. Feral, even.

I can endure one more evening. At least one more. But please, I beg you — I pray without knowing whom I'm praying to — give me rest from these thoughts.

Via Olgettina

Lips: thin, fat. Peach fuzz, enlarged pores. Eyelashes crusted with mascara. Asymmetrical nostrils, cheeks spotted with freckles, or pimples: dry, ripe. Piercings, tattoos, lipstick, no lipstick. Teeth glimpsed between lips, or concealed behind lips. Handcuffed wrists, a patch of sky streaked with clouds, hemmed with barbed wire. Small birds against the blue.

The faces all belong to women. White, Black, Asian, Latina. Some very young, some older, some hard to categorise. A stream of faces blinking on and off like fairy lights as we lie, embracing, on the sinking mattress. He's little spoon, I'm big spoon. The title appears on the laptop screen in front of us: *Orange Is the New Black.* The new series everyone is talking about, freshly downloaded from The Pirate Bay.

Do you mind if we start watching it? he'd asked after washing the dishes, when our paths crossed again in the bedroom. When I agreed, he'd laughed. *You'll just fall asleep again anyway, like last time.*

I'm pulled in two directions, first by an impulse to detach myself from him, to put an end to this confusing closeness, then by a desire to stay. I want to stay. Despite my initial resistance, physical contact with his body makes the voice grow quieter.

Bodies speak more loudly than our brains would like them to. They are not always wise. Bodies keep keening and wanting, like insolent animals, seeking each other out until the bitter end. Sometimes all they crave is a modicum of warmth.

The protagonists of Episode One are in love, like us. Their love is an unbearable reminder of what we had — of what we could still have. How do we get back there? I cleave more closely to his body, hoping it will answer me. My knees cradled by the backs of his knees, our bodies knitted. The protagonists are in love, but they are separated when the blonde one, the Katy Perry look-alike, goes to prison. This is what awaits us: unavoidable, ineluctable division. This series, which I half-watch as the thoughts continue to swirl inside me, is the perfect metaphor for our life.

Why did I agree to watch this thing? My eyes drift closed involuntarily, then a little after three in the morning they reopen. What wakes me is a weight on my chest, like a sack of sand against my sternum, pushing on my lungs. It grows steadily worse, and I see now that the voice has its body back and is crouching on my ribs like a goblin. I feel awful, hungry for oxygen. I want to call an ambulance; how to tell a panic attack from a heart attack? *If you don't love him anymore, you have to leave him. Why haven't you done it yet?* I can't breathe. I want to wake him, I want to shake him awake, but then what would I say? I can't. I have to manage this on my own.

I sit on the edge of the deflated mattress, feeling the tiles against my bones, and open and close my fingers like neurotic flowers. I don't know what to do. I lie back down. I need to sleep.

The minutes pass: three fifteen, three eighteen. Marius is sunk in sleep, breathing heavily, grunting. My love sleeps like a pig. I plug my ears. The room seems brighter than usual, as though lit through the window by a streetlamp, or a floodlight over a construction site. Since when has there been a construction site on our street? How can they be building something new when I'm about to raze everything to the ground? I reach down to find my phone, and type into Google: *how do I know if I still love him.* Then: *how do you know if you're in love.*

I click on a link that takes me to a forum — there are so many discussion threads, a whole community of lovers burning not with passion but with guilt and doubt. A subculture of people suffering from post-love delirium. Variations on the same questions pop up again and again. Some users let months, even years go by before making a decision. Many are still in denial.

Curled at the far edge of the mattress — as far as possible from Marius, for fear of being caught in the act — I bounce from thread to thread.

The fact that you're even asking this question means you don't love him anymore.

You know how it feels to be in love. When you love someone, all you want to do is be with them all the time.

Eight sure signs that you're in love: 1) you can't stop thinking about the person. 2) you feel like you're floating on a cloud. 3) your heart beats faster or you get butterflies when you're around them. 4) you find it hard to sleep. 5) nothing else seems to matter anymore. 6) you feel less stressed. 7) you feel full of energy. 8) you and the person are making long-term plans together.

Every sentence feels like a stab wound, a blow to the throat.

I get to my feet, walk out of the bedroom and into the kitchen. I pick up last night's bottle of wine, still practically full, and down the whole thing. If only my brain were in my stomach and

I could simply flood it with drink. I lock myself in the bathroom and sit on the floor, in the dark, with my head between my knees. I press my forehead into my kneecaps, hard, harder, trying to find a hiding place inside the sensation. The cats start mewling at the door, so I open it. As soon as they're in, they meow to get out. Fucking cats. I feel like kicking them, or grabbing them by their necks and smashing them against the wall until they're quiet, until their bodies are wet rags. I need silence.

I lean down and pick them up, cradle them to my chest, kiss them.

I'm sorry, I whisper. Come on, I'll give you something to eat.

With nowhere else to go, I return to the one place that is unbearable to me. I lie my body back down on the mattress, next to him. For a while, I manage to disappear, to feel nothing, but the moment I return to myself, the same questions are there to meet me. They repeat and repeat until my alarm goes off — *shit* — and I remember I have a compulsory political-philosophy seminar this morning. I desperately need the credits if I want to salvage anything of this master's degree. So I put myself back together, and leave the apartment while he's still asleep.

I drag my body along the street, into the bus, onto the Metro, all the way to Cascina Gobba. I spend the interminable commute typing more sentences into Google: *how to know if you've fallen out of love. when is it normal to stop loving someone.* An hour, more, bent over the tiny browser window on the screen of my phone. Dozens and dozens of identical testimonies can't be wrong. For once, the internet seems to agree on something: true love is incompatible with uncertainty. One person writes: *So many couples stay together out of affection, not love.* Another: *Don't do what I did. I wasted six years of my life.*

Love is not to be confused with affection; affection is not to be confused with habit. And what about sex? We used to have it three times a day, now it's twice a week, at best. Is that normal? What are the parameters of normal?

Without warning, it seems, the train arrives at my stop.

Cascina Gobba. Today I'm taking the shuttle train — I don't give a fuck about the money. I board a carriage containing a small clutch of hospital patients: a woman with oxygen tubes emerging from her nostrils, a mother holding a child with bandaged eyes, an old woman leaning on a walker. I make my way through the hospital's basement maze of immaculate corridors, and into the university building.

As I'm looking up the classroom for this morning's seminar, a voice calls my name from behind. It's Sarah, an old classmate from my undergraduate course. She's enrolled in a doctorate now, having taken the correct steps at the correct pace.

How's Marius?

Why did she have to say his name? Why is she asking after him, today of all days? I need time to process everything, to understand what's happening, but no one will give me any peace. I keep being reminded of him. Of *us.* I need a break from the plural.

Good, I answer, he's good, and as I speak I feel my face slipping away, the skin sliding off like a mask.

Faceless, I enter the classroom and try to take notes, concentrating all my energy on being here, despite the endless barrage of questions still firing in my mind: *Do you love him, or don't you? If you close your eyes and visualise his face, how does it make you feel?*

I try to bring his features into my mind, one by one, and track the emotional response they trigger.

When you think of his eyes, do you feel that same euphoria you felt when you first met?

What about his hair?

He had such beautiful hair, but already he's beginning to lose it. Six months — that's all it took for his beauty to begin to wither.

That's enough; I don't want to do this right now. *Please*, I beg myself, *I need a break.*

But there's no stopping now.

The voice keeps instructing me: *Open your eyes and look around. I want you to compare him with the boys in this room. That one there, the cute redhead with the tortoiseshell glasses and the light beard. Would you swap Marius for him? He's better looking, admit it. What about that one? Look at his arms, those biceps. Look at that round arse, imagine what it would be like to open it and put your tongue inside, imagine fucking him right here, against the white wood of his desk.*

I want to scream, inside I am screaming, because if it were true love then these crowding, swarming thoughts would be powerless, they would mean nothing. I wish there were an objective way to quantify my feelings, a machine that could estimate how much I love him and tell me if it's enough. I need a value, and a scale to compare it against. Isn't there a lab somewhere that could do it? Neuroscience works miracles these days. Or maybe I need a mystic — surely it's not so different from photographing auras. I wish I could walk through a museum of other boys, examine their faces in close-up, their bodies in 3D, enormous, sculpted like a hundred Colossi of Rhodes. *Look at this; do you desire this?*

If the answer is yes, then it's proof that the person I'm with is not enough, that he's not the right one. I've aways believed that when you fall in love, everything else should disappear. There is no more desire, no more need, because true love completes you: he or she or they fill every empty space, feed every appetite, satisfy all urges.

True love doesn't degrade over time — *love is not love which alters when it alteration finds.*

Let's count the months: April, May, June, July, August, September, October, November, now December. Eight months of him as my sole focus. But he is no longer enough. All I want is to be enthralled by someone, and he no longer enthrals me.

Desperate to move, to shirk the voice in my head, I gather up my things — notepad, pencil case, jacket — and walk out of the classroom, pausing before I leave to sign my name on the attendance sheet.

Are you leaving? asks a random voice behind me.

I'm not feeling well, I answer, without turning around.

I exit the building through the back and reverse my steps from earlier: shuttle train, Metro, bus.

During the commute, I open the group chat whose notifications I've been ignoring for the past twelve hours. It's the art historians.

Hey, you okay? You haven't replied since yesterday. How are things with Marius?

Marius Marius

Marius — *how are things with Marius?*

Has something happened?

It's not like you to be offline, we're worried!

I don't want to keep this to myself. I want help, I want to talk to someone, even if it's just Melissa. But I feel like a fool, after eight months of gloating online, eight months of love-heart emojis and soppy photos and smug affirmations of our overwhelming, unbreakable, miraculous love. Our Shakespearean love, a love written in the stars. How do I look her in the eyes now, with egg on my face, and say: *You know what? I thought about it, and I was wrong.* Even thinking about that conversation I already feel hunted, exposed, guilty. I can imagine her response: *This is so typical. You always give up on everything.*

Confiding in someone makes it real. Then again, a burden that isn't shared grows exponentially heavier. Unwanted thoughts are a bit like oysters: they take a grain of sand and worry it into something larger, harder. Or maybe they're like that zombie fungus that infects ants, taking control of their movements. Colonising their bodies. I start to doubt myself. *Maybe this is just a phase. Maybe it will pass.* But it's been days now. Two whole days.

Two days become four. December is trickling away before my eyes, but my focus on the thoughts is unwavering. Is this really how it goes? Can the most beautiful thing I've ever felt, the strongest conviction I've ever had, simply disintegrate without warning into a pile of ash? The sense of urgency returns, the feeling of the walls closing in, a trap constricting. I want to grab myself by the shoulders and shake as hard as I can. I want to hit myself until I'm unconscious, and when I wake up I want to be back with you, the way we were. The way I thought you were.

Why can't we just go back? Why can't you make all this go away? There's no other place I can exist, nowhere else I feel safe.

I spy on you, scan your body, analysing it from different angles, rating it, comparing it, *yes or no.* Hands, fingernails, feet, back — a slight arch, mild scoliosis. Could that be the root of the problem? A new haircut: better or worse? Which do you prefer: full beard or no beard?

I'm teetering on a threshold, too scared to step off into either direction: stay or go, love or the death of love. What about that scar at the top of your lip? Is it new or old? I examine it in detail: a keloid, an excessive proliferation of scar tissue. That must be it. Our love story ended by an unnoticed scar.

It's as though there's a collective force, hundreds and thousands of newtons of force, a whole crowd of powerful arms trying to pull me towards the edge, beyond the point of no return, and my feet are clenching in opposition, heels driving into the earth, fingers clawing at whatever they can, palms turning red, then purple, my hands skinned by the friction of resistance. But I'm losing the fight, ceding ground centimetre by centimetre. It's becoming clear that these past eight months were a kind of delirium, a kind of ecstatic insanity.

Either he is different or he's the same. Either he has changed or something has changed in me. As I move closer to the cliff edge, I want to embrace him one more time, so that we fall together, entwined.

Love is dead. Milan has betrayed me. The centre did not hold; the centre was empty, and I am numb.

I'm leaving you.

Iuby, don't leave me.

Here we are at the edge, and it's me who has to push you off.

Via Rogoredo

Sounds crazy to me, but do what you want.

It's not like I can stop you, I tell myself, as I desperately try to think of a way to stop you.

Marius's parents have insisted — demanded — that he visit them in Umbria for Christmas. For the sacred Christian and Orthodox celebrations, the holy feasts they hope will wipe the slate clean. I am methodical, persistent, in my counterarguments. *How dare they? They haven't sent you a single euro in the past four months. You could be starving to death for all they care.* Then, changing tack: *You'll save money if you stay in Milan.*

Accusations and criticisms and excuses pour out of me, because I'm afraid of being alone. Of not missing you, of detaching completely, of using your absence to get back on Grindr and fuck half of Milan. Because I'm afraid of myself. Now the source of danger, the wild element to be restrained, is me. I need you to tie me down, handcuff me, so that I don't ruin this, ruin everything — us, our past, our future. It's not about making a decision anymore; it's about containing my incontinence, taming the animal inside me.

When I'm with you, I'm scared of not feeling what I should. When I'm alone, I'm terrified of cheating, of watching on helplessly as my body exercises its sexual impulses. Any other body would do: a construction worker, a bartender, the first body I come across. All I need is a parking lot, a dark alleyway. The solution, I think, is to *be less*, to dial everything down. A kind of ontological *capitis deminutio*; the elimination of the will, in order to resolve the conflicts arising from the will.

The season progresses. December 18, 19, 20. Mariah Carey starts singing *make my wish come true*

all I want for Christmas

is you.

The moment I wake up in the morning is always the worst. The fear is at its peak, at crisis point, as if hardened overnight into a great stone. By evening, it feels a little looser, more mobile.

I get up early, as usual, while he's still sleeping — thank god he's still sleeping — and escape to the kitchen where I empty ten, eleven, twelve drops of Bach Rescue Remedy into a large glass of water and drink it down, washing the guilt from my insides with magic liquid. The point isn't to medicate myself, in any official or scientific sense. I developed this routine as a way of managing the panic: wake up, go to the kitchen, drink the remedy. A repeatable set of actions that, while failing to solve anything, at least establishes a sequence of predictable moments, three fixed points like a constellation in the raw mush of my confusion.

Unless I have to teach a class — an unavoidable obligation — I don't leave the house. I spend all day with him, on our uninflatable mattress, suspended in a strange kind of undertow, a state of being with no purpose beyond its own preservation. Stillness can conceal all manner of struggles. We watch tv series and YouTube videos, wasting time, marking time, keeping time standing still. His body, once a miracle, is now a perpetually pyjamaed shape that lies beside me, inert. This sad teenager's bedroom reveals us for what we are: a couple of failures who chose misery.

In the end, my objections count for nothing. You've made up your mind. On the morning of December 21, I accompany you to Rogoredo Station, wheeling your battered silver suitcase so you don't have to. I say nothing as we negotiate the obstacles of the city, its stairs and ramps and barriers, simulating the peace I will need to survive your absence. What a beautiful day — the sun is out. You ask if I'll miss you, and I say yes, a lot, when what I should say is *I don't know*, and that not-knowing is all I can think about. This is a test. When you're in love, and your beloved goes away, you should cry, pine. Instead, I feel desolate, swirling somewhere between guilt and loneliness.

You step onto the FlixBus, already crammed with bodies and scarves and jackets, and we wave our hands at each other until the mechanical green giant rumbles into motion and disappears behind a curve in the road.

A week without you might as well be forever.

I let myself be washed along by the journey home, but when I step through the front door, the pounding anxiety returns with a vengeance. In front of me stretches the reality of six whole days alone — enough time to reveal my indifference. If I still loved him, what would I be feeling right now? Not this, surely. I miss the surges of light, the wings, the ecstasy of our early days together. I know it's not a fantasy, I know it's real because I was there, I felt it.

I go straight to bed, burying myself under the covers, and call the cats to me. Their little marsupial faces. I'm resigned, now, to the thoughts. *Sleep*, I tell myself. *Try to sleep*. I want to sleep until you return, a loveless sleeping beauty, protected from the dark thistles in my head by a glass coffin.

I manage to nap for a few hours before a voice wakes me. A moaning. A soft cry.

Yes, yes.

Coño. Then again: *Coño.*

Estoy venendo.

Vee is holed up in her bedroom, as usual. Since her mother's departure, she's hardly left the house. She doesn't seem to have gone to university in weeks. The truth is, we don't even know if she's still studying. She orders takeaway over the phone every day for lunch. Two pizzas and a family-sized bottle of Coke, all for her. Occasionally sushi, three of four bags full. The food is taken into her bedroom, and nothing ever comes back out. She stockpiles the pizza boxes, the empty bottles, the plastic bags and packaging under her bed, along with a stash of sex toys and lubricant — I know because I periodically poke my head in when she's in the bathroom, spying rat that I am. She hoards everything, eventually filling the balcony with mounds of bulging black garbage bags, our shame on display for the whole street to see.

It's unusual to hear sounds from her room, but that's where they're coming from now. They are unmistakably the sounds of sex. But she's alone. Could she be using the webcam?

Yes, she must be. Now she's giving instructions: *Drink your water. Go on, lap it up like the dog you are.* Then more excited moaning, a scream unsuccessfully smothered by a pillow. In the background, a mechanical hum, an electric device slapping against sweaty flesh. Then, for a moment, perfect silence, broken by her suddenly sober voice saying: *Yes, PayPal is good.*

It's not entirely true that she never leaves the house. Sometimes, in the evenings, she bolts from her gastronomic sex bunker like a horse from a starting stall, racing to the bathroom. From our bedroom, I can hear her bowel movements, the vigorous lapping of the bidet. When she emerges, the perennial Little Mermaid pyjamas have been replaced with leather miniskirts, bustiers, enormous shoes moulded from transparent plastic. She barrels through the front door and down the stairs, clattering like a herd of beasts, only to return ten or fifteen minutes later.

Months later, she'll explain that guys come by to pick her up. Guys with fetishes, mostly. They have sex once or twice, then never see each other again. She doesn't charge the nice ones, but others she does.

One day, returning from a rare daytime outing, she reports that someone has graffitied the word WHORE on the front of our building, in green spray paint.

Must have been an acquaintance of mine, she says, laughing.

Evening arrives, and Marius texts me. I wish he wouldn't. I never want him to write to me again. Or rather, I don't want him to write to this version of me. I can't figure out what is required of me, how to negotiate this interaction. I notice my thoughts, and pin each one down like a butterfly on a lepidopterist's board. I agonise over each word in my reply, second-guessing every expression of interest or affection — my fingers type them spontaneously, automatically — for fear of prolonging a false, now-meaningless language.

Then, a startling realisation: it's Christmas. I have to give him something. I want to give him something. But how to navigate the unwritten law: the greater the love, the greater the gift?

I had an idea, before everything changed: tickets to see Miley Cyrus. Marius has loved her ever since her Hannah Montana days. She's playing at the Forum di Assago next September. That's nine months away. Will we last nine more months?

Lately, Marius has been playing the same music video on repeat while we eat breakfast. It was directed by Terry Richardson, and involves a naked Miley clinging to a huge iron wrecking ball. Concrete walls smash, collapse. Tears roll down Miley's white cheeks.

I choose to defy the poisonous murmurings inside my head, and buy the Miley Cyrus tickets. It's morning when I take the tram and Metro to Mariposa, the music store at Duomo station. As I'm handing over the money, a thought says: *Keep the tickets. You can take whoever you want.*

Buying them is only half the battle — a real boyfriend would wrap his beloved's gift with reverence, with loving attention. My solar plexus curls into itself at the idea: ischemia of the fourth chakra. I walk into the Danish stationery shop on Via Meravigli and wander the endless aisles of wrapping paper and greeting cards, a thousand shimmering hearts in red, yellow, silver. I can't afford hearts. After the hearts comes a wall of bears and reindeer, beady eyes glaring at me, seeing right through me, mocking me, reminding me how futile this all is.

If you loved him, I think, you'd place the slim envelope of tickets inside a pretty little box, and that box would go inside a bigger box, boxes within boxes, and you'd wrap the whole thing in a monumental bow, like this one. The week you met him, that's what you would have done, no question.

Now the pomp and sparkles seem false, ridiculous. Go for something spare, minimalist, so as not to arouse suspicion. No need to go over the top with ribbons. Avoid shades of red and pink. Nothing too loud. Go for cold colours, to reflect your insincerity: impassive blue.

As quickly as possible, I'm out of the claustrophobic shop and into the buzzing street. It's here, pressed between the lunchtime Christmas crowds, that I finally accept I need to talk to someone.

Easier said than done: psychotherapists aren't cheap. In this city, self-care is a hobby for the wealthy. After some digging online, however, I discover a network of mental-health professionals who offer discounted rates to people of limited income. Thirty-five, forty euros a session, instead of eighty or ninety. They call themselves the Accessible Therapy Network. A bunch of quacks, I think. This must be a last-ditch effort to snare clients. Nevertheless, I write to one of them, who turns out to have a background in family and systemic psychotherapy and sports psychology. The photo that accompanies her write-up shows her on the sidelines of a soccer field, floodlights illuminating an asymmetrical haircut, shaved on one side. In my head, I hear the sneering voice of my nonna Lilli: *'nu masculone.*

The therapist replies to my enquiry quickly: *How does Wednesday 8 January work for you, at 6.30 pm? If it's urgent, we can speak on the phone before then.*

I write back: *Can't you just tell me, in your professional opinion, what's happening to me?*

It's best if we discuss it in person, she answers. *Try to stay calm, and be patient with yourself.*

I persist: *How long will it take me to work through this?*

Everyone is different — an easy, one-size-fits-all response. *If you feel the need, please don't hesitate to call me.*

When I google the location of the clinic, a space she shares with five other therapists, I discover it's in Lambrate, about two or three doors down from the first apartment I shared with Pietro.

I prepare to enter the dark tunnel of days that separates me from our session. My resistance softens as I begin to place something like trust, or hope, in the idea of a resolution, whatever that may look like — a new beginning. A last resort.

The season's festivities flow around me soundlessly, as though the audio has been turned off and my brain has overdubbed the familiar scenes with its own, funereal soundtrack. My all-consuming thoughts make words impossible, so I stay silent. At lunch in Rozzano, amid the green and pink Christmas lights and the proudly displayed nativity scenes, baby Jesus still safe under his bed of cotton wool, my mother is suspicious.

What's up with you? You seem off. Everything okay?

Marius's return from Umbria quells something in me, but inflames something else. I can't stand being close to him and I can't stand being away from him. Still, the evenings offer some relief; the setting sun promises sleep, my only refuge from the exhausting litany inside my head.

It takes two whole days before I can muster the courage to give him his gift. I feel like an imposter.

Marius holds the concert tickets in his hand and says: Iuby, this is too much. You're crazy. I'll buy you something with the money my parents gave me for Christmas.

Don't worry about it, I say. You can get me something once you're earning money.

What I don't say is that a gift from him, now, would be unbearable. This way, at least, I can imagine I'm atoning for my sins.

△

December comes to a close, and January arrives.

I still can't bring myself to talk to Marius about what's going on inside me. The day of my appointment with the psychotherapist, I tell him I'm going to a singing lesson.

Oh? How much is it?

Not much, the instructor teaches from home, it's like a passion project for her.

The appointment is on a Wednesday: the day of Hermes, armed with his winged caduceus. As if pushed along by a benevolent wave, I find myself at the door of the clinic, my finger pushing the gold button of the intercom. The machine croaks gently in response: *Just a moment*.

I'm buzzed in. I go upstairs. I don't have to wait long before the therapist calls me in.

I deposit my weight in an apple-green pleather armchair, still tasting the licorice gummies I took from the big glass bowl in the waiting room. The therapist has a Tuscan accent and is wearing Doc Martens. A purple motorcycle jacket hangs from the back of her chair.

I recite the opening phrase I've prepared: Good evening, doctor. I hope you can help me. I've been in a relationship for nine months, but I don't know —

Let's start from the beginning, she says. Tell me everything.

She exudes a calm that bounces right off me; I find it patronising, taunting.

Tell me everything, she is saying, *and I will make it real.*

On the coffee table between us, a box of tissues waves a tiny white flag.

Piazzale Susa

Two sessions in, and we're still only playing in the shallows.

Before the third, she asks me to bring along some photos.

Childhood photos, she says. You as a child. And, if possible, one for each of the key figures in your life. Parents, grandparents, aunts and uncles. Pets, if you like.

A treasure hunt in my mother's wardrobe yields a number of candidates. Shoulder pads and perms. Birthday parties. Millefoglie cream cakes and gâteau St-Honoré. Oversized overalls. My first communion, at which mamma resembled Lady Gaga in her *Just Dance* phase.

I have no idea how the photos will be used. I imagine us constructing a magnificent family tree, tracing the trauma down every branch, a kind of Jodorowsky-inspired psychogenealogy. Although, I do recall saying that this is an emergency. I wonder if she knows I haven't paid the gas bill this month so I can afford her sessions. I try not to think about how behind we are on rent.

Normally, I'd love this kind of thing, but right now I'm in crisis mode. I don't feel in control. What I need from her are tools, rules to follow, new remedies to replace the ones I've outwitted. My current avoidance-based coping technique isn't cutting it.

When Marius is out with friends — or, more rarely, out looking for work — and I'm at home alone, I don't budge from underneath the covers, skipping meals so as not to abandon the safety of my sad little hideout. I'm afraid that any sense of open space, physical or mental, could topple the fragile structure of my self-restraint. That structure is essential, it's all I have. All that matters is staying inside it. Alone under the covers, I binge-watch recordings of the philosophy seminars I've missed since giving up on the Wollstonecraft essay and ghosting my thesis supervisor. Sometimes, when I'm too spooked by the apartment and its possibilities, I go out into the street and walk nonstop for five or six hours: Via Tito Vignoli, Duomo, Loreto, Porta Romana, Corso Lodi, then back again, until my legs are annihilated, my feet covered in cuts and blisters. A pilgrimage with no sanctuary. I studiously avoid watching films or series centred on sentimental relationships. The same goes for music — no love songs, no break-up songs. I steer clear of couples and archetypes who aggravate the *cittavṛiti*, those mental whirlpools that suck me in and carry me away. I perform a social-media cleanse, unfollowing all the guys I find attractive, even celebrities. Any male who engages with me online — a greeting, an emoji, an innocent *congratulations* — is immediately blocked, erased from the face of the Earth.

I attempt to exorcise the demon of concupiscence by resisting masturbation, even though I still find myself incapable of seeking out Marius's body. The times when he takes the initiative, I concentrate on the kernel of my sensations, which oscillate between fear and pleasure. In the end, there's only a paper-thin line separating attraction from repulsion, desire from the impulse to flee.

I decide that my therapy sessions are too impractical. This bargain-basement psychologist has to go. Any reasonable patient would bring up their doubts in session, initiate a conversation about outcomes and expectations, navigating a way around the obstacle as a team. Not me. I ditch her with all the incivility of a scorned teenage lover. I cancel our next session at short notice and block her on every possible platform: phone, apps, email. I leave scathing reviews online. *Charlatan*, I write. *Occultist*. This is how I'll take my revenge. *Conspiracy theorist*. It's better to burn bridges, so I can't come crawling back later.

Once I've dispatched with the photo fetishist, I turn my attention to finding a replacement. This time, I decide to go for something more traditional. None of this modern avant-garde bullshit. I want old-school psychoanalysis. But Freud is passé, possibly even cancelled at this point: a reductionist sex addict. After a day spent researching online, I decide Jung is the way to go. I track down a Jungian therapist who conducts her sessions from home; I imagine her as a character from an American tv show. After some back and forth, I manage to negotiate a lower price. Then, one cool but not cold morning, I make my way to her apartment on a street near Piazzale Susa.

The building is elegant, and a concierge in a watermelon-pink coat immediately deduces why I'm there.

Fourth floor, she says, barely raising her eyes to look at me.

A jovial middle-aged woman opens the door to greet me. Her voice is bright but powerful; she speaks from her diaphragm. She wears a long cardigan embroidered with owls and crescent moons, so long it gets tangled around her legs. She has the air of a clarinet player, or a trombonist. After ushering me into the hallway, she gestures to the first door on the left.

Please, she says, her tone informal. Come in. Tell me what's going on.

The room is well lit and woody, like the living room of a Swiss chalet. A large Persian rug absorbs our footsteps. Shamanic objects hang from the walls: masks, drums, cosmological maps. I sense them watching our encounter, their eyes small hollows of shadow. I am more than willing to follow wherever this matriarch of archetypes wants to take me. She will be my guide.

These guys are the masters of the house, she says, smiling in the direction of the three European Shorthair cats that share the room with us, one in her lap, the other two curled at the foot of her teak armchair. Around us, on shelves and surfaces, I notice a collection of figurines: Smurfs, Moomins, toy soldiers from various eras, realistic and anthropomorphised animals. Dylan would lose his mind in here. In front of a large bookcase, I see a box full of sand — a miniature Zen garden?

They're all devices to help free the unconscious, she explains. I'll let you try some of them later.

As it turns out, we'll never end up using any of it. Mainly because, after briefly asking *how I've been feeling since we last met*, she spends our sessions talking about herself: the novel she's writing, her mother, her brother-in-law, old patients of hers, her degree in economics, her passion for Inter Milan. She must be bored, I decide, of me repeating the same complaints over and over again. Her anecdotes and memoirs spin around us, growing like fairy floss, and all I can do is sit and nod.

At the end of each session, she concludes: Keep engaging that cognitive filter, and you'll be fine.

I try to envision the imaginary mesh, a perforated metal disc floating above my head, protecting me from intrusive thoughts.

Just remember, she says as she walks me to the front door, her hand ever so gently pushing my hip, *cognitive filter*.

I mustn't be paying her enough.

Viale Abruzzi

Two fingers swing left, right, left, right, a blessing in motion.

Follow my fingers.

The same instruction every time, delivered in the same softly downward-curving voice.

Follow my fingers.

The therapist is on a chair, the patient on a couch. The patient's attention is absolute — they want to be good at this. The therapist's fingers move back and forth through the same small patch of space as he asks the patient to bring the episode to mind, conjuring not so much a visual image but a sensory memory of it.

Follow my fingers as you return to that feeling of terror, that burn of anxiety, that compulsion to end the relationship.

Stay with that feeling. Stay with it.

The patient's pupils move side to side for ten, twenty seconds before the therapist prompts the eyes to close.

What are you noticing now?

The patient reports sensations with precision: tightness in a particular part of the neck, a heaviness in the pit of the stomach.

Then it begins again: *Follow my fingers.*

Ten seconds, more, then another pause. The patient bathing in the trembling depths of their body, eyelids sealed.

△

Futile, I think, to try and fix something that can only be accepted. All things come to an end. It's childish to oppose the natural evolutions of physiology, the biochemical changes that come with falling and staying in love. Those early hormones inevitably drain away. They must: in the first throes of romance, the brain produces amphetamines, particularly phenethylamine, along with copious amounts of oxytocin and adrenaline. What goes up must come down. Every take-off must be followed by a landing. The earth opening up to swallow us whole.

My first session goes well. There is a second, then a third, fourth, tenth. I hand over thirty-five euros each time. A tithe for my soured love, an offering at the feet of a crumbling chryselephantine sculpture ready to collapse and bury us under a howl of dust. (The death of a deity always implies extinction.)

The sessions, which I attend one morning a week — as frequently as I can afford to — soon become my one remaining interest. I haven't opened a book in weeks, I've stopped attending university, my yoga practice has stalled. I am acutely aware of the changes happening in my mind and body. The weekly pilgrimage to this first-floor clinic on Viale Abruzzi is my final effort to save myself. To save us.

My new therapist — this time I've chosen a man, to get right to the heart of the problem — says my fixation on leaving Marius stems from my fear of being left by him. Abandonment issues in prevention mode. If I'm honest, I'm not entirely convinced by his hypothesis. In one of our sessions, I submit another for consideration, duly researched on the internet: relationship obsessive-compulsive disorder. ROCD. The theory doesn't seem to be popular in Italy; it was first proposed by two Israeli researchers, and there hasn't yet been a great deal of literature produced on the topic. I do most of my digging on online forums, reading pages and pages of overlapping testimonies. None of it is enough to convince my therapist. In fact, he'd never even heard of ROCD.

In any case, he says, I prefer to avoid labels like that. They can obscure personality traits, reify experiences. Sometimes they can even feel like a prison sentence. So let's just stick with what you're feeling, and work with that.

In our first session, and every subsequent session, he says the same thing, his tone unbearably cool, detached: *You will either leave him* (please, no, my hands virtually raised in prayer) *or you will stay with him. But you will make that decision when your mind is calmer.*

These thoughts that go through your mind, he continues now, are clouding the way you really feel.

So I'm trying to avoid the way I really feel?

He explains further: In the presence of anxiety, no other emotions can make themselves heard.

He believes firmly, with conviction, that I will get better, in time. I will come back to myself, I will make it out of this in one piece. Optimism is a requirement of his profession, I suppose. I'm less inclined to think that way. As early as our second session, I raise the possibility of medication.

Aren't there drugs that can make this go away?

It's too early for that conversation, he says. But down the track, if you're still interested, I can pass you the details of some psychiatrist colleagues of mine. Let's see how the therapy goes.

We alternate talk therapy with the EMDR sessions, in which he instructs me to follow his finger with my eyes, aiming to re-establish equilibrium between the two hemispheres of my brain. Critics of EMDR liken it to hypnosis, claiming the effects are transient at best. Personally, I prefer these sessions to the conversation-based ones — after so many years of honing the mind–body connection through yoga, I've learnt that the only way to recalibrate the mind is to forge different paths with the body, repeating certain movements, reducing myself to the purely physical, and rebuilding the mind from there.

I need to *do* something.

I've neglected my personal asana practice, even though I'm still working as a yoga instructor — a grave violation of the first precept of yoga teaching. Now EMDR emerges as an unlikely replacement. The technique was developed in the Eighties by Dr Francine Shapiro, to treat trauma victims: survivors of war, tsunamis, earthquakes. Strange, and cruel, that love can be its own kind of disaster. It uproots us, ruins us. What begins as a gentle caress ends up tearing the roof off, shattering every window, leaving us exposed. Why wasn't I warned that love — real love — always draws you into waters deeper than you can swim? Love is a kind of madness: a thousand poems and films and songs and paintings will tell you that. But is it possible to be driven mad by the absence of love?

Before we begin, my therapist asks me to envision a place where I would like to be. A real place, a place that actually exists, where I feel at ease.

When the sensations we work with become too intense, he says — on closer inspection, he looks a lot like my father — *you can always return to this safe place.*

My safe place is between the shelves of an independent bookstore.

Δ

I heard about the Viale Abruzzi clinic through my friend Lucio. Lucio and I met online, not long after I started living with Dylan, and we still chat every now and then on Messenger. When we first started talking, he was in Shanghai for work. We'd share secret video calls, his phone hidden between beer glasses or beneath the rim of a satiny metal tabletop. We never did anything. Not even when he returned to Milan a month later. Unless you count the brief kiss in his car outside my apartment. The next morning, he texted: *I had to go straight to the pharmacy after you left, I couldn't breathe.* Panic attack? Allergic reaction? Coincidence? Then he adds: *There's something about you I find terrifying.*

Lucio is the only person I've spoken to about my Marius crisis. He's in therapy, too. Again. (Still?) At the moment, he's seeing a kind of psychoanalyst/astrologist who charges him a fortune for cryptic advice, like: *Don't cut your hair until you're fully healed.*

I imagine his garden of growing curls falling over his eyes as he texts me daily for updates: *How's it going? How are things today?*

I sense, in the heartfelt regularity of his questions, an echo of his own pain, and his own hope for recovery.

He likes to send me meditation videos by spiritual teachers from Germany and Canada. The last thing he sent was a link to an ebook called *A Course in Miracles*, a text written by two US psychologists, Helen Schucman and William Thetford, in 1975. It's half New Age spiritualism, half Catholic fundamentalism.

More often than not, Lucio's recommendations sit unread in my inbox. But it helps to know that I can write to him when I'm feeling worse than usual, on those days when the voice bares its teeth and puffs out its chest, or else recruits allies, malevolent sisters with black bile foaming at their mouths, who sometimes ambush me in the middle of a walk, or during a late-morning lull, which I naïvely mistake for a rare moment of relief, but is only the calm before another suffocating storm.

Our first anniversary approaches, and I want to be able to celebrate it.

19 April 2013–19 April 2014. A milestone, or a tombstone?

One by one, grand plans are shelved, or buried: the surprise party, the romantic dinner, the day trip to a delightful town in the mountains. When the day arrives, we make do with a meal at the all-you-can-eat restaurant down the street. I feel like an imposter; the only way to dispel the sensation is to forget the reason we're there. I convince myself that this is just a regular meal, nothing special. Afterwards, I resume my usual state of quiet inner turmoil.

Soon, May is upon us. Branches start to bud, petals unfurl, and suddenly the world is pink and white, but mostly pink. The return of spring finds me shaken and stubborn, my eyes still darting back and forth in time with the fingers of my therapist, my healer, my saviour — let's not forget how much he looks like my father — in the hope that, somehow, my dedication to this practice will be enough to stop the slow dismembering of my love.

Relationship obsessive-compulsive disorder works a little like Husserl's eidetic variation: you start with a phenomenon, a mental object, and in an attempt to discover its essence, its unalterable structures, you begin to imagine its characteristics changing, one by one, each time asking yourself if the object could survive that change. Is a chair with three legs still a chair? What about a chair made of clay? Could a chair survive as paper, as air, as nitrogen? You imagine altering its shape, its dimensions, its composition. What about its appearance and function is unalterable? What makes a chair a chair? At what point does the object, the phenomenon, become impossible? At what point does it disappear?

These are the questions I am asking repeatedly, obsessively, about love. Is a love that no longer takes your breath away still love? Is it still love when it leaves room in your heart for other things? Is it still love when it no longer saturates every inch of you?

What makes love *love*?

Via San Vittore

Aldebaran. Elnath. Alcyone.

It's Taurus season when an interstice finally opens in my mind, providing enough space and clarity to read. Not fiction — I'm still not ready to read for pleasure or entertainment — but guides, handbooks. I'm seeking understanding. I start with books that offer alternative philosophies of desire, laying bare the fantasy of our Western understanding of love: the kind of love we learn from fairytales, a shimmering, dreamlike thing that is wished for, then granted, often with the help of magic. Desire is nostalgia for the stars. Now I think of it as a devious beast, an animal capable of digging itself out of any enclosure. One day it might simply disappear from the place you thought you'd left it, and reappear somewhere it shouldn't. It is dangerous, violent, biting the hands that feed it, launching sneak attacks, raging even against itself. I desire, therefore I devour. The appetite of desire is insatiable.

Desire is that basic, aggressive drive that exists in all of us, the psychic fang that longs to sink into the flesh of those we love. Love is always accompanied by the faint hum of hate.

Between my psychotherapy and EMDR sessions, I read about the morphology of desire: the possibility of cultivating a separation between the feeling of desire and the desired object/subject. I find my way back to Simone Weil, who writes: *The great trouble in human life is that looking and eating are two different operations … Children feel this trouble already, when they look at a cake for a long time, almost regretting that it should have to be eaten, and yet are unable to help eating it. It may be that vice, depravity, and crime are nearly always, or even perhaps always, in their essence, attempts to eat beauty, to eat what we should only look at. Eve began it. If she caused humanity to be lost by eating the fruit, the opposite attitude, looking at fruit without eating it, should be what is required to save it. 'Two winged companions,' says an Upanishad, 'two birds are on the branch of a tree. One eats the fruit, the other looks at it.' These two birds are the two parts of our soul.*

I return, too, to the teachings of Chandra Candiani, a child-voiced poet in her sixties or seventies whose meditation circles I attended for a time, in her Sant'Ambrogio apartment, not long before I met Marius. During our first meeting — a kind of interview, in which Chandra sounds out the motivations and intentions of potential students — she asked me a question I've never forgotten: *What is the shape of your pain?* At the time, I didn't know how to answer her. I wasn't aware of any pain. Small troubles, yes; passing spells of melancholy, just like everyone else. But *pain?* The word seemed too onerous, too definitive. Pain presupposes fidelity, I thought. Obstinacy. Pain is a kind of insistence. I, on the other hand, am fluid, mobile.

I stopped attending Chandra's meditation circles after a few months, shaking her off the way a wet dog shakes off water, ready for the next thing. Now, though, I've lost the gift of teleportation, and I find myself recalling her lessons. I sit in half lotus, an island of calm amid the piles of cardboard boxes and dirty clothes, and observe my thoughts, the same way I observe the sensations in my body: the points of contact with the floor, the weight of one leg against the other, a tension or tiredness in the muscles of my shoulders (the trapezius, deltoids, sternocleidomastoids). I inhale. I exhale. I notice myself growing broader, wider, with the inhale. I try to feel my thoughts as only thoughts: they advance, then recede, like the breath, and around them there is space, invisible expanses where my mind can rest. Each day, I try to pitch a tent inside that spaciousness, and remain there for at least a few minutes, suspended above the fizzing network of connections and impulses. Eventually, though, a sharp sword of anguish rises up again to puncture my little refuge — I am untrained in the art of transcendence.

I manage to keep all the reading and meditation a secret from Marius. He notices nothing, and I'm proud of that. I wonder if love is always like this, will always be like this. They say to love is to give what you don't have, so I offer you the illusion of certainty, a sense of security I no longer feel.

Some days are pure fiction, the monster inside me muzzled.

Hands held over mouths — his, mine, ours. Mouths kissing, repetition, compulsion. Mouths invigorated by the kisses — *pupic, sărut* — that I now fear, and delay at every opportunity, releasing them like butterflies into that too-distant future in which everything will be as it was, firm and undeniable, a future in which Miley Cyrus sings her heart out and we have a home just for the two of us, and we take trains and planes and bake birthday cakes, and wrap each other's Christmas presents in enormous pink bows, and somersault together in the pool again, and visit museums, and eat pizza. And gelato, mountains and mountains of gelato.

If I can find a way to fix all this stuff in my head, I promise I will learn your language.

My secret regime of reading, walking, and meditation doesn't cure me, but I do begin to receive flashes of insight. I sense new and unexpected rivers of intuition flowing inside me. For instance, I start to notice that the guys I'm attracted to — working out in the gyms where I work, sitting opposite me on the tram — all look the same. They have the same facial features, the same face shape, the same sized ears. They are rendered in the same colours. They are poor facsimiles of Marius, all of them. I realise that I am looking for Marius outside himself; I am seeking Marius without me, the Marius that existed before I met him.

When I sit with this realisation, it deflates me. I shrink back to my true form: a capricious, heartless little creature. Hanging around until the novelty wears off, then moving on to the next thing. A conditioned reflex. Setting up idols and knocking them down, one after the other. A samsara of erotic renaissances.

I wonder how many people have renounced love altogether in order to free themselves from this torturous cycle.

With my yoga, my meditation, my therapy, my self-help books by Pema Chödrön and Eckhart Tolle and Krishnamurti, my self-flagellation in the form of long, lonely walks on an empty stomach through this hard-faced city I'd hoped so badly would solve all my problems, what I'm really doing is asking a question: Is what's happening to me a sickness, or a rite of passage? How many people before me have surrendered to the physio-chemical processes that mark the shift between infatuation and whatever lies on the other side of it? What I'm looking for is someone to say: *Don't give up. Keep holding on.*

As I work to maintain this strange state of turbulent stasis, a modest improvement is made in our domestic space: we acquire a bed. Now I can read in luxury, bathing in the soft spring sunlight on a real bed with a proper mattress and a sturdy wood frame.

The bed comes from my father. I interpret it as a kind of peace offering. My father is moving out of his luxury apartment in Milano 3 — a ghetto for rich people, built by Berlusconi in the 1980s — into a rental in a depressing little village near Pavia. He's already bought a new king-size bed, so he's getting rid of the old double bed. He heard from his mother, my nonna — ever persistent in her refusal to let the relationship between us collapse — that I was bedless, and could use the charity.

My father comes over to deliver and help assemble the bed. That's what fathers do: they help out. They fix problems.

I know he knows that I live with my boyfriend, but the two of us have never spoken about it. A conversation of that sort — a *coming out* — presupposes a level of parental involvement that he has never shown, and a level of trust I've never felt. Unsurprising, after twenty years of hearing him crack jokes about faggots and fairies. As far as I'm concerned, my father's decades of homophobia are not erased by the big smile he gives Marius at the front door, or the playful charisma with which he helps him screw the headboard to the bed frame.

I take a photo of the two of them, backs turned, labouring over the joins of wood, and upload it to Instagram with the caption: *the men in my life.* I immediately regret it, and delete the image from my feed.

My father doesn't come alone. He brings his girlfriend with him. I'm surprised to see that it's the same one, Noemi, the ex-cheese and salami merchant. She accompanies my father upstairs, then stands next to the window overlooking the street — my father has ordered her to keep an eye on his new car, which is parked out the front on Via Giambellino.

Would it kill you to live in a less dodgy neighbourhood, kid?

Noemi keeps vigil by the window for a good hour, in silence. My father's women — the ones that stick around, at least — are more like companion animals than people. All is well, as long as they're obedient.

Why don't the two of you come to our new place for lunch one day, my father says as he's returning his collection of pliers and screwdrivers to their green-and-orange toolbox. He is talented at crafting enthusiastic, imaginary futures, perfect worlds in which every broken thing is put back together nicely, the past forgotten. But we both know there will be no lunch.

At any rate, we now have a bed. A real bed.

Vee is still living with us, and her presence becomes more and more offensive. She begins taking greater liberties with the shared space, bringing men home without introducing them or even mentioning them, as if they didn't exist. Often there are three or four guys in the apartment at once, a clutch of silhouettes — I only ever glimpse them from behind, as they gather in the hallway — wearing caps and bomber jackets. The conversations I overhear are always about money: someone hasn't paid, someone still owes her. I don't have the strength to get involved, let alone confront her about it. I tell myself it's not for long, we'll move out soon. Another of the many promises I make to our grand future.

While I'm at it, I fantasise about a life that is more aligned with who I am, with the things that ignite me spiritually and intellectually. I don't want to be a glorified fitness instructor anymore. I add professional angst to the eddy of intrusive thoughts swirling in my head: *What can I do? Who can I be?* I'm twenty-eight years old and I have nothing to show for it. It's not exactly that I haven't found my place yet; rather, I don't know if there *is* a place for me. I lost my university scholarship because I missed too many exams and ghosted too many professors, which means the prospect of a PhD is off the table.

I fill the void by typing things into my Facebook status: entire essays on the patrons of the bar down the street, yoga teachers I work with, random passers-by. It is through writing that I come to an important realisation: I haven't *lived*. I have only *witnessed*. I write about Vee, and Dylan, and Minnie, and Pietro, and Melissa, layering fact over fiction, simultaneously confessing and fabricating everything. It's like a form of verbal voodoo. I write several times a day, a ceaseless ritual. ENTER, publish, start all over again. It's not unusual for me to spend three hours on ten or twenty lines. Marius is confused: why so much effort over a Facebook status? I mimic the styles of my favourite authors: Joyce Carol Oates, Rosa Matteucci, Teresa Ciabatti. I am bitter, hurtful. A poetics of shot nerves.

I write so that I don't have to think. I write so that I can see beyond my thoughts. I've tried everything — art, music, yoga, theory — and each time, like clockwork, I have given up on it. Now writing opens up the possibility of synthesis, untangling the dichotomies that have troubled me since high school: art/philosophy, abstraction/expression, reason/feeling.

People start commenting on my posts: *You should write a*

book. I'd buy it. Adopting their conviction in lieu of my own, I sketch out the bones of a novel: a synopsis, an index, character notes based on figures from my childhood. I decide to dedicate a chapter to each character. The book will be about the place where I grew up. Working title: *Family Album.*

Some writers are great inventors, capable of spinning plots and characters out of thin air. Others are too faithful to names and faces, their ideas too firmly embodied. I am interested in telling the reality that lies beyond the plainly visible, a reality that exists on an already narrative plane, a kind of literary shadow, superimposed on the everyday world but never touching it. I am fascinated by the places where fact intersects with the distortions of subjectivity, by the ambiguous overlap between fact and fiction, person and character. The in-between is a place of provocation.

I want to rewrite the world, combining the real with some other version of the real, twinning actual people with their more spectacular avatars. I want to demolish everything in order to rebuild it. I want to collapse the walls between genres and let everything spill together: reportage, dishonesty, delirium, memory.

The distinction between a *novel* and an *autobiography* — or even *fiction* and *autofiction* — is trivial, a marketing strategy. My experiences, when they are presented in the form of literature, are already external, expropriated, in the sense that I am positioning myself as a spectator of my own life. Don't be fooled by the sleights of the first-person form. I am not reducible to a set of narratable facts and events. I am — we are — nothing more or less than the neutral, transparent point that observes, only observes.

To put it another way: the only human truth is the truth offered by a story.

Writing makes something clear to me: seen through the lens of desire, all bodies are minor bodies. Minor is the desiring body that runs, rises, gravitates towards larger, brighter, more dazzling bodies, that bestows on other bodies the status of suns and planets, fires to be orbited, the reason for everything.

There is no centre of the universe except the one we invent for ourselves.

Corso Venezia

We're halfway through May when it happens. After what seems like years of printing, hand-delivering, emailing (*please see attached*) and posting CVs all across Milan, Marius is contacted by a large international fashion company. He is invited to attend a group interview. Rumour has it they're looking for four candidates, each of whom will be offered a three-month trial contract. The store is in San Babila, at the bottom end of Corso Venezia, on the fringe of the fashion district.

There are several stages to the recruitment process, and Marius sails through all of them. He gets the job. Part-time, starting tomorrow. A sigh of relief, a beam of light, though still not enough to silence the reproachful voice in my head. *Bravo*, it says, *you're dating a part-time sales assistant.*

More accurately: I'm dating a part-time sales assistant at a minimalist fashion outlet that sells shapeless tunics and stark apron dresses (you pay extra for the lack of detail). The look is convent fashion, catechism chic. The store managers are a clique of sadistic man-children and haughty, bitchy homosexuals, hailing mostly from the South or from Eastern Europe. They take to bullying Marius, imposing a kind of boutique hazing ritual. His tender age, and the precarity of his employment, makes him the perfect victim. It doesn't help that he's so malleable, so tolerant, especially around people he doesn't know well.

Marius doesn't tell me about the bullying for some time. When he does, I make fantastic plans to avenge him (surely that's a good sign?): I'll come into the store wearing a hoodie, sleeves obscuring the blue utility knife Marius uses to cut fabric into patterns, and walk up to the second floor, where I'll leave a couple of them bleeding among the headless mannequins and the austere, half-empty clothes racks. Then again: why get my hands dirty when I could just pay some of Vee's new friends to do it for me? I imagine them waiting at the back exit at closing time, ready to deliver their brute justice. *Don't do too much damage*, I'll instruct them. *Just enough to scare them.*

Around the same time he starts working, Marius also returns to university. His Christmas trip to Umbria yielded family quarrels (chief among them an argument with his father, who was horrified to learn that his son, probably in imitation of that new 'housemate' of his, no longer eats meat, a decision that augurs even graver disobediences — men are meant to hunt, women to gather) but it also yielded money. His parents resolved to give him two thousand euros for a short course in professional styling, at the same university he attended last year. (*So they can afford to keep sending him money after all*, I think, but don't say.) The course, which entails one day a week for three months, is patently pointless, but I keep my mouth shut. This isn't the moment for hard truths.

As predicted, the brief afternoon classes, attended mostly by middle-aged *Marie Claire* addicts with pipe dreams, are a waste of time. Marius learns nothing. Becoming a professional stylist has nothing to do with training and everything to do with who you know. It requires networking, bootlicking. Still, Marius remains optimistic about his future, adamant he won't be folding shirts for the rest of his life.

The same month, a long white envelope appears in our letterbox. It looks important — registered mail. I start opening it as we ascend the stairs to the apartment, me leading, Marius behind.

Are you expecting mail?

I don't think so, are you?

I tear the edge of the envelope and slip my fingers inside. There, folded, neatly into three, is our first tenant warning letter. It's nothing too concerning, just a bureaucrat in an office somewhere doing their job. Still, we take it as a sign. In any case, we weren't intending to stay much longer.

Now that Marius has an income — a meagre, temporary income, but an income all the same — the dream factory is back up and running. We start looking for apartments. Somewhere more comfortable, somewhere just for the two of us, somewhere near the Metro. There's Milan, and then there's *Milan*. I have only one objective: to be closer to the centre, back where I belong. This desire works like a cushion against my fear; the pull towards the centre is a counterforce against the compulsion to leave.

We resume the demoralising travails of house hunting: the lunchtime phone calls, the Saturday inspections of overpriced one-bedroom apartments (a thousand euros a month, paid quarterly, plus a security deposit, plus the agent's commission) that, in any case, result only in rejected applications. The promising conversations that end, abruptly, in babbled excuses when the landlord discovers we're a couple (*You know what? I'm so sorry but my husband has changed his mind*). Some places are genuine dumps, old janitor's quarters with faulty heating, glorified shipping containers rented out by wealthy old ladies who own half the building.

Then we find it: the 'loft'. Seventy square metres in Palestro for seven hundred euros a month, cash in hand. I can barely contain my joy. I write to my friends to tell them the good news: *Palestro. Can you believe it?*

Palestro Palestro Palestro Palestro Palestro.

My new address is an incantation, a mantra.

I was wrong to doubt us. Time heals everything. All is repaired.

The owner, a bull-necked photographer with a flat cap and a folding bike, calls the apartment a loft, but when we arrive for the inspection, we find ourselves in a sparsely furnished one-room basement, accessed by an inconspicuous door next to the building's bin room. A windowless underground warehouse. The only light that enters has to fight its way through the sooty glass of a miniature clerestory, out of arm's reach and therefore impossible to clean. A plump layer of dust dims even the brassy afternoon sun to a blear suggestion of daylight.

There's a bit of humidity, the owner warns.

A digital hygrometer propped up on the scruffy vintage dining table confirms it: eighty-nine per cent. The place is practically an aquarium.

Then again: the closest Metro station is *Palestro*.

We decide to take it. We agree to move in in August. My fifth home since coming to Milan. We tell Vee the news only when it's a fait accompli; she says she can stay with a friend in the south-east.

With a date set, and everything in place, the old thoughts come bubbling back: *You won't live together in that house. When you break up, one of you will keep it and the other will have to find somewhere else.* But who will be *the other*, me or him? The cats and I can't seriously be expected to find a room in a share house. And so it begins again, the same noxious river, the same cascade of worst-case scenarios.

Let the voice speak, I tell myself. Let's hear what it has to say. And I cede the stage. I stand back as the voice rants and raves, separate from me now, never touching me. I'm learning, I think. Learning how to wait for the drops to evaporate, for the winds to change. I am looking down on my thoughts as if through a skylight, observing their churning patterns through a layer of glass.

I remain as still as possible as I watch the deluge, a typhoon conjured up for the sole purpose of imagining the limits of its own destruction. The pathologically anxious have excellent imaginations. If I keep still — as in EMDR, as in meditation — then I eventually grow bored of watching this simulated crisis, this storm in a bell jar. Look: the lightning is a toy, I can hold it between my hands and stretch it with my fingers. Violet plasma, like playful St Elmo's fire. There's a chance it could kill me (cardiac arrest, respiratory paralysis), or at the very least burn me. But so far, I'm unscathed. Its violence is purely luminary.

June comes around, and with it my twenty-eighth birthday. I feel like a phoenix — new plumage is born from my skin. As we prepare to move apartments, I also make plans to return to

La Statale. Paradoxically, giving up on San Raffaele has allowed me to reclaim control over my studies. I'm not far off getting my master's. I've only missed a handful of exams. Once that's rectified, everything can flow again as it should.

The only real obstacle is money. The transfer and tuition fees, as low as they are, are still unaffordable at short notice. In the grips of a fleeting euphoria, I open a Facebook chat group full of my relatives: close, distant, maternal, paternal, whatever it takes. All the wrongs and humiliations of the past are set aside. I summon everyone together and ask them to contribute what they can. *Ten, twenty euros, whatever you can afford. This is so important to me.*

My mother takes it badly. She feels belittled, undermined. Her son, a digital beggar. Revealing my neediness in public, and to this audience in particular, makes her look like a failure.

You're not a little boy anymore, she texts me. *Act like a grown-up, save your money and wait until next year.*

I write back: *That's rich, coming from you. And no, I can't wait until next year. This has to happen now, right now, in this exact moment, or it will never happen.*

I'm worked up now. I keep typing: *You do realise that you created me, right? I am the product of your inattention, a plant you left to grow in the shade, hunchbacked and stunted. Maturity and autonomy aren't qualities that just magically appear in a person. How can I be expected to grow if no one ever helped me dream?*

This is true not just of my potential as a human being, but also of my potential as a partner. I never had a model of a healthy relationship, much less a prototype of true love that I could try to replicate. Who am I meant to look to, who am I meant to draw inspiration from? In the part of my brain that forms romantic attachments, all I have is a big black cross, a burnt field of withered mirror neurons.

After several minutes of ellipses appearing and disappearing, appearing and disappearing, my mother writes back: *It's easy to place the blame on others.*

Then: *I know I made mistakes. But when the fuck are you going to grow up and take some responsibility for your own life?*

We'll never see eye to eye on this. She can't let go of the idea that children should simply transform into adults, emerging like larvae from a chrysalis at a certain age; despite all the mistakes, despite the lack of guidance, life finds a way. And I, engrossed in the causal lines traced during my psychotherapy sessions, am convinced everyone is just a product of their upbringing.

I wield the full arsenal of my education against my mother's eighth-grade logic, slinging arrow after arrow of pompous terminology: *affective deprivation*, *disorganised attachment*, *enmeshment*. What I'm really doing, when I use these words, is summoning the past as a witness in the prosecution of my parents. In the perpetual compensation hearing that is my life.

Mothers make for easy scapegoats. Like witches, we string them up by the hair, leave them dangling from the bony branches of our cold, wasted hearts. The child that once could only cry and stamp his feet in protest now holds a flame to the sagging dress of his exhausted mother and watches it catch alight, first glowing, then crackling. Burn, mamma; this is the moment in which I let you burn.

I don't hear from her for several days. She leaves my last message unanswered, and I don't write to follow up. The days accumulate into weeks — two, four. If this goes on, the weeks will soon turn into months. Years. Are we really going to spend the rest of our lives estranged, in stony silence? The concept of an apology is alien in our family.

In the meantime, my mother's sister responds to my call for crowdfunding and promises to help. *Don't worry*, she writes, *you can always count on your uncle and me.* My mother's two younger siblings, still teenagers when I was a child, are now in their forties, with kids of their own. I grew up watching tv with them — *Twin Peaks*, *Nightmare on Elm Street* — on the bedroom floor. My aunt tells me to get in touch with my uncle. *He'll give you as much you need*, she assures me.

I am comforted, briefly, by the idea that bonds can extend horizontally as well as vertically, that a family can remain a family despite years of mutual indifference, despite all the birthdays that pass unremarked.

I write to my uncle, and his response brings me back down to earth: *Do you realise your mother has been crying for the past two weeks straight? You won't be getting shit from us, sweetheart. Time for you to be a big boy and earn your own money.*

Corso Vittorio Emanuele

Towards the end of our last week in the Via Tito Vignoli apartment, I invite Dylan over. With no specific plans or intentions, at some point I'd unblocked him on Messenger and WhatsApp. A few weeks later, he'd started sending me old photos from our two years as housemates. Every few days, a new photo. Our last dinner party in Via Lulli. León, eyes at half-mast, crouched beside one of the many toy robots that patrolled the shelves of our apartment. The latter photo came with a comment: *Look at that little willy.* I left every message unanswered. *Okay, I'll leave you alone now*, he wrote, after enough time had passed.

He can hardly believe it when I write back: *Spina and León have asked if you would like to come visit them.*

His reply is tentative: *Really?*

The enemy inside me, the one curled inside my bones, eventually reveals the falseness of my external enemies — in the end, they were nothing but cardboard cut-outs, antagonists crafted outside myself in order to isolate the object of my desire from everything around it, from anything that might threaten or contaminate it. As my infatuation cooled, so did my hostility towards Dylan, leaving space for the possibility of making peace.

I'll come for afternoon tea, he writes. Then he adds: *Can I bring something?*

Marius is at work when Dylan arrives. It's just the two of us at the white kitchen table, surrounded by cabinets filled with utensils we haven't even started packing yet. Between us sits the cherry crostata he brought with him, almost too beautiful to eat, and the two cups of bancha tea I prepared in honour of his Japanophilia. I avoid touching on the topic of our falling-out, my awful behaviour. I steer as clear as possible from anything like an apology or an admission of guilt. The shame, the embarrassment, are still frozen lakes inside me.

I keep the conversation light at first: small talk, gossip of the kind we always used to indulge in. Then I tell him about my fight with my family, and Pietro's illness, which I've only just learnt of.

I hadn't heard from Pietro in at least a year, I say, bar the odd comment under a Facebook post. Then the other day he sent a photo of himself in a wheelchair, so I wrote back to him.

I read Pietro's words out loud to Dylan, a message no doubt copy-pasted to all of his Facebook contacts: *For a few months now I've had pain and weakness in my leg …*

It sounds horrific, like a terrifying ordeal. After seemingly endless tests and hypotheses, specialists in Sydney believe he has a rare autoimmune condition. They suspect he has a degenerative disease that affects the joints: his hands, wrists, feet, and knees will gradually swell until they no longer function properly. At least money is no object: his new boyfriend will ensure he gets the best medical advice available.

I find some recent photos on Pietro's Facebook page and show them to Dylan. Dylan mutters under his breath: Poor bastard.

I'm grateful for the sombre mood, which is a perfect

distraction from the elephant in the room. Tragedy takes up all available space, silences all other conversations, no matter how necessary. Feeling like the bullet has been dodged, I ask Dylan about work.

Any news?

I've already heard a few things through the grapevine: a few months ago, he got a job at the Disney Store on Corso Vittorio Emanuele. A literal dream come true. He tells me he's only working part-time for now, but hopes that will change. From a plastic bag emblazoned with the face of Elsa from *Frozen*, he produces a tangle of gifts for the cats: clusters of long, metallic pearls, strings of plastic rubies. Spina and León tolerate the game of dress-up long enough for us to take some photos for Instagram. In compensation for their suffering, I lean over to fill their dinner bowl with kibble, taking advantage of the break in eye contact to ask Dylan: So, are you still in Via Lulli?

A rhetorical question.

Yes, he answers. For the time being.

He's thinking of moving out. Finding somewhere smaller, less central. That is: somewhere less expensive.

Although it'd be a pity to leave, he adds. It's such a great apartment.

Since Marius and I moved out, he's been renting out the spare bedroom on Airbnb. During peak season — summer, fashion week — he can make two or three months' rent in just a few days. As he's talking, I clear the empty teacups and stack them in the sink.

I can give you a hand with the move, if you want, he says.

In the absence of an enthusiastic response, he adds: Or have you already got it sorted?

We don't have too much stuff, I say.

To change the topic, I play him some audios of Vee, surreptitiously recorded from inside our bedroom: first a loud fake orgasm, no doubt performed in front of the webcam, then the baritone roar when her country's football team scores a goal at three in the morning.

He laughs: Is that your housemate?

Come with me, I say. I'll show you her room.

What if she catches us in there?

She won't. She's gone to look at her new apartment.

I push open her bedroom door, and inside it's even worse than I'd expected. In addition to the usual deposits, organic and otherwise — sex toys, pizza boxes, plastic containers of leftovers — is a red plastic bucket filled almost to the brim with a foul-smelling, brown-orange liquid. Dylan's hands move protectively to his nose and mouth.

As we return to the safety of the corridor, he picks up the thread I'd tried to abandon.

Seriously though, I'm happy to give you a hand with the move if you need it. Where did you say the new place is?

At that moment, the front doorhandle turns. Marius is home, earlier than expected. Dylan's face lights up.

Well good afternoon! How are you?

A crashing hug, a proper reunion, nothing like our muted greeting. Dylan rubs my boyfriend's head, cooing: Look at you, you're more handsome than ever.

Not an inkling of jealousy stirs inside me. I feel nothing. At the bottom of the hole where my emotions should be shines the possibility that I am no longer capable of feeling anything but apathy or absolute despair. The whole middle spectrum is missing; only the hard ends remain.

We should hang out one night, the three of us, Dylan says.

Definitely, I hear myself answer, as I wonder if perhaps this lack of reaction, this protective emotional dormancy, could in fact be a sign of my recovery.

Via Pisacane

I turn the cracked spines in my hand, assessing the damage. They look irreparable — utterly deformed, misshapen — but I'm surprised to learn that everything can still be gently massaged back into place. One by one, I submit my neglected community of books to this tender treatment. Poor things, scarred and cobwebbed, dragged from place to place, only to be left tumbled in a dark box in the corner of a room.

Marius tried to dissuade me from taking them to the new apartment. You could at least get rid of the university ones, he said, if you've already passed the exam.

This latest move could be the death of them. Already, after a month in the basement-loft, I can see that they're suffering. They won't survive the environment down here, the endless cycle of damp and heat. The humidity seeps into the pages and bends them into waves, warping the covers, turning the white paper yellow, then ochre, forming urine-like stains. My beloved books are autumn leaves turning to humus.

And that's only the beginning.

I soon start to notice spots expanding on the walls, marshy growths in blue and green-brown, like algal artwork. I read up on the respiratory risks of household mould for humans, cats. *What happens if you breathe mould?* The internet replies with a host of horrifying suggestions: inhaled antigens, fatigue, skin conditions. Not to mention the potentially deadly ones: aspergillosis, bronchial asthma, pulmonary fibrosis, pneumonia. Didn't mould kill Brittany Murphy and her husband, Simon Monjack, back in 2009?

We cook, eat, and sleep surrounded by toxic, living stains. Then there are the insects, little fistfuls of them seething in the damp corners of the floor: *Psocoptera*, otherwise known as booklice. They reproduce quickly. I launch a bleach- and ammonia-based counterattack, terrified they'll establish colonies in the cats' ears and eyes and mouths. What I really need is an exterminator, a professional, someone who knows what they're doing. I call the landlord, who advises us to leave the heaters on day and night in 'dehumidifier' mode. That should help, he says. We try it, but the hygrometer only registers a two per cent decrease.

There's no way to drain this swamp, no way to stem the rapid proliferation of spores and hyphae.

I call him back, furious: This is unsafe, we can't live like this.

I want to scream in his face: *We're dying in here.*

Don't worry, he says. We'll figure something out. I'll swing by tomorrow.

I believe him. He's in the habit of 'swinging by' to see how we're getting on in 'the space' (instead of a *loft*, he now refers to it as a *space*). He drops in without warning at all hours of the day and night — seven in the morning, ten in the evening. The formal nature of our relationship, symbolised by the rent we pay him punctually each month (it's hard not to be punctual when he collects it in person), is not enough to erect a boundary between us, to designate this space as ours. He is deeply bonded to these weeping walls, these furnishings, these artworks, and they remain his, available for him to access whenever he pleases. The apartment, and by extension the amicable young men who inhabit it, are always at his disposal.

When he visits, the landlord tells us all about his many projects. The man is a volcano of ideas, an unstoppable force of nature. He recently left his wife and children for an Irish model he met on set (the model is already pregnant with his next child). Next up on his to-do list is the renovation of his open-plan studio, whose large, armoured door stands directly opposite our entrance. The studio is a mirror image of the space we live in. He talks us through the myriad possibilities for remodelling: pillars, mezzanines, a ping-pong table. He takes to swapping our furniture around, relocating certain pieces to the studio, replacing an armchair with a potted plant. I only protest when he tries to take the table. Please, we need that, I say, spreading my arms across its marble expanse.

The table is the only surface I have to study on. I sit there for hours at a time, underlining notes, preparing summaries of my pre-enrolment reading. Against all odds, my family crowdfunding efforts were successful. I even patched things up with my mother. The next step is to download course guides from the university's website, and figure out which exam to take first.

I fill the lightless afternoons and evenings with pages and pages of bioethics, trying to ignore our landlord's voice sailing through the door: *Santiago! Santiago, where the hell are you?* Every day the same name, like a curse. Santiago is the landlord's peon, a jack-of-all-trades, generally tasked with knocking down walls and fixing the plumbing, but often assigned more menial labour, like collecting parcels and paying bills at the post office.

Santiago completes every task asked of him quietly and dutifully, with his head bowed. When the landlord loses patience and raises his voice, Santiago says nothing. Abolition didn't reach this particular corner of Milan, it would seem.

In August 2014, I resume my studies at La Statale. At the same time, I start getting paid to write online articles.

It starts with a couple of trial pieces for a website, then quickly snowballs. I manage to catch the attention of a few online-magazine editors, and they sign me up as a 'collaborator'. The word *journalist* means nothing anymore — the internet has made it too fluid, too expansive. The endless, rapid-fire requests of my 'clients' force me to abandon work on my family-album book. Accelerated by the pace of demand, the words explode from me like ribbons, bending easily to current events and trends. My only aim is to take up space, to circulate. I want my name to be on everyone's lips.

I'm paid next to nothing for each article — usually somewhere between eighteen and twenty-five euros, although some editors offer as little as four euros. The trick is to have several articles on the go at once, preferably with a range of different deadlines. I pump them out quickly then send them off without proofreading, sloppy and riddled with typos. I turn to repetition, recycling ideas and syntax and openings. I write the same article over and over, changing the theme but retaining the basic structure. With practice, I start producing five or six articles a day. I stoop to plagiarism, copy-pasting entire paragraphs from Wikipedia without even bothering to edit them. To avoid being discovered, I steal from lesser-known sites whenever possible: *Biografie Online*, *Accadde Oggi*.

Making a living from this kind of work requires not just speed but initiative. As well as meeting editors' requests, I'm also expected to pitch them a constant stream of ideas. I would like to tell them I have no ideas. I simply have no space in my brain for ideas. My brain is a vacuum. *There are no more fucking ideas*: the collective scream of the atomised arts workforce, one giant network of knotted, frazzled nerves, tenuously connected by the hustle of the internet.

We — the copywriters, the clickbaiters, the verbose scribes of the digital age — are asked to feign expertise on an improbable range of topics. People who did degrees in modern literature or art history find themselves writing pop-psychology listicles and reviews for sushi restaurants. Still, I manage to scratch out a niche for myself: I become a specialist in stoking controversy. I grow adept at digging up divisive topics and framing them just so, to elicit the most powerful sting. The best way to keep an editor happy is to write articles that readers engage with. The more antagonising the piece, the longer the threads of comments unspooling beneath it, the better. I'm not bothered by the threats of legal action, or the packs of rabid dogs unleashed by angry influencers. Nothing can stop me. *I am a writer.*

I reduce my yoga teaching hours to the bare minimum, and spend every other waking hour writing. My identity, if I have one, fades away to make room for an ever-changing façade, a cloak continually spun and unravelled by the black or white magic of words. I won't be hindered by values, by my conscience. I'm a mercenary, willing to deliver my soul to the highest bidder. I work for ostensibly feminist platforms whose female writers earn half as much as I do. I work for LGBT publications run by straight white men who publish gossip columns and clickbait quizzes with titles like *How Gay Are You?* I am a device into which a goal is entered — a number of clicks, likes, shares, comments — and, in response, thousands of words come tumbling out. The strength of my writing lies in its blunt force, its lack of nuance. It is hard and fast and provocative. I write about the world without looking around me. I write about things I don't understand, things I lack both the time and the motivation to educate myself about.

We, the pyjamaed freelancers of the 2010s, are interchangeable gears in the online publishing machine. Our job is to produce content, produce without thinking, without asking questions. Serial production. Instant, constant. We're not paid to research or report the facts. There's no time for that, and no budget. We're paid to enhance SEO. The only metrics of quality are those provided by Google Analytics.

If I take no pride in my work, I still get a kick out of its performance. There's a certain thrill associated with an article gaining traction, a kind of intoxication that comes from being seen and consumed, piece by piece, by the world. This feeling becomes my main source of endorphins. It tells me: *I exist. I am here.* The opposite is also true; when an article fizzles, sinking into the timeline unnoticed like a sad stone, I feel myself disappearing, fading into irrelevancy.

Money is still tight, so I find it hard to refuse the landlord's offer to teach yoga from his newly renovated studio.

His grand plan is to gather a group of friends — he already has ten, twelve people lined up, he assures me — to practise yoga together on a weekly basis. Fellow photographers, illustrators, interior designers, artistic professionals who live and work in the area. Soon, though, the promised group shrinks to one. It's just my landlord and me, before dinner on a Tuesday. Fifteen euros for a private yoga class. As I'm waiting for him to change in the studio's minuscule bathroom, I wander under the neon lights, among the tables of photographs and paperwork. I swear I'm not snooping; the invoices are right there, in plain sight. He's making fifty, seventy thousand euros per shoot.

These numbers are still rolling around in my head when, about a month into our arrangement, the landlord requests a different kind of meeting.

I need to talk to you, the text message reads. *Can we meet for a coffee?*

Then: *Actually, I'll just swing by later today.*

When we sit down to talk, the three of us, his voice is unserious, minimising.

I wanted to tell you, he says, that I crunched the numbers, and at seven hundred a month I'm not breaking even. I'm going to have to raise the rent to nine hundred. If you can't make it work, I completely understand, but I'll have to ask you to look elsewhere.

As he speaks, Marius and I remain impassive. Later, when we're alone, we let our rage fly.

Then, three days later, the landlord shows up again, this time without warning. He is repentant. He thought about it, and he understands how hard it is to find a place in Milan at the moment, especially at such short notice. He has an offer for us, a generous proposal — we can take our time to think about it, of course. A studio apartment has just been vacated in his building, on the top floor, the third floor. It's only small, but it should do us for a few months, while we find somewhere else.

You're young, he says. I want to help you out.

After a pause, he gestures to the front door with both index fingers, pointing them like two little guns: Do you want to come and see it now?

The apartment is just a short walk away. It's a one-room attic with a microscopic bathroom. Fifteen square metres for two humans and two cats. My sixth home since I moved to Milan: a walk-in closet in the city centre.

Via Felice Casati

The new apartment feels like a coffin. In the early September sun, the attic is unbearable. The air conditioner churns ceaselessly; without it, our clothes and sheets are drenched in a matter of minutes. The nights are even worse than the days — summer evenings in Milan are sultry, interminable.

I have to go. I start shoving things into my bag: keys, phone, glasses, lip balm, a fresh pack of tissues. Something to eat, I suppose. If I get hungry later, there's no guarantee I'll find something vegan.

I slide into the narrow shower, and the water seems to amplify the voice, embolden it: *Leave him. You have to leave him.* The usual song. But I can't leave him, I think. Not right now. He's just lost his job.

I was with Melissa when I heard the news, in a café on Via Felice Casati. Coffee, almond shortbread, pistachio frangipane tart. *Hi, excuse me, are any of these cakes vegan?* I hadn't seen Melissa in almost three months, since she started her new job as a 'collection custodian' at a museum. In practice, she's a glorified security guard. Two university degrees to work as a security guard in a museum. Art history is a competitive field in Milan.

It's only temporary, of course, she assured me. I'll find something else.

It was the middle of the morning. Marius should have been at work, but he called me.

Hey, where are you?

What's wrong?

They're not renewing my contract. They told me I can just go home now, without finishing my shift.

His three-month trial was over, and they'd decided to let him go.

Did they tell you why? I asked. You deserve an explanation, at least.

The truth is, I had been expecting this. I knew it was coming. Marius is a bad worker: too slow and careful in folding the clothes, too meticulous with the displays, too indulgent with the customers. Doing things properly is important to him.

So what now?

They advised me to apply for unemployment benefits.

This happened only a week ago. Now, brushing my teeth in front of the bathroom mirror, drying the dark hair that covers most of my body, the voice is more resolute than ever. *Look around you*, it says. *You have to leave all of this behind.* I laugh in its face, in the many faces of its vile, multiplied heads, rooted in the walls of my skull. I laugh and I fear I'll regret it, scared I'll be punished for my arrogance. I turn my thoughts elsewhere: Do the cats have water? Let's clean up the litter tray, while we're at it. I empty the synthetic sand into the plastic tray, releasing a feeble cloud of dust.

Maybe all we can do is laugh at the evil spirits inside us. What ghost can persist in the face of laughter, the body thrilling, the contortions of the face and breath, the cynical bliss of it?

I laugh because there is no evil spirit. I laugh because at last I understand the game.

Love was never going to save me. There is no blessing, no magic portal to Wonderland. There is only this moment, right here.

I am back in my own body and I have a job to do. When I look at Marius, I no longer search for the otherworldly glow I thought we'd lost. I find his eyes when they're directed elsewhere: towards a screen, at his hands as we prepare dinner. Every other part of his face triggers the same old obsessive thought patterns, but his eyes — the grey, sage-green, hazelnut crescents of his eyes — do not.

I'm beginning to suspect that things were aways going to turn out the way they did. I'm not the kind of person who can fall in love and hold steady. I am, was, always have been, the kind of person who doubts, who second-guesses, who rejects what is in front of them and craves whatever it is they don't have. There is no realm of experience people like me can exist in without hearing the disorienting whispers of our own uneasy minds.

And so my job is to find a way to live at the ambiguous edge of things. To identify the private micro-strategies that allow me to live with the threat of my compulsions. To abandon my obsession with purity, to float inside the chaos of my mind even as it screams: *Heaven or bust! Raze it all to the ground!* My job is to learn how to stay loyal to dreams even when they are troubled.

Laughter helps; it creates a space for feelings to pass through me. Like dancing through pain.

∆

Right now, though, I have to go.

What's the time? It's late. Quite late. I slip one arm into the sleeve of a t-shirt, then the other. Socks, shoes, then suddenly I'm on the street. The air is sweet, kissing my suffering body with little gusts of freedom.

I start running, the strap of my bag slipping from my shoulder. To the casual observer, it must look like I'm fleeing something, or someone, but in fact I'm running because I must, because my body is asking me to. I whirl down the Metro stairs, suddenly unsure if there are trains running — was the strike happening today or tomorrow? Tomorrow, it must be tomorrow; there's a train arriving in two minutes.

On board, I'm faster than ever, slicing through the roots of entire neighbourhoods, speeding beneath the foundations of buildings and the intersections clotted with cars. Red line — Duomo, Cadorna — then green line: Porta Genova, *next stop Romolo*, then Famagosta, or is it Barona? The past seven years moving through me in reverse, unravelling metre by metre, kilometre by kilometre. Sometimes in life we get stuck, that's all. That's all this is: a bottleneck, a path that grew a little narrow, stopping the flow of movement. A body that dreamt of blazing through space in a thousand colours, but instead turned in on itself. There's no failure here, no defeat. Once we shed the ideas we've inherited, the patterns we've borrowed from others, we're left with the possibility of inventing something new.

I peer through the doors at the next stop, squinting against my myopia. I'm moving in the right direction — for a moment I thought I might be on the wrong train.

The carriage speeds through more roaring tunnels and past more platforms until it emerges into the twilight. The city is behind me now. I'm going back, coming home. We race through empty fields that have somehow resisted being turned into mirror-faced condominiums and office buildings. The Milanese countryside where I was born. I only recently discovered that Rozzano's public housing towers lie under the path of migrating white storks. This is the unknown, empty space that dwells between known places. The connective tissue; the transit zone.

The artificial firmament of the Forum di Assago grows closer and clearer, a pulsing duet in red and blue. Feeling a flicker of apprehension, I get out my phone and text him: *What time does it start again?* He doesn't reply.

As the train reaches its terminus and slows, softly shifting tracks, he still hasn't replied.

As the doors open and I head to the emergency-exit doors, following a small clutch of fare-evading fourteen-year-olds who, like me, want to avoid the turnstiles, he still hasn't replied.

I'm wondering if I should write to him again as I emerge from the metal stairwell into the noise and wind of the A7 highway, Autostrada dei Giovi.

City Limits

Everyone is screaming.

Her face rises from the darkness at the back of the stage. Ten, fifteen metres of digital aurora. With her blonde crown, she is a rising sun. The screams grow louder, heavier. Her blue eyes are wide open and rotating in their sockets, like something out of a carnival fun house. One ear is pierced with a safety pin, the other with a collection of small round studs.

Once the screen has risen completely, the video starts to change: now she's winking, now her mouth is wide open and smiling, chin extending downwards, deep furrows forming in her cheeks like the hinges on a ventriloquist's dummy. Her mouth opens wider, unnaturally wide, an almost reptilian disarticulation, bubble-gum pink tongue unfolding into a giant slide. And then she appears.

Heralded by a skull-shattering wall of screams, Miley Cyrus glides towards us, emerging from her own throat. A miniature Miley spat out by a giant Miley. She dances her way, waving, towards the rows of young girls decked out in their *Bangerz* merch.

This, tonight, at the Forum di Assago, is her only Italian tour date. And we're here. You and I, standing side by side in the ecstatic crowd, with our seventy-euro general-admission tickets. We're really here.

Look, my love — we made it.

I got you a beer, you say, and I snake my fingers between yours. Our whole story could be told through the chaotic migrations of our hands, the interlocking and separating of our palms and fingertips. As I hold your hand now, I look at you in profile: your eyes, your beard, the line of your nose. They are the same as they were when all this began.

This is it. I've decided.

But that's not true. I have only allowed enough time and space to flow between me and the need to decide.

Inhale, *I love you.*

Exhale, *I hope I'll keep loving you.*

Once I worked through the sense of urgency, letting the compulsion to measure and inquire slowly dissipate, that space could be filled with new images. What is love, after all, if not a constant, confused exchange of images? Those first infatuating impressions continue to live in us, only changing shape slightly. They are never erased.

I spent the months between December 2013 and September 2014 searching for a solution, a way out. I desperately wanted to go back to the past, to correct whatever had gone wrong. But there was, there is, no threshold to cross. There is no going back, and there is no repairing the past, because the past is self-healing. I believe even the worst crises are capable of dissolving, with time. Sometimes for no particular reason, which means no recipe or handbook will help.

I don't have the answers. I don't know what changed, or how it happened. It could very well not have happened. Now I think:

we're just two kids, two people who didn't know what they were doing but found a way to be together. This is not a story about our dysfunctions, or our pathologies — it's just a story, a carousel of common, recurring properties, of fears that return for known or unknown reasons, with which we continually have to grapple, again and again, never *once and for all.* The fact is, nothing that is alive can ever be pinned down.

Over and around our heads, there are balloons, and giant inflated spheres that bounce back and forth between the stage and the crowd.

Milan! Are you having fun?

So make some motherfucking noiiiiiise!

Her super-high-cut leotard gleams under the lights, incongruous with her white cowboy boots. A pair of red Rolling Stones tongue-and-lips flap from her chest and lower back. Miley the child prodigy, the Disney heroine, the slut, the queen of country. Miley, one hand on her pigtails and the other on her crotch. Miley, who in a few years' time will share photos of the new tattoo on her forearm: a *biscione*, a blue serpent swallowing the body of a man. The heraldic symbol of the city of Milan.

Five oversized furries twerk beside her like monstrous childhood toys: a fuchsia monkey, a blue dog, a purple shark. The other dancers wear glitter tracksuits, except for two: one, only four foot tall, is dressed as Britney Spears in the *Oops! I Did It Again* film clip. The other, around seven foot tall, is dressed like Jessica Rabbit. Later, Miley simulates oral sex with Abraham Lincoln, takes flight astride a giant hot dog, and rolls around on a monumental bed with lovers of all genders — Hannah Montana is pansexual.

There is a kind of knowledge that only comes with distance.

This holds true for emotion, and perhaps especially for love, that most powerful of all emotions, the one most loaded with expectation, with dreams of redemption or transformation. There is something surprising and disturbing about love, the way it changes with perspective. It's a little like a painting that offers one complete image from afar, but up close you find that the figure, or the scene, has vanished into a sea of wild brushstrokes. The initial phases of love depend on this figurative sense, this impression-from-a-distance, which is also an act of faith, a conceptual leap. The image cannot be reconstructed from up close — those individual brushstrokes cannot be teased apart and reshaped. Taking a step backwards is the only thing that brings you closer.

Miley brings a bottle of water to her lips and takes a long slug, catching her breath, then spits an explosion of spray onto the front row, like a profane blessing. Marius kisses me, taking me by surprise, and I try not to invite in the swarm of conflicting feelings — maximum good, maximum evil — that his touch still provokes in me. In their place, I recall a sentence my therapist once said to me: *You summoned the pain and disaster of separation in order to feel something as absolute, as undeniable, as that first sense of infatuation*. A self-inflicted lightning bolt, only heavy, joyless — more like a fist, or a hammer.

Whether my therapist was right or not is beside the point. It doesn't solve anything. It's possible nothing will ever solve the problem of *you*. But I can use his words to carve a little hollow of refuge, a place to shelter from the questions that have given me little peace since they began. The daily repetition of instability itself creates a new kind of stability, a new normal. All I can do is take things as they come, choosing at each moment not to be swept away by the current. I can lodge myself in the earth with the living roots of my sensations, assisting gravity, and, in this way, I can remain. I can stay, room after room, meal after meal, year after year. I can stay for our second year together, our fifth, our eighth, and now our ninth, pinballing across the city from Via Lulli to Tito Vignoli to Palestro, then on to the next place, where we'll continue making ends meet, where you'll keep trying to become the person you feel you are and I'll keep doing piecework and reading philosophy.

Miley twerks on the hood of a car in a leotard made of dollar bills, and I think about how I don't want to have wasted this time together. Counting backwards, I realise that the months of resistance now outnumber the months of perfection.

I never would have believed it a year ago, but this daily reaffirmation of loyalty is also a way of loving.

I take your hand again, and together we jump: up and down on the soil of crushed plastic cups and straws, above and against this mind game I have invented for myself, and which I will never reveal to you, because I don't want you to be scared. I leap past the sea of happy, dancing heads, past the bouncing ponytails in blonde, brown, black, red, past the backwards-turned caps, past even the wild, raised arms of the superfans, soaring higher and higher, buoyed by the effortless bellows of my lungs. Way up there, floating above the crowd, I eat up every last molecule of carbon dioxide.

We Can't Stop concludes with a roar, and the arena is plunged back into darkness.

You bring your lips to my ear and ask: Do you think that was the last one?

Acknowledgements

Thank you to the real Marius, for allowing me to bring this fictional Marius into being. Without your generosity, this book would never have been possible.

To my mother, herself a master of resistance, for passing her secrets down to me. And to my sister, who knows me better than I know myself: the future is yours.

Thank you to Beppe Cottafavi, who, one now-distant summer, offered a home to this second novel when it was still just a concept floating in some other dimension. To Marilena Rossi, who handled the book with a passionate eye and a steady hand, and helped me believe in it. To Alessandra Maffiolini, for diagnosing the text using her superhuman subatomic and aerial vision. And to Giovanni Francesio, for making me feel at home in the publishing house of my dreams, and for trusting from a distance — with patience and respect, for many months — in my vision and process.

To my agents, Chiara Melloni and Irene Pepiciello, for the countless phone calls and messages and coffees, for the cruelty-free pasta lunches and the trips to the emergency department for my anxiety attacks, and, above all, for your intuition and ideas, which never fail to feed (or, when necessary, calm) my own.

To Roberta De Monticelli, for the best philosophical initiation imaginable, and for the luminous frameworks I still use, to this day, to decipher the human experience. To Laura Boella, for teaching me about thinking hearts, and for introducing the possibility of a different kind of philosophy — one that feels more *me*. To Chandra Candiani, for the evenings of meditation and the wise things she whispered to me, which I was never worthy of. And to Teresa Ciabatti, whose writing and speech and silence never fail to awaken me, and remind me that, despite the passing of time and the mess of life, words still have the capacity to set us on fire and move us forward, together.

To my friends Simona Maniello, Gianfranco Petriglieri, and Alessandro Wegher, who were the first to read everything — and not by chance.

And finally, to my cats, Mirtilla and Purè, for being the purest, most human thing that has ever happened to me. You have turned me from a gaggle of reveries into a real person, from a collection of moments into a lasting presence. You taught me, too, to feel life outside myself. You are my dharma.